About the Author

I was born in Coventry, the youngest of six children. We were amongst other hard-working families in a clean, caring, supportive home which offered few frills but provided a very necessary safe haven from the outside world. The thread of blood linked the differing personalities and aspirations of us siblings and as I've grown older, I've learnt to appreciate their friendship more and more.

I've always made up stories, a legacy from my dad who delighted in telling me scary tales; I create poems, spiritual philosophies, relaxation scripts, either on paper or mostly in my head, and have a tendency to drift into my own little world during conversation, a habit that used to annoy my teachers and my very busy mum immensely, and understandably so!

I haven't changed in this respect!

KEEP THEM CLOSE

Betty R Rose

KEEP THEM CLOSE

Vanguard Press

VANGUARD PAPERBACK

© Copyright 2020
Betty R Rose

The right of Betty R Rose to be identified as author of
this work has been asserted by her in accordance with the
Copyright, Designs and Patents Act 1988.

All Rights Reserved

No reproduction, copy or transmission of this publication
may be made without written permission.
No paragraph of this publication may be reproduced,
copied or transmitted save with the written permission of the
publisher, or in accordance with the provisions
of the Copyright Act 1956 (as amended).

Any person who commits any unauthorised act in relation to
this publication may be liable to criminal
prosecution and civil claims for damages.

A CIP catalogue record for this title is
available from the British Library.

ISBN 9781784656 94-2

*Vanguard Press is an imprint of
Pegasus Elliot MacKenzie Publishers Ltd.*
www.pegasuspublishers.com

First Published in 2020

**Vanguard Press
Sheraton House Castle Park
Cambridge England**

Printed & Bound in Great Britain

Dedication

To my family and friends, here and in heaven, with love.
To those who self-doubt, with love.
To those who read this book, with love.
To my guardian angel, the teacher angels, and my guide, with love.
For everyone who has ever lost their home, with love.

All my Love

Bett

Acknowledgements

Thanks to Pegasus for believing in me.
Thanks to my granddaughter, Chloe, and my niece, Joanne, for being my beta readers.
Thanks to my sister, Maureen, for her thoughts on the ending.
Thanks to my husband for the use of his songs. © Clive Rose Music, songs released on Horus record label.

PREFACE

I took a walk with my daughter through my home town one cold afternoon in November 2017.

As we chatted and gazed around, I became increasingly aware of the many youngsters sitting out in the open on blankets or coats on the pavements, their vulnerability exposed for all the world to see. A few were already bedded down for the night amongst the shoppers, not making any effort to find privacy or shelter; their plight touched my heart, I hurt, physically, tears welled up inside me and I couldn't swallow because of an uncomfortable lump in my throat.

I hadn't walked through the city centre for nearly two years; not since I'd retired from nursing.

Yes, I was aware of the shortages of affordable housing, why? I couldn't listen to the news without becoming aware of the situation in the UK, but being physically confronted with the reality in this way was very different to half listening to the political debates on TV.

I stopped and chatted. They were boys in their late teens, polite and thankful of the few pound coins that I gave them. One immediately grabbed his few belongings and rushed off to buy a takeaway; he could get a meal for £3.00! The second lad tucked the money down inside his trousers, dismissing me. He turned his head, dragging the blanket around him.

I asked him, "Why are you sitting out in the open?"

"The police and centre security moved us on from council-owned car parks and from inside the shopping centres; people like me are a nuisance, we're bad for business."

At home I couldn't shake off the afternoon's experience. I spent the next few days chatting to anyone that would listen. I took some time out to investigate the help that was available for the homeless in my city; there were various charitable organisations and council services available. So why were they out there? Why didn't they ask for help? Were their appeals refused? Were they turned away? The local churches and religious centres offered support; some volunteers walked the streets at night to help — what did I do? Look after my own I suppose. It seemed the sheer volume of need was overwhelming.

I listened to many people from different backgrounds and generations; I asked why they think there were so many homeless? Most answers were blaming and damning; some were complacent, insisting that there is a lot of 'help out there' but I didn't accept this. In the 1980s, when I was going through a divorce in a time of escalating interest rates and a housing crisis, I knew from my own experience that any of us, even those who hold down a job, can find themselves in tricky situation.

Without being political, I know that, for many, this isn't the affluent West anymore and the plight of the homeless has been with us for many centuries, for many reasons, but I've never been so sure as now that, in this present climate, without a good supportive family, any of us could find ourselves in trouble.

It's a frightening prospect and a very miserable reality that many find themselves without a safe place to live. One aspect that bothers me are the many youngsters who are working, but still not earning a high enough wage to cover the cost of private renting; or even then, will never be able to save a deposit to buy their own property.

And so, the importance of family and the very basic need we all share of having a roof over our heads is my theme for this story. I also hope to include a powerful reminder that none of us should be complacent, for the hard truth is that this could happen to you, or me, or 'any of ours'.

Forgive me if I preach, but everyone needs to belong, somewhere!

PROLOGUE

It's the third week in November, it's late afternoon and the cold has started to bite. The dull grey sky looms overhead, bringing with it a sense of foreboding. He spreads out his blanket underneath him in a futile effort to insulate himself from the freezing cold and the hardness of the pavement; shivering, he pulls the hood of his duffle coat forward over his face. The young man sits, head down, vulnerable to the elements and open spaces, without the separation of 'boundaries or moat' to shield his physicality and fears; not for him the security of a front door to close behind him. His body aches for the solidness of a wall to lean on and for some protection from the dampness and the wind. Perhaps, when the shopping centre closes for the night, he might find shelter in a shop doorway and hopefully be able to 'bed down' with some sort of privacy.

So many times today, he had been moved on by the retail centre's security, or by the local constabulary. The businesses don't want vagrants sitting outside their glitzy window displays. It's nearly Christmas; they want to spread good cheer, and even more they need the shoppers to spend good money. This 'sort of carry on' couldn't be ignored, could it? Customers would walk past the shop instead, maybe not wanting to be reminded of what? That all is not tinsel and fairy lights? No, the staff were asked to make a phone call, and make it snappy, call the security team, get him moved on, and quickly; it's bad for business!

Today a few coins had been dropped into his lap or thrown onto his red blanket; glancing down he saw a heap of coppers, maybe a little silver. In the Christmas rush, many looked without seeing; a few shoppers walked by quickly, looking away from the uncomfortable, ugly truth of homelessness. Other 'respectable' folks sighed, and 'tutted' their disapproval; some shoppers returned with a sandwich or a can of fizzy drink, usually following on with a reprimand that they wouldn't give away money to be spent on 'drink or them drugs'.

A middle-aged plump lady, well wrapped up in a purple coat against the elements, paused, her cheeks and nose almost the same shade as the hand-knitted scarf and matching woolly hat that was pulled tightly around her ears. Hovering in indecision, she nervously wiped her watery eyes and gazed down at him. Her dumpy figure hung over him; he caught the aroma of coffee and some sort of perfume; it reminded him of candy floss. Smiling, she dropped a 50p coin onto his blanket.

Gazing down at him, she mumbled to herself, "Why, he's just a young boy, can't be more than, I don't know, more than twenty!"

Moving on, she suddenly turned, hesitating. Seemingly distressed by his plight, she pushed a crinkled £5.00 note into his hand and slowly walked away, still feeling troubled. Her children had 'flown the nest' and it 'didn't sit easily' that she had a warm comfortable home, all to herself, with two empty bedrooms; her family grown and moved out, and no one to share it with.

Did the gift of cash satisfy her conscience or calm her distress? Not really, she took away his image as he smiled and whispered thanks through chattering teeth. The sorrow and misery, and the wretchedness of the young lad's situation as he sat shivering, his face 'pinched' and grey, engulfed her in a dark cloud of negativity. Waves of uncertainty and unease washed over her; she was helpless to intervene in his situation, wasn't she?

"What can I do?"

Attempting to ease her conscience, she reminded herself of organisations such as the Salvation Army, the local council housing offices, or shelter? Yes, they were all very good, he could go to them, that was their job wasn't it? To help?

She sat on the bus, pushed up against the window by a large man sharing the double seat, his thick overcoat encroaching into her space. Very carefully she turned her face away from him to avoid the unpleasant whiff of sweet whiskey and unwashed body creases. As the bus trundled and lurched along, she pondered on her Sunday school teachings. One in particular came to mind: 'The Parable of the Good Samaritan'. In the story, the Good Samaritan had crossed the road to help the injured man lying at the roadside, and bravely ignoring his fears and the very real risk of being attacked in a similar way, he'd stepped in, offering compassion and practical assistance.

Perhaps she would have a word with her elder son when he called in this evening, and then she could return to town tomorrow and have a look around. If he was still there, then she and her lad Jimmy would have a word with the youngster, and maybe even offer him a home.

Popping a sherbet lemon into her mouth, she counted down the stops before she would be able to remove herself from the confines of the dusty window glass and the greasy leather seating. At last the bus approached her stop, and nervously excusing herself she pushed and squeezed past the occupier of the seat next to her. Offering up a sly smile he craftily pressed himself forward and pinched her ample bottom.

That night, still troubled, she had a word with Jimmy. They made the decision to return tomorrow, being a Saturday, and they would find out more. He'd advised caution, of course. To take a stranger into her home needed careful consideration, but despite his gentle warning she was strangely elated.

"Kindness brings its own rewards," she had countered.

She waited to listen to the evening news broadcast and then climbed the stairs to bed, pulling the heavy curtains across to shut out the cold draft of air. She snuggled down into her soft duvet, whispering her prayers, and a final "Yes, that lad needs a home." Comforted, she dropped off to a sound sleep.

For some it was a different story.

Another long night beckoned. Filled with a strong sense of foreboding, he watched as, one by one, the shutters were pulled down and the staff left for home after the first late night Christmas opening. Voices carried through the darkness, calling out their goodnights; they pulled up their jacket collars against the cold and hurried home to rest their aching feet. Home to fresh bubbling coffee, maybe a beef stew and a pot of tea or, for some, the pub and a Chinese takeaway or fish and chips.

For him, there'd be no cheery welcome and warm hall beckoning, not for him the enticing heat and cooking smells from the kitchen. No one shouting at him to "hang your coat up", no noise from the telly.

The lights from the shops dimmed one by one. He shook with a familiar dread and emptiness as the icy darkness approached, the only comfort now being from the street lamps and the flickering glow from the few shops that had left subdued lighting on in their front displays.

He was trembling — why? Was it the fear of being alone in the darkness? Or that someone would steal from him again, or maybe someone would have a bit of fun and 'smack him about'? He screwed his eyes up tightly. No, his mind screamed out, don't think about it, don't go there, lad, don't think about it!

As the pubs emptied, he knew from experience that most would walk past, not even notice him or give him a second thought, and that's just what he wanted — invisibility. His worst anxiety wasn't that he would catch the interest of an inquisitive or nasty- tempered drunk, someone who saw him as fair game or a target for verbal abuse. No, it was the dread of another sort of demand, because once, just once; he'd been approached for sex and offered money. His stomach churned as he remembered. He'd been woken by a shadow leaning over him, a hand gripping his collar, a whisper in his ear and a quiet, 'well spoken' invite; the threatening undertone was clear, the words carried on spicy, cigarette-fuelled breath.

"Come on, you're a delightful young lad, I noticed you earlier on today. Let's go back to mine for a warm cuppa and some fun. Are you hungry? I'll make it worth your while." There was a pause. "Or I may, well, I could make things awkward for you!"

He forced the memory of that night to the back of his consciousness. What had happened to him was so dreadful and degrading. He knew that he would never speak of it again!

As a child, his fears were of the 'bogey man' hiding under his bed, or of the ghost that lived in the wardrobe behind the coat hangers, and of the banshee waiting outside in the dark. He ached for the security of his mam's hug and for the laughter of his sisters, and for his grandad, Michael.

His stomach growling with hunger, he knew he'd wait until the 'takeaways' and night clubs closed. Then he'd scavenge through the discarded foam cartons and chip papers for his supper. The £5.00 note was tucked away in his boxer shorts. He pushed his hand down inside to feel the shiny paper, just to reassure himself that he hadn't dreamt it. He knew he'd invite attention if he were to venture into the crowded precinct just now. He would stand out like a sore thumb amongst the revellers in their nightclub finery.

Thinking ahead, he crept back into the pharmacy doorway. The noise and screams and commotion from the closing of the entertainment venues had settled. Tugging the damp blanket around his shoulders, he was hopeful he wouldn't be disturbed until the morning.

Eyes heavy with lack of sleep he dozed, 'closing the shutters' against reality. He drifted back to his soft, squashy bed with the freshly washed sheets heavily scented with Mam's favourite washing powder; to bath night and the orangey-scented glycerine soap that Mam had crafted with love; to the sweet smell of Grandad Michael's horses and the waxy polish that they used to clean and shine the harnesses and saddles. How he longed to be in Ireland now, in his grandad's barn, singing their songs and soothing the horses.

The sound of footsteps and laughter nearby woke him. His stomach tensed with fear, the bile burned as it rose into his throat; shrinking back into the doorway, he waited. This time they passed him by!

He shivered, whispering into the darkness, "Perhaps God will take me tonight; maybe I'll just drift into sleep and the cold will take me. Mam always talked of angels and heaven — I know she'll be waiting for me, she promised."

Scratching around in his pocket he felt for the 'little something' that was wrapped in tissue paper and then in a cellophane bag to keep it from the damp. He couldn't bear to take it out and gaze at it at this precise moment.

The loneliness and longing that doing so would, he knew from recent experience, be too much for his broken heart to take. But he needed to know that he had it safe — Mam's lock of red hair, a physical reminder of her love.

Head drooping forward, his eyes closed, he was unable to fight off the heaviness of body and mind, but his hunger kept him away from the peaceful oblivion that his spirit craved for. Slowly he drifted into the twilight world of his childhood, of his grandad Michael and grannie Mary, of his mother, Robina, and his sisters Adamma and Kamaria. And then his great grandparents Eamon and Faith, Brendon and Elizabeth, Uncle James and Uncle Samuel; and for some reason, Moses, the dad that was a stranger to him. They were all there with him.

For young Finn did have family. He had grandparents, uncles, aunts and cousins living back in Ireland, and his two older sisters living in the UK; one in London and the other in Edinburgh. He'd been raised with the belief that family should 'stick together'. They may not always like each other, but as blood relatives they needed to 'watch each other backs' when times were hard. The family had an obligation to care for each other, and each one of them must protect the younger and weaker members from the predators who were 'outside of their pack'; it was family first, and then the rest of the world!

But now he was alone, leading a primitive existence in a secret world of uncertainty and unease, surviving by stealing a pack of biscuits, a carton of milk, a pack of corned beef. Anything that, out of necessity, would keep him fed, and warm, and alive.

He had no address, no bank account, (at least not one with money in it), no benefits, 'they'd' smashed his mobile phone. He was too frightened to return to his old neighbourhood; he had no way of knowing if 'they' were still hanging around, waiting.

He'd been fine until then — everything was going to plan. Sitting alone in the kitchen, he thought he heard voices outside; there was a quiet knock on the door. Maybe it was Nellie — she would say that she was lonely. He smiled — she'd promised his gran she would 'keep her eye on him'.

"Come on in, Nellie."

They didn't need an invitation.

There'd been three of them; they'd ransacked the house, wanted to know where his sister was, where the 'stuff' was.

"We want our money, she owes us."

They could find nothing of interest. He was living simply; Adamma had taken her expensive 'stuff' with her to London. Kamaria had the laptop; and how they'd laughed when they saw his simple mobile, and then smashed it.

They'd tipped him upside down and laughed when a few coins fell out of his pockets. The tall blonde lad clamped him tight — he could still smell the oil from his jacket; he'd wriggled as his mate grazed his face with a penknife. It slipped, cutting from just under his eye down to the corner of his mouth.

The older guy in the cap shouted, "Enough, stop!" The blood trickled down Finn's cheek as he stared into the sweaty face. Gripping him by his throat, he rasped in horrifying detail how he would rape that 'bitch of a sister' of his when he found her.

He'd squeezed until Finn's legs gave way underneath him, and then threw him outside in a heap, in the cold, in the blackness.

The last thing that he remembered from that night were screams of laughter as they threw burning paper into the house and threatened to set him alight if he didn't move fast.

Finn knew that he had to warn Adamma. How could he? Maybe it was best that he stayed away. She was in London; she didn't come home often, may not come home for ages, he reasoned. And hadn't they warned him? Stay away or something terrible will happen to the rest of his family and look what they'd done to old Joseph and Aneta — they'd petrified them. He couldn't think straight, and now the voices were there again. They were back, whispering — he couldn't make out what they were saying; he wouldn't listen. "Don't tinker with the darkness," his mam had always told him. "Say your prayers, son, ask your guardian angel for help — he's always there."

CHAPTER 1

The Story of the Moran family, Brendon and Elizabeth Moran, Parents of Michael, Finn's Grandad

Michael was born to Brendon and Elizabeth in the year 1930, following the Irish War of Independence and the Irish Civil War, just a few years after the time when Ireland became politically divided from the UK. He was born into the free state or Republic of Ireland.

The six states remained part of the UK, Northern Ireland.

Grandad Michael Moran was the first born and he was followed by his three brothers. They all shared the same jet-black hair and grew into the tall, lean men that his family were known for. Michael and his brothers had similar temperaments, easy going and warm like the mild, forested South West climate that they grew up in.

Michael, John, Patrick and James had a charmed and uneventful childhood. They worked on their father's smallholding from a young age, where they helped their father with his large herd of cows, and with their many geese, ducks and chickens. They were strong, useful boys and the money they brought in from helping others round and about, with their animals, repairing fencing and such and, when they were old enough, washing dishes and collecting glasses in the nearby pubs, provided much-needed cash for the family coffers.

Although the family cash tin was often empty, their clothes were warm and functional. They were well fed on their mam's meat and potatoes and turnips, leek and potato soup, roast chicken and eggs from their hens and bantams, and warm soda bread which was cooked on a stone on top of the fire, and when they were lucky a bit of salmon or trout or char. In season they had apple and potato cake, and for a special treat they had porter cake.

The boys had warm shelter and freedom, and they grew into tall, strong young men, nurtured by the surrounded beauty of the native forests and the clean running waters from the bubbling streams. The lushness of the 'blanket bogs' provided warmth — the family had their own patch and they cut the peat for fuel for cooking and heating. Their home was a simple, low, white stone cottage with two bedrooms, a kitchen and small family room. They had running water in the kitchen and an outside lavatory and they still used a tin bath which hung up just inside Mam's cleaning cupboard.

As young boys they enjoyed their weekends together, cycling out to the most western point where the mountains reached up into the endless sky. The brothers enjoyed climbing in all weathers; their thick, coarse, woollen jumpers protected them from the constant mizzle of soft rain. When the humidity brought thunder and lightning, and it often did, they would dash for shelter inside an abandoned stone cottage nearby; or just jump back on their bikes, shouting and laughing as the rain lashed their faces and ran in rivulets off their coarse, woollen jumpers and down their skinny, gangly legs.

They were undisturbed by the troubles around them; they had a wildness which their father, Brendon, encouraged, whilst their mother Elizabeth directed it into their music. Michael learnt to play the tin whistle and then the flute, James taught himself to play the guitar, John had the singing voice of an angel and Patrick played the Bodhrán drum and the fiddle.

The four brothers remained close, bickering as siblings do, sometimes arguing or having a scuffle, but it never came to anything serious. It was never allowed to escalate into anything that would threaten the sanctity of their home; their mother, Elizabeth, had raised them to believe in the gift and blessedness of family life, and of the importance of being loyal to one another.

For Elizabeth was grateful for the family and the security that Brendon had provided, and she never forgot for a moment how her life could have taken a very different turn. After working as a lady's maid in London from the age of seventeen, Elizabeth had accompanied her mistress of three years and her new, wealthy husband, the squire, when he had decided, on a whim, to take up the old life back on his lands in Ireland. Becoming bored with his life in London, he had 'a fancy' to take up a simpler life on his estate and to show his new English wife his home.

"You will find that the countryside in Ireland is nothing but a 'work of art', my dear. We have castles and ancient ruins and acres of lush green that are a delight, and the hunting and riding are excellent; the herds of native Red Deer are a wonder to behold."

His new English wife did not need any persuading, for it was expedient to be away from London and her creditors. Her previous husband had left her in a difficult financial predicament after his sudden death, and confiding to her close friends that, "It's a terrible thing to always be in debt, for I can't sleep owing all the money that I do," she had closed up her house with an eagerness that had surprised few.

Unfortunately, after a short while in his new home, the squire took another 'strong fancy' to his wife's lady's maid, Elizabeth. She was petite and slender and very pretty. She wore her pale blonde hair platted and wrapped around her head in a golden halo which framed her delicate features and set off her lovely deep blue eyes, fringed with long, copper lashes. The squire took one look into those eyes and he was smitten.

One evening after a riotous dinner party, when the couple and their guests had taken much wine and brandy, he had crept up to the attic rooms of the servants and had 'slunk' into his wife's lady's' maids' room and forced himself on the vulnerable young Elizabeth. The squire had been too drunk and clumsy not to have alerted any of the other occupants on the same floor; however, none of them chose to investigate the muffled sobs and murmurings for they knew better than to get out of their beds. The staff were very aware whose room was along the corridor, and they had all noticed their employer's interest in the pretty English maid.

His visits didn't stop there. He continued to creep up to Elizabeth's bed at regular intervals whenever the opportunity arose. Whether his wife knew was a matter of opinion, for in her circles it wasn't so unusual for a bored husband to take an interest the family servants. Elizabeth was young and far from home and family, but her gentle nature belied a deep inner strength and stubborn resolve, and a determination that her vulnerable situation would not result in dismissal.

She was aware that if her mistress was openly confronted with the circumstances, then she would not take any responsibility for the welfare of a young girl who she saw as culpable, and she would quickly dismiss her and then where would Elizabeth be — homeless with no means of income, and with no letter of recommendation for new employment. Knowing that the squire was not a cruel man, she forced herself to tolerate his clumsy advances. She was not ignorant of the social behaviours of 'the rich and privileged'. She'd been employed in the houses in London from the age of twelve years, and she knew better than to even dream that such behaviour would be other than an amusing titbit in giggled conversations behind manicured hands. She was in no doubt that if 'word got out', her mistress would be smarting with indignation and spite.

Eventually the inevitable happened. When Elizabeth warily confronted the squire, he had surprised her with such remonstrations of remorse and apologies, as to give her some hope that he would not abandon her plight.

'What to do'? He had paced, wrung his hands, and deliberated. For he was no fool, and was very aware that his wife would accuse her maid of deliberately enticing her husband, and she would then further justify his behaviour, as was often the way of privileged women faced with such a situation — he could hear her now!

"My husband is a red-blooded man, and of course he would take what was offered to him."

No, he couldn't allow that. He'd grown fond of Elizabeth; he wouldn't be responsible for her being thrown out in the middle of the night with nothing but the clothes that she stood in. Then, as soon as the house were out of their beds, she would be the source of the latest bit of tasty scandal.

The squire mulled over Elizabeth's pregnancy for a day or two. He walked, and ambled with his two hounds until he returned exhausted and, with his clothes damp and his stomach rumbling with hunger, he would take himself off to the kitchens. Collapsing down into a chair he would complain to his butler that he had 'walked as many miles as if he had travelled from 'Malin Head' to 'Mizen Point'.

Still troubled, he had taken his problem to 'a Mass', and he had tried to ease his conscience in his confession to the young priest. Following his visit to the church, Father John had visited, and suggested that they take a walk. He hoped that the squire would again talk of the young woman's predicament. When the subject was broached, feeling justified and safe to do so as a 'man of cloth', he'd angrily scolded his elder and better on his immoral behaviour. At the same time, he'd carefully enquired if maybe there was another honest man that would be prepared to take Elizabeth on, for she was a 'fetching' young woman.

At that very moment, as fate would have it, the stable manager, Brendon happened to walk by, and humming and whistling to himself quietly, he stopped short when he saw his employer with Father John. Doffing his cap he wished them a good evening, and sauntered on as if without a care in the world.

Brendon had managed the stables and the squire's fine horses for the last seven years whilst his employer had been living in London. He was a likeable, handsome chancer, very fond of his porter and a whiskey when he had the funds and, when he didn't, he would play his fiddle at the nearby inn. That would always provide him with a few full glasses. But he was a loyal and very skilled worker, and the squire had a respect for the man; for he took great care of his horses and stables and he had never disappointed him in any way.

Waiting until the priest left, he called Brendon over. He 'sounded him out' and asked him what he thought of the young maid Elizabeth — he'd noticed the two of them chatting from time to time. The squire cautiously put his proposition to his stable manager; he offered Brendon a few acres of land and a dowry for Elizabeth if she kept quiet and married Brendon. The pair of them seized the opportunity; the squire even 'threw in a gold band' for the marriage. Elizabeth knew that this was her only way out and, besides, she liked the handsome, tall stable manager with his sense of fun and confident personality. Brendon could not believe his luck; a gift of money and a beauty? Why? It wasn't her fault after all — he knew that she was a decent young woman who had been placed in an intolerable position.

The clergy was summoned and made aware of the agreement, and the wedding was arranged quietly, and the ceremony completed with little fuss.

The newly married couple moved away south to their land and made a home in the small dwelling left empty by the previous occupants. It wasn't in a bad state of repair and Brendon was confident that he was 'up to it'. Elizabeth's dowry paid for materials for the roof and enabled Brendon to purchase livestock. Elizabeth proudly placed a Saint Brigid's Cross outside the entrance of their new home, above the door, and they began their married life.

Elizabeth's baby girl was born six months later. The squire made discreet enquiries and on discovering that his child was female he withdrew. Despite Brendon's love of alcohol and his tendency to brag and tell tall tales, he was wary of the possible implications if he told of the arrangement, and he would frequently reassure his wife that he would ever do so.

"Do you think that I'm weak in the head woman? For sure, he's a powerful man, and that missis of his is a force to be reckoned with. I would never give her the opportunity to take her spite out on you."

Brendon kept his silence and the squire never visited again.

The girl child had been born sickly. She had arrived into the world as a tiny scrap of a new born, and

Elizabeth fretted that the child had suffered from the shame and the worry that she had experienced when carrying her. The baby didn't survive past nine months. She left this earth following complications brought on by teething, which led to fever and a bout of convulsions which 'took her off'.

She was christened Catherine Elizabeth, and quietly buried in the churchyard without a headstone. Brendon had shaped a small cross out of willow, and Elizabeth continued to visit her alone on each anniversary of her passing. She found comfort in tidying the small plot, and before leaving she would lay a bunch of violets or snowdrops in remembrance.

Elizabeth went on to bear her husband four healthy sons — James, John, Patrick and Michael — but God never gave her another daughter; she knew this was her punishment.

Brendon and Elizabeth kept the secret to their grave. Their sons never knew how their parents had managed to buy their own land. Sometimes Brendon would tease that he'd found the 'Leprechaun's pot of gold' and caution them never to mock or speak a word of it, or they would bring down the wrath of the little people on the family.

Elizabeth took solace in her four sons, who were born quickly in yearly succession of each other, and she worked hard with her husband to build up their small farm. Brendon, who despite his loudness and wiliness in his business affairs, and having a too fond a liking for his alcohol, proved himself to be a gentle and caring husband.

In the late 1940s and early 1950s, the brothers began playing regularly in the local pubs, or travelled to Dublin or Cork to perform where the tourists had started coming through. They still helped their parents on the land, and continued earning 'what they could', working in the local food industries or labouring on construction sites around the country. Meanwhile they dreamed of farther fields. They planned to try and get work on the passenger and freight liners that sailed on routes to Europe and America, and even one day to Canada and Australia.

They had grown into fine sons that Elizabeth and Brendon were proud of. Patrick and John, particularly, had a hankering to escape the confines of their island home, set in the farthest west of Europe. When they played their music in the cities on the east coast, such as Dublin or Belfast in the northern states, they would mix with other travellers and tourists, and they were all in agreement that they would try their luck in America one day. All, that is, except Michael, who had a notion to try London or Liverpool or one of the midlands cities in the UK first.

Fate stepped in. Following an offer of a very well-paid gig at a big wedding in Dublin, it being a rare engagement that covered their travelling costs and provided a stay at the hotel where they were to play; the brothers were introduced to a fellow guest who was an agent for a shipping company. He offered them work on one of the many cruise ships which had started to replace the traditional passenger/freight liners. The middle two brothers, John and Patrick, eagerly snatched at this opportunity. This was an enticing offer of steady employment and travel. Without looking back, or further consideration about leaving James, the youngest brother, and Michael, the middle son, at home to manage the land and animals, or bearing in mind their now elderly parents, they said their goodbyes.

"They were off, like 'a ball shot out of a cannon," complained James, who was a little nervous about making changes. Now that he was faced with the reality of leaving his home, he found that the land had a pull on him that was too strong to ignore. He stayed!

CHAPTER 2

Michael Moran Meets Mary Boyle

Michael turned down the offer of the cruise ship for another reason, for he had 'lost his head and his heart' to a guest at the wedding, Mary Boyle, who was one of the two bridesmaids.

He was no stranger to the comforts of a female, but this young woman did not exude comfort. Somehow, he knew that this lady would be the love of his life, the darling of his heart, the woman who would drive him crazy with passion and a protectiveness that shook him.

And Mary returned the glances of the tall, lean man, whose intensive, challenging gaze cut straight through her with a message that was primeval, and she welcomed him, invited him.

He was everything that she had dreamt of in her man; from his deep set, steel-blue eyes, and his weathered complexion, his coal- black, curly hair, and wide smile with very white teeth, to the broadness of his shoulders and tall, lean length. Why, 'heavens above', he'd made her knees all of a tremble. Later in the evening, when they danced and chatted, she noticed that he wasn't actually perfect, for he had a tooth missing at the top side, which he'd lost when he and his brothers had become too enthusiastic in a brawl. It added to his attractiveness in a strange way. When Mary returned the light and fire in his eyes, with a trembling smile and a flushed complexion that communicated her need, she ignited a fire in his belly.

For this woman was handsome; she was a rare beauty with her dark auburn hair that curled around her face and cascaded down to her waist in a thick, luxurious mantle. Her soft grey eyes had flecks of gold in them and her complexion was creamy white, whilst her cheeks were a becoming pink from the heat in the crowded room. She was tall, just a few inches less than himself, and her full breasts and wide hips were complemented by a slim waist.

Firmly taking hold of her by her shoulders, he guided her towards the outside door. His hand caressed the silky softness of her neck as he turned her away from the raucous laughter and cigarette smoke and the heat from the sweating, dancing bodies. They passed by the pungent smell of sour grease and onions wafting through from the kitchen and, as she walked ahead of him into the soft damp darkness of a new moon, she heard the shriek of an owl. She smiled — to hear the call of the owl at this moment was a sign; for the women in Mary's family believed that to have a sighting or to hear the call of the owl was an omen, an omen of change, of wisdom and prophecy, of good luck and protection. Mary knew that a barn owl mates for life. She heard the long, soft answer of its mate calling back and felt the soft fluttering of wings so close to her that she took a sharp intake of breath as her heart missed a beat.

As she looked up at Michael, her dove-grey eyes sparkled with excitement. She raised her fine, arched eyebrows and laughed softly; she was no stranger to the happenings between men and women. Hadn't her own mother bore seven children? She'd heard the noises from the bedroom in the still of the night, the cries of protest and slaps and grunts and groans that she would try to smother by hiding under her covers. What happened in that big double bed of mammie's had been no secret to any of them.

But for Mary, she wanted something different! She didn't want to be 'the someone' who her partner just settled for, knowing that he never really cherished her, or knew the essence of her as a woman. She wouldn't be the placid wife who was not too opinionated or loud, who would be a good homemaker and who was pleasant-looking enough. She would not settle for being the equivalent of a comfy chair, a companion to clean his house and to provide a warm backside when his smutty jokes at the pub excited his need.

She had quietly observed her mother being an expert in practicality, wondering why she always stayed in the background in company. She knew that over the years she had pushed the reality of her marriage away, stifling the nagging doubts that arose in her breast every now and then by smothering her pain with food: warm soda bread, leftover pie or potatoes, seedy cake, oh, with anything at hand! And Faith had grown to be rounded and fat — another reason to hide away in her home whilst her husband made derisive comments about "the huge size of your arse woman."

This evening, Mary was a million miles away from the restrictions and memories of her childhood. She was excited, she knew her own power as a woman and she was keenly aware that once a man had succeeded in the chase, he would become complacent or, even worse, indifferent. Neither was she going to bargain for love, playing a game of respectability.

Mary wanted to see the world, to travel. She had a wildness in her blood that was seeded in the wildness of the north westerly coast. She was away from home, away from the confines of her brother's overpowering protection, she knew what Michael wanted and so did she.

Michael hugged her close to him — her long auburn hair was scented with geranium and rose water and she clung to him tightly. Closing her eyes and making no move to pull away from him, she placed her hand on his backside and laughed softly. She was going to throw caution to the wind, not in the way of putting her trust in God, or the priest, or Michael — she knew just how far she would allow things to go!

CHAPTER 3

Mary was Born to Eamon and Faith Boyle in 1933. She and Her Family Lived on the North West Coast of Ireland.

Mary was born a twin. The older of the two was stillborn — she was named Susan. She was the only daughter in the Boyle family that survived her childhood. Two of her other female siblings, Bernadette and Margaret, died of TB at the ages of eleven years and thirteen years. Her other siblings, Anthony, Daniel and Thomas, all grew into fine, strong men. Mary was adored and protected by her brothers and her father Eamon and mother, Faith.

She was raised on the wild north west coast of Ireland. Her father had land and a small farm. He was able to make enough to keep his family, and Faith did a little traditional weaving and knitting and sewing. When she was able, Faith sold the shawls and tweeds for a good price in the local shop in a nearby town to the few visitors that came their way. She always ensured that she gave a more reasonable price to the locals.

Sometimes, when times were lean, her father Eamon would join his three elder brothers fishing. They made a reasonable living catching herring, mussels, winkles and oysters, and sometimes salmon, but generally Eamon preferred to work his land — he had a fear of the sea.

The livestock on the land comprised of a small, specialist herd of cows, a large flock of sheep, chickens, four goats and two geese that were really Mary's pets. To Eamon's amusement, she named them Sybil and Sid, after a visit to town and a brief encounter with two English tourists that fuelled her imagination. There was never a shortage of fresh eggs and milk for breakfast. Mary was given the responsibility of letting the hens out in the morning and chasing them into the hen house at night. She enjoyed feeding the squabbling chickens and running away from the strutting cockerels that sometimes flew at her with their spurs held in front of them in a boxing pose. She would help Faith with the goats and enjoyed the times when her mother brought home a billy goat as a mating partner for a goat that was in season and was 'calling'.

Her brothers all toiled with their father on the land, but they also took work wherever they could find it locally, either labouring on building sites away from home, or on neighbouring farms. As they matured one by one, they ventured further, and eventually only Daniel stayed at home on the farm.

Faith had no idea how her own marriage had shaped her daughter's expectations or views on relationships. She was mostly accepting of her husband's need to dominate and own her; it was part of the culture that she had grown up in. Eamon wasn't a cruel man, but he accepted and never questioned the church's teaching of 'married duties', and he genuinely believed that 'he had the right', and that although children were always a blessing from God, they were the work of the wife whilst the men had to provide. The few times when Faith had asserted herself, he'd sometimes slapped her in frustration; his attachment to her was always played out with a need to either dominate or protect her.

Faith quietly endured but she was clear that there would be no more pregnancies after her twin girls were born — 'church or no church, she had done her bit'. Using her innate womanly wiles, she always ensured that her man had money for drink. An overindulgence of porter always ensured that even if he had the inclination, he was physically unable to complete the task. She encouraged him to pop out with the boys of an evening. The aches in his joints from his oncoming arthritis, aggravated by the dampness of the night air and the long walk home, meant that on most occasions he would thankfully fall into bed, asleep and snoring within minutes. This avoided conflict in the home for, as she had grown older and wiser, she'd realised that meeting Eamon 'head on' was as hopeless as trying to swim upstream.

Being content with having a man that provided for the family, and thankful for the land and cottage, she didn't question 'her lot'.

"Sure, wasn't it a blessing" that they could put their head on their pillow knowing that they were one of the few families around these parts that owned their own land.

Faith had inherited the land and cottage after her parents' death. One by one her brothers had all emigrated to America to join the other descendants of the family who'd escaped the starving poverty of the great potato famine which had hit Ireland in 1846. They'd not written or kept in touch; they had 'broken free' and ventured into an exciting world, hopeful of finding gold or land and becoming rich.

Being the youngest child, she'd taken care of her elderly parents; it was expected. At the age of sixteen she had met Eamon at a Mass. She was tall and slim, and her mane of fiery, red hair and soft, hazel gaze had 'taken his fancy' in a way that hadn't happened in a long while. Her parents had encouraged him, they had married after a short courtship of only six months and she never questioned her duty.

Eamon was an older man who had lost his first wife and son during childbirth. He was strong and steady in his manner and outlook. Her parents had been relieved that their daughter was settled, and they were also appreciative of having a strong son-in- law to take over the heavy work on the land. Faith saw that she was blessed with a good man, and she was thankful and secure in the knowledge that a landlord could not come knocking and demand a higher rent or even throw them off the land, as had happened to many not so many years back. She didn't ask for, or expect any more — it was enough!

When the mood 'took her', she would sometimes walk around her home, humming, and caressing the rough stone walls lovingly, knowing that she would grow old there and die peacefully, 'God willing', in her own bed. She knew that the children who had passed early from this world were here with her; she fancied that she could hear their laughter. Sometimes she would catch the scent of rosemary and earth, and the spikey herbs that they used to collect together. Yes, she loved her home.

Eamon was at a time of his life when he was thankful to be past the excitements and agitations of his youth. Often to be found in front of his smoking peat fire after a 'draught or two', his mind would return to when he was a boy, to 'that day', which had started with such promise; a rare day, when he and his brother had been released from the school routine and duties around the home, and they had ventured a bit farther than usual.

It wasn't the first time that the north Atlantic had claimed one of their family, but Eamon still fretted that, as the elder brother, it had been expected of him to keep his brother safe, that he should have been able to save his younger brother, John, from being pulled back from him, down into the sea, and drowned.

He still had nightmares after 'all of these years', in which his brother would be calling him, calling him and crying out.

That day the rest of the family had been preoccupied with 'some sort of troubles', and Mammie had waved them off. "Get you'selves off, but make sure that you little 'uns' don't get into any trouble, for isn't there enough in this house at this time."

They knew that their uncle had been 'taken off', but nothing more, other than Mammie crying, and Father muttering, "The dam British," under his breath.

They had been packed off before breakfast, and John had complained that his stomach was 'growlin', and so they had been given a lump of hard cheese and warm, thick triangles of soda bread straight from Mam's heavy frying pan, before their sister Marion had clipped Eamon's ear, laughing. "Be off with you now and stop your whining."

They had munched on thick slices of bread and cheese, they'd launched themselves off, wildly shouting and running, and frightening the 'coos', before they had finally found themselves down at the sea.

Eamon had been engrossed, poking about in a rock pool with a stick, concentrating hard on pulling out a sea anemone to join his collection back home. John had been standing in the shallows, mesmerised by the tide sweeping in and sliding back out. He'd ventured farther and farther out into the waves.

Neither brother took heed of the darkening of the sky, and the strange yellow light above them, until the storm broke in 'all of its ferocity'.

John was taken — he had been 'lifted up' and pulled under the deep waters in an instant before he had the chance to catch his breath and scream.

When Eamon turned, his brother had disappeared. Only his boots were visible, laying along the beach where he had hastily tugged them off before wandering down to the sea edge for a paddle. For John had damaged many a pair of boots with sea water, and he hadn't been keen to do this again after the pasting that he'd received from his father after the last episode.

Eamon still trembled when he remembered that day; how could he ever forget? Oh! how he had shouted and screamed in terror, until he was hoarse and sobbing, but the thunder of the waves had drowned out his desperate calls.

Yes, Eamon had a fear of the ocean, a fear that it would once again claim one of his family, one of his own!

His children never challenged him — they knew better than to question him.

CHAPTER 4

1958
Mary's Married Life with Michael

Mary was twenty-five years old when she met and married Michael. who was just three years older, and after a speedy courtship of three months, which set tongues wagging? Her ma' was pleased and surprised; she'd had nagging doubts whether her daughter would marry at all because she had been so spoilt being the only girl in the family. Eamon created hell; he had been happy to keep 'his girl' at home, and wasn't it traditional, he argued, that as the youngest daughter she would stay with her parents and take care of them in their old age?

She stood her ground with her father; she wasn't intimidated by 'the old goat'. Marrying Michael didn't mean that she was ready for a family just yet; she had a yearn to explore other lands and cultures before she settled for a traditional married life, and she certainly did not have any yearning for children today, despite her being 'almost an old maid', as some might have it.

The couple were of the same mind. They initially thought of taking a sea passage to Canada or Australia, but then decided to combine their dream of travelling the world together with earning money on the cruise ships, each of them being flexible enough to take on the various roles that were available.

The years together were happy and unrestricted. They saw the sights, spent a little money, enjoyed the Mediterranean, New York, the Caribbean Islands, Malta, Cyprus, and when closer to home they took advantage of their leave to visit London or the other big cities around the UK, before signing up again for a new post on a different cruise ship.

They didn't neglect their family ties. They would send money home, always pay a visit to 'the old ones', when it was possible, usually staying a little longer with Mary's parents. Michael had a hankering to settle there — the wildness of the north west coast appealed to him, rather than the softer, heavier, climate of his boyhood home.

On social occasions they were a popular couple. Michael would play his flute or strum on an old guitar and Mary would join him; she relished any opportunity to show off her Irish step dancing or to sing along with a melodic haunting ballad; she was always full of song and vitality.

Michael found that her maturity enhanced her beauty. 'She had a way with her', lighting up any company with her confidence and open manner, and Michael's charm and dark handsome looks attracted many a female, but they remained true to each other. They both enjoyed a 'good drink', for Mary could 'hold her own' with any man. Life was good, they enjoyed the freedom and the many friendships that developed.

Inside each adult remained the child of the church. The teachings, the social expectations and obligations of their religion were central, and always would be, but they had decided early on that if they followed all the rules of the parish priest and the Catholic Church then they would miss out on too much 'living' and fun. Aware that one day they would return and live a decent Catholic life, they saved hard, for their outgoings were small; with their living accommodation and meals all covered whilst they were working on board the liner, they quickly managed to accumulate a 'nice little nest egg'.

During their time away, Mary ensured that there were no additions to their family, taking full control of the family planning. She had no intention of risking all on her husband's willpower. The favoured withdrawal method of contraception had failed her mammie, and most of her girlfriends too, when alcohol came into the equation and she dismissed the 'so called rhythm method' which, on enquiry, had proved to be highly ineffective. At school they had not been taught sex education and most of her friends' houses had been full of children, well, that was when they all survived! For many of their neighbours, the mothers had an equal number of children on earth as in heaven. Mary had made it her business to 'slink around'. She listened at key holes; there were herbs that could help, or stranger still to her young ears they soaked sponges in vinegar, then put them into their private parts; many of them were so desperate to avoid another pregnancy. She'd seen her friends' mothers with a child at her breast long past the toddler's first hesitant step, hoping to prevent the return of menstruation and fertility.

Mary was a determined and intelligent young woman and had found an acceptable solution. Back home, the conservative elements in the government and the Roman Catholic Church were not willing to consider artificial contraception, but she was able to buy condoms in Belfast and the UK, just in time for her marriage in 1958. Attitudes amongst her friends back home stopped her sharing her use of contraception with them. Many still feared they were committing a grave sin if they ignored the church's advice, and so she was aware of the whispers, when she returned home, about the lack of children in her marriage, and the disappointment that 'poor, wretched, Michael' must be feeling. Michael was nothing of the sort!

Nonetheless, there came a time when they were both ready to 'lower the anchor'. Following Michael's dream, they settled on the north west coast. With the money that they had saved they bought a few acres of land and Michael built a lovely home. The money that they had worked hard for and saved meant that neither had to work on the land as tenant farmers as many still did.

Both sets of parents had unusually succeeded in owning their own land, and they wanted to 'continue on' in the same fashion, for they knew that if they owned the roof over their own head, even if they had little resources at first, they would not be at the mercy of unscrupulous agents or absent landowners.

Within months of moving into their home, at forty years of age, Mary allowed herself to become pregnant. Michael was forty-three, proud as punch to at last be proving his manhood, and the jollifications carried on until the early hours of the morning at The Long Horse, whilst Mary enjoyed a small glass of porter in the privacy of the 'snug'. Mary's pals hadn't travelled far from home and were shy of taking a drink in the pub. The local drinking establishments were still very much the domain of men. She found that she sat on her own for an hour and left her husband to his celebrations.

Mary had a difficult confinement. It was a long and painful birth, but their daughter was born healthy and strong, and following his vigil of long anxious hours, Michael rushed inside, kissed Mary soundly and then, tenderly taking his new born in his arms, he sobbed. He thanked the Lord for Mary's safety, and for the gift of his very own child. They were both enchanted with their daughter and named her Robina, on Mary's insistence that the robin which had perched on the window ledge outside during the birth had been a sign!

After Robina was born, life was good. Michael continued working in the local pubs for two evenings a week, playing his music with James. It brought a little cash in and it also gave him an opportunity to 'have the crack', and 'get out from under Mary's feet', as 'she would have it'. Michael enjoyed going out on the boats when he was given the chance. It brought in enough fish to sell at the local market and for their own table and he was proud to own his property, maintaining the fencing and the barns. His land was a joy to him; she was the only a mistress, other than Mary, that he never tired of.

He'd also allowed himself one, or you could say, two, extravagances. Following the celebrations of his daughter's birth in the pub that evening he'd met an old friend from his past, a chap that he'd grown up with as a young boy in the south west, and, following that meeting, he'd purchased two stunning foals, a pure white, and a tawny chestnut. They were never meant to work on the land — they were for pleasure — it was a delight to possess something beautiful. When he was able to get away, he enjoyed the horseracing. He was careful to have only a 'little flutter'; nothing that would make a hole in his finances. Mary would dress in her Sunday best and join him when she could, but these occasions were rare, for these days she was content to focus on her family and her child and the responsibilities that came with them.

Mary enjoyed being a mother, raising her child, sewing, baking, making a home. She worked hard on their land, slowly building up their own small compliment of ducks and chickens and planting a few fruit trees in sheltered spots at the back of their new home. Michael took care of their cattle, his beloved horses, and any maintenance or drainage issues, digging ditches, repairing the roof of the barn, fencing and marketing. Life was good and Mary counted her blessings each day.

In the early days of their marriage, two of Mary's brothers lived nearby, and Mary's brother Anthony was still living with her parents at the family home. He'd never met a girl that he liked enough to marry, and her ma' and da' were only too pleased to have his company and help on the farm. The family were a close-knit unit — they all enjoyed the blessings of having family nearby for support and companionship. They attended Mass on Sundays and on 'Holy days,' and Michael would drive into town, 'mid-week', with the eggs for the butcher, and then he and Robina, and sometimes Mary, would travel down and visit Michael's parents every now and then. They found comfort and security living in the traditional ways handed down by their families. There was laughter and plenty of love, they had all that they needed, it was enough!

Mass on Sundays was always an anchor for the two families. It had always sustained Faith during the hard times, and it taught Mary trust. She realised that despite the priest's outward grimness, he listened; he explained to her that God didn't expect her to have all the answers. For Michael, the teachings were a way of life, they told of a forgiving God and a heaven that he never doubted; for Eamon, Mass provided a discipline and a form of protection and offered him a blind, comforting acceptance and a way of belonging.

And for Robina, whilst she grew into a winsome 'fey' child, it helped her remain grounded. The christenings, confirmations, readings of the last rights, the respect and fear for the priest, the confessional that forgave their weaknesses — it was part of their core being. Sometimes, yes, it was boundary to be pushed against, but it gave them a sense of belonging and security.

CHAPTER 5

1973
Robina, Born to Michael and Mary Moran

Robina (1973), was raised as an only child, a precious only child, who spent much of her solitary youth looking for grey seals or staring up into the sky at the sea birds; twirling and spreading her arms, mimicking their flight as they screeched and whirled their way through the racing clouds. The seas around the north west coast were often dark and turbulent; she was exhilarated by the waves which were fierce and exciting, she loved the freedom and wildness of the coastline. The vastness of the sea touched her soul, it was her friend. The beach welcomed her, freed her from the stifling conventions of school and church and home. She would fly out at every opportunity and, when the waters were calm, her father took her with him on the motor boat. If the sea was too rough for 'his precious', then she would occupy the time curled up in one of the wooden shacks until his return, oblivious of time, popping the strings of sea weed pods, lining the sea snails up in a row for a race, watching for mermaids swimming on the crests of the waves or chatting to the spirits who were a part of her life, always in the shadows or sometimes solidly physical. Absorbed in her own reality, alone with the sea and sand and crashing of the waves, she would pass the hours in peace and comfort, unaware of being cold or hungry.

As a child, her mother had not been allowed to wander down to the sea alone. Her father Eamon had a fear of the ocean; he had refused to talk about it and when she pushed him too hard with her pleading he would shoot out of his chair and yell at her.

"I've told 'ya' so, now that's it."

That always put a stomach-churning stop to her hopes of joining her friends on an outing to the beach. He never chastised her with his belt as he did the boys — Faith would have taken it herself if it came to that — but Mary was resentful that she'd not been allowed the same freedoms as the boys had. Robina was given the freedom that her mother never had, whilst Michael made sure that she was raised with a healthy respect for the ocean's moods and the changing of the tides.

Robina treasured the land and her home. She loved the sweet scents of the grasses, the muskiness of the earth, the sweet hay, fragrance of the horses, and the way that they would munch away at their oats first thing in the morning. She was a help to her mother; often found amongst the hens and ducks, she would laughingly chase away the spiteful cockerel when he flew at her with his spurs in mid-flight. Mary would mutter "that bird will be having a date with my cooking pot if he carries on like this," but Robina would protest, "Mam, no."

A sensitive child, she struggled with the harshness and realities of nature and animal husbandry; when it all got too much she would run to her startled mother, frantically waving her arms in distress, and Mary would rush outside in panic, only to find one of the ducks waddling up from the stream with the wriggling legs of a frog hanging out of his greedy beak. At other times she refused to eat when she realised that the roast chicken dinner was the hen that had stopped producing eggs.

A child of the sea and the earth, Robina wandered in the fields around her home, losing all sense of time until the darkening skies or a whisper from her guardian angel cautioned her to make her way home. Very often she would return with an injured bird, or rabbit, or maybe a hedgehog that she'd found lying on the side of the lane. Michael would quietly look on as his daughter stroked and crooned softly to the creatures; he was amazed at the tender way that she handled them and wondered how he and Mary had produced 'such a child'. Lost in earnest healing and prayer she would need a prompt from her father to 'leave them be'. Wrapping them in her woolly jumper, she'd place them in a cardboard box, safe and warm, and put the box near the side of her bed, and she would cry heartily and bury them when they died.

Even as a baby she had a way of stopping passers-by, then a placid toddler that gave no trouble, and finally a delightful, fairy child, as delicate as gossamer; she shone her spiritual light on all around her.

And as from a young age, when Robina had struggled to understand the cruelty in the world or questioned the priest why God allowed people and animals to suffer and be in pain, she continued searching for answers.

Grannie Faith Boyle, Mary's mother, knew that her granddaughter was gifted, or 'fey' as she would have it. Robina was able to see the 'little people' as she once could as a young girl, but she had never questioned the child, believing that her granddaughter would share with her when she was ready.

It was clear to Mary too, that her daughter happily lived between the world of earth and spirit, but she was cautious about talking about such things with her husband, Michael, who'd himself noticed 'an oddness'. He'd laughingly explained away Robina's 'ways' as being the result of a vivid imagination; they were just the fancies of a child, and he took care not to laugh in front of her. He didn't want to make the child feel awkward or inhibited.

When Robina visited Faith and Eamon with her mother, as much as she loved her grandparents, she sometimes found the energy in their home to be full of sadness and tears and, finding it unbearable, she would hurriedly excuse herself and dash outside of the dark confines of their home into the cold air, where she would twirl with her arms outstretched until she became dizzy. The breeze would whip her long red hair around her, and she would lift her young face upwards to the vast skies and take deep breaths of clean air, instinctively boosting her energies.

Grandfather Eamon would look on in wonder and he would mutter and tut, "This child spends too much time on her own, our Mary". Grannie would laughingly dismiss his concern and Mary would hurriedly try to downplay her daughter's wildness.

"Ah, she's just a child, Father," and then quickly introduce a new snippet of gossip to distract his attention away from her daughter, and any further worrying speculation.

But Mary did have concerns and she ensured that she had some long talks with her only child about protecting herself with white light, reminding her that she could always stop and take charge if she became uncomfortable or uneasy. Mary was careful to emphasise that some folks would not understand Robina's ways, and that they may even be frightened or distressed by them.

Robina would listen impatiently for a short while, fidgeting, before exclaiming in frustration, "I hear voices in the wind mammie, listen! The fairies and elves, they call my name, they are calling me" and she'd be off, out of the door in a flash of excitement, without heeding the need of warm clothes, or whether it was 'lashing down with rain or no'.

Mary had respect for the Irish folklore that she grew up with; she was careful not to mock, and, in truth, she had some belief in the many tales whispered about the elemental kingdom. She had been raised to be wary, and Faith had warned her that to disregard the 'little people' would invite mischief or trouble into her home. Her beliefs were a mixture of God and his angels and all things fairy, as were many of those around.

She knew that Robina would not be happy unless she was able to channel her caring nature, and as Robina grew into a woman, she understood that her ability to recognise when a family pet or wildlife were sick was not shared by all. In public, to protect her daughter, Mary would quietly downplay Robina's ability to bring healing and comfort. Robina's experiences with the fourth dimension didn't diminish as she grew. They continued, but she was protective of her 'friends' and she tried to follow her mother's example, avoiding any behaviours that attracted attention or her Grandad Eamon's scorn.

Robina developed into a lovely young woman, graceful and slender, and she turned many a young man's head. With the pureness of her milky-white complexion dusted with amber freckles on the bridge of her small nose, her flowing, red, wavy hair that tumbled down her back and over her shoulders, her twinkling turquoise-blue eyes that held their gaze in all innocence, and her father's wide generous smile, she was stunning.

At the age of sixteen, after achieving good results in all her chosen ten subjects, and receiving her Junior Certificate, she continued to study with determination and interest. She skipped her transition year, sailed through her senior cycle of learning and at the age of eighteen she passed her finals and was ready to begin her training as a student nurse. It was all that she wanted to be, for Robina viewed that there was no greater privilege than to serve and to help bring some comfort into a world of suffering and conflict. Michael and Mary agreed with her choice, although with some reservations; for their daughter was caring, yes, but they knew that a nursing career would demand stamina and a strong mental disposition, and Robina had always been such a delicate and protected child.

What did shake them was their daughter's resolve to study and train in the UK, and no amount of discussion and persuasion was effective enough to change her initial choice to, instead, taking up her nurse training at home.

Michael was very unhappy with this situation but a strange coincidence, or some might call it synchronicity, led to a change of heart and some lessening of their unease. Michael and James were playing a 'gig' at a local hotel when they happened to bump into an old school friend of Michael's. The men hadn't been in each other's company for few good years. Over a few drinks Michael listened intently to the story of the many opportunities at university in England, and how his pal's daughter had been one of the first student nurses to take up the new nurse training curriculum, instead of taking one of the old apprentice- type training courses at the local hospitals.

"Why, our Claire will finish with a diploma or even a degree after her three years," he'd boasted. "It's a great opportunity and I would only encourage your daughter to take this road, that is, if she has the grades to be accepted," he'd added smugly.

Michael did not have any concerns that Robina's qualifications would not be accepted. That evening, on his return, he and Mary had discussed the surprising 'meeting up'. The result was that both parents concluded that, at some level, this was a confirmation or a guidance that Robina had made the right choice. Robina was relieved that her parents had finally relented and applied immediately to three different universities in England. Following an anxious wait, she was delighted to be offered a place at Liverpool University, where she would be joining Claire on a Nursing Diploma course starting in September that same year.

The family met up for a small going away party at Robina's home, with both sets of grandparents; Michael's parents Brendon and Elizabeth, and Mary's parents Eamon and Faith, the now elderly priest, Father John, Michael's brother James and Mary's brother Daniel, and a few of the nearby neighbours and two of Robina's school friends. They celebrated far into the night. The fiddles played wildly, the jigging was lively, the food was tasty and plentiful, and finally, just before dawn, Mary sang a high, clear, haunting ballad accompanied by Michael strumming on his guitar, which brought the night of celebration to an end.

They left for Dublin at six a.m. — the whole family, including the elderly grandparents, were squashed into two old farm vehicles, but spirits were high even though there were a few with sore heads. Robina's uncle, Daniel, took the wheel of the first car, Grandad Eamon sat in the front passenger seat, giving his son directions which were quietly ignored, and Faith and her granddaughter sat immediately behind him.

"Now Robina, just a few words of advice for you, because you'll be meeting all sorts of folks in this big city of Liverpool. Keep good company, keep your own counsel when you see or hear anything that you don't like, listen enough so that you are in the picture, so to speak, then, if you have too, get yourself away, otherwise there are some that'll drag you down."

Leaning forward she hugged him close to her, the lemon- scented, waxy gel that he used to settle his still unruly head of wiry hair was greasy against her face and for a moment she was filled with a moment of panic. Faith sensed her granddaughter's reaction and she caressed the softness of her granddaughter's hand and gave it a reassuring squeeze,

"You'll be fine, Robina, you are going to train at Liverpool University Hospital and you will be staying with your father's friend's daughter Claire — she's doing well and already in her second year. There will be a lot to learn but you are a bright young lady, and you can always telephone or write; your home and family are only eight hours away at that," she comforted.

Robina took in a deep breath. "That's right, Grandma and Grandad, I'll be fine, and I'm going to work hard and make the world a better place. You'll be proud of me."

Uncle Daniel started to hum a tune and the conversations halted as the car bumped over the potholes in the narrow road, each lost in their own thoughts as they stared out of the dusty windows at the dark early morning sky slowly developing into a pale watery shade of pink and orange. They stopped for a break and Mary passed around coffee and thick, buttered sandwiches, for they were determined to make a day of it. With 'the old ones' becoming older, and the rest of them being busy with the animals and land it was rare that both sides of the family ever met up together, let alone took a trip into Dublin, well, the women folk at least. Once the food was eaten up, they chatted about the great British city of Liverpool and how it was home to two of the most famous Premier League football clubs, Liverpool FC and Everton FC, and Aintree Racecourse, which famously hosted the Grand National horse race every year.

Finally, Robina left Ireland on the ferry from the busy Port of Dublin the following afternoon. She and her grandparents, her parents and both uncles James and Daniel, stood waiting together in the cold, crisp air, made colder by the icy breeze blowing in from the Irish sea. Michael and Mary held hands to calm any last-minute doubts that they had about Robina's choice to venture away from all that she had known for the last eighteen years. Their cherished, protected daughter was shaking with excitement, she was bubbling with chatter, confident and ready to make the world a better place, and blindly accepting her family's blessing, she did not presuppose that life in a city in the UK would be so very different. Michael clasped her baggage close to him as if to reassure himself in some way. He was reluctant to release her spanking new collection of red suitcases and her holdall, heavily packed with her favourite keepsakes, clothes, books, gifts of cash from both sets of grandparents, and hidden in the corner, with Michael's insistence, his Bible.

PART 2

Robina's Life and Family in the UK

CHAPTER 6

Robina, Moses, Liverpool

Robina's ferry arrived at the Port of Liverpool on the eastern side of the river Mersey at nine p.m. that evening. When she eventually disembarked thirty minutes later it was cold and dark, and the breeze drove sharp needles of rain into her face and hair as she anxiously looked around for Claire, the student nurse who she was expecting to meet her off the ferry. She suddenly realised that she had no idea what Claire looked like, for it was her father that had made the travel arrangements. Worried and shivering, it seemed an age before she heard a welcoming shout from behind her!

"Hello there, Robina, I'm truly sorry that I'm late. I had planned to get off my shift early, but things turned upside down at the last minute."

Robina spun around in relief and was met by a plump dark-haired female wearing a very wet raincoat and spectacles that were misted up with rain. She rushed forward and shook her hand.

"I'm Claire — come on, let's get ourselves out of this weather. We've a lift over there with Moses; he's one of the hospital porters and he took pity on me and gave me a lift when he saw the wet state I was in. I'd been standing at that bus stop for ages."

A tall, dark young man rushed forward and, smiling broadly, he shook Robina's cold hand before grabbing hold of her luggage and piling it into the boot of his car. Claire opened the back-passenger door and ushered Robina inside; laughing sheepishly she climbed in the front passenger seat next to Moses.

The journey to the centre of Liverpool was exciting. Robina continually wiped the moisture from the window as she looked out into the lights and the heavy traffic. Moses hummed along with the radio and Claire carried on a shouted, excited, conversation from her seat in the front of the car, proudly relating the responsibilities that she held as a second-year student nurse, expressing her relief that she had passed her assignments so far, and finally how very pleased she was to have a friend from home to join her and of the fun that they would both have sharing in the same house.

"One word of warning, Robina, my father's not to know of my partying; he wouldn't approve, so no tales back home," she laughingly cautioned.

Suddenly the car screeched to a halt on the wet road and Moses pulled up outside a small end terraced property.

"I'll help you in then; open up, Claire, and I'll bring the suitcase in."

It was late in the evening when they finally pushed their way into the small hallway. Moses dumped the cases down at the bottom of the stairs before turning to take his leave. It was the first time that Robina had managed to see him clearly. She was struck by the physical appearance of this handsome, golden guy; he was tall and brown and almost beautiful, and his rich, deep voice and warm, shining brown eyes were full of laughter and welcome.

Moses was equally captivated by the delicate young women standing in front of him. Her turquoise eyes met his briefly as she gazed up at him, bashfully, and thanked him sincerely in a lilting Irish accent, whilst shaking her thick flowing red locks out of her jacket.

Claire bustled in, unaware of the sudden awkwardness between them.

"Right then, we'll have some cocoa and then I'll show you to your room. It's late and I'm on an early shift tomorrow; I'll see you out Moses, thanks again. 'I'll see you right' at the pub tomorrow".

The girls sat together at the kitchen table, happily munching ginger biscuits and drinking mugs of hot cocoa. Robina liked what she saw of Claire, who, now she had dried off, had the bushiest, curliest, black hair that seemed to have a life of its own and thick, shapely eyebrows that expressed every emotion as she chatted and laughed with a cigarette in one hand and a biscuit in the other. Robina was almost mesmerised by the energy that exuded from her new companion, and she wandered how Claire would ever be up and ready in the morning for her nursing duties.

It was near midnight before Robina climbed into bed. Leaving her suitcases opened but unpacked in the corner of the room, she took what she needed: her towel and toothbrush, pink pyjamas and her father's bible that she discovered hidden under her dressing gown in the corner. She hugged it next to her; the brown leather cover was faded and worn and the pages tissue thin and yellowed, but despite her tiredness she decided that she would read a little just for a short while, for she loved the beauty of the Psalms. It had been her 'father's way' to read his bible at the kitchen table each night before he turned in, and as a child she had often crept out of bed and joined him.

Back home Michael and Mary were tucked up in their own bed. For the first time in years they were alone, and the house was missing the energy of its absent third inhabitant.

Moses was sitting alone in his bedsit, listening to the late radio broadcast and thinking of the 'angel' that had arrived tonight. He was in no rush to sleep; he was not due into work until the afternoon — it was his turn on the late shift. Closing his eyes as he drew on his cigarette, he pictured her milky-white complexion and shy, gentle smile, her turquoise-blue eyes framed by thick, curled lashes, and the way in which she had placed her small hand gently on his arm when she had gazed directly into his eyes and thanked him in her sing-song, clear Irish lilt.

Moses was almost twenty-one years old. Unlike Robina, with her extended family, he had been raised in an orphanage with his younger brother Samuel, following the sudden death of their father, Samson, who was killed in an accident at the docks.

CHAPTER 7

Moses and His Parents, Samson and Alannah

In 1960, Moses's father, Samson, was just twenty years of age when he joined thousands of others from the Commonwealth countries, on the invitation of the British government, to emigrate to Britain and help build post war Britain. Samson was given his British citizenship and was keen to find the well-paid work and riches that so many other Caribbean immigrants had been promised before him. He'd left his parents and extended family back in the West Indies and had never found the time or money to visit home since his arrival in Britain. He moved from the Midlands up to Liverpool to find better paid work on the docks, where he'd met Alannah, who was living-in with a middle-class family and working as a 'mothers help' and housemaid.

Neither of them had any other family in England.

Alannah was born out of wedlock and raised by nuns back in Ireland who had found her a post and, at the age of eighteen, she'd joined a family in Liverpool where she had been settled and happy until she met Samson.

Her employers disapproved of the mixed-race relationship. Samson was black and she Irish, and when gossip began in their middle-class neighbourhood,

Alannah was promptly asked to leave her employment and not given any references. Her employers were keen to keep 'this shocking news' away from their three children and associates. The relationship was doubly disapproved of in a middle-class society that looked down on Irish and Black immigrants. The family, being aware that their help had been born illegitimate, had thought themselves to be doing their Christian duty in taking her in, and 'Mother' now declared that Alannah's bad blood was outing.

Defiant, and in the face of the narrow-minded judgements and prejudice, they married in 1969, Alannah now twenty-four, and Samson twenty-nine. Not having any other family in England, they cleaved together, cherished each other, a young couple so much in love, and determined to make a life together in the face of the bigotry and ignorance that they faced each day.

The couple rented a room in a terraced house shared with three other couples, sharing a toilet and kitchen and a tin bath, but in a short time, with Samson's wages, they were able to improve their lot and rent two rooms and a kitchen and bathroom. They were making a good start for themselves. They didn't mix with other 'whites' but built up their own circle of friends amongst the other West Indian families, working and living happily together.

They had their two sons, Moses and then Samuel, within the first two years of their marriage. Both boys were under the age of three when Samson was tragically killed in an accident at work — crushed by a falling crate dropped from an overhead crane. Alannah was bereft and frightened, a widow, without any income and without family support. Unable to find work whilst she had to care for the boys, her only option had been to take them to the Catholic orphanage; accept their disapproval and beg for help.

With full intentions of returning, she'd hugged her boys, promising to take them out when she 'was set up'. But despite sending letters and leaving them photographs of herself and their father, she never did collect them. From the ages of two years and twenty months, the orphanage was the only home and family that Moses and his brother Samuel knew.

Moses had lived independently since he was 'put out' into the adult world at the age of sixteen, and his brother had joined him a year later for a short while until, searching for security again, Samuel had joined the armed forces at the age of eighteen. Despite his brother's encouragement to enlist with him, this choice was not to Moses's personal liking. He enjoyed his independence. Free from the restrictions and institutionalised living of the orphanage, he now only had himself to please and care about, and he was keen to stay this way; earning a wage as a porter gave him enough for all that he needed, and he was never short of female company. But this meeting with Robina, and the intenseness of emotion that had followed, or 'whatever it was' that he was feeling, was new to him.

"Easy, and always ready to have fun," that was Moses, and he was careful to present this persona to the world. He lived from payday to payday, staying on the hospital site in the porters' lodge. He allowed life to flow around him, confident in his ability to deal with whatever life placed in front of him. The patients and staff adored him; he brought warmth and graciousness to the sometimes cold, clinical settings. His generous spirit and caring heart led him into difficulties when he became too emotionally attached to patients, and staff would sometimes have to 'have a firm word' with him when he was showing too keen an interest. On occasions, these behaviours would bring him to the notice of matron, especially when he was found sneaking in food or cigarettes. He was always most apologetic and eventually forgiven. The elderly matron was sure that this wonderful young man, with his bright spirit and easy manner, meant no harm, and his sunny nature and dedication to his work made him indispensable as a member of her ancillary team.

Moses was very aware of his magnetism, especially amongst the women that shared his working environment, but his need for freedom and independence up to now had taken precedence over any inclination to tangle in anything deep and meaningful. He was never involved with any female for more than two or three dates.

Alone in his bedsit, he reached for another cigarette. Moses found that he just couldn't shake off the image of this almost ethereal female that he had met up with tonight. His intuition whispered that there was going to be a powerful happening in his life; it would not be ignored. He drew on his cigarette deeply, as waves of excitement and unease washed over him.

Laughingly, he spoke out into the empty room. "Man, something strange is going on here — what's happening to me?"

CHAPTER 8

Robina, Claire and Teddy

Robina couldn't fight sleep any longer. The Bible dropped onto the rug beside the bed. She was oblivious of the impact that she had made this evening, but she did hope, just a little maybe, that 'he' had noticed her. Gazing out of the tiny window, she stared up at the night sky and whispered, "Mammie, oh, my heart! He is 'soooo' beautiful."

The slam of the front door closing downstairs woke Robina with a start and she turned over sleepily and glanced at her wristwatch on the bedside table — six thirty a.m.! Realising that it was Claire leaving for a seven thirty a.m. start on the medical ward, she slid back down the bed and pulled the duvet over her head.

It wasn't long before the din of the buses trundling past and the windowpanes vibrating at an alarming rate woke her for a second time. So, pushing her feet into a pair of fluffy socks she ventured downstairs and into the tiny kitchen. Switching to BBC Radio 1, she made herself a pot of tea and toasted two crumpets, and then sat herself down at the kitchen table, lost in thought. She could hardly believe that she was here at last, eager and ready to begin her nursing career.

Robina would be one of the September intake of student nurses at the university; she'd just two days until the term began. Today she would visit the campus and the university library and probably have coffee in town after unpacking her cases. She was restless and keen to explore the town.

Claire had offered to introduce her to a few friends, and they were going to 'drop in' at the local at the corner of the road this evening. Robina was nervous — she enjoyed socializing when she was familiar with the people or surroundings but meeting a crowd of strangers in one setting was daunting. She'd always been very protected at home. The possibility that Moses might be in their company too set her pulse racing, and with a surge of energy she jumped up and ran up the stairs two at a time, hurriedly pulled jeans and jumper and underwear out of her case and switched the shower on high.

The hot water streamed down her face and lithe body as she prayed earnestly. "I'm going to be the best nurse ever. Mighty God, thank you for this opportunity to bring healing and love into people's lives. I won't let you down, dear angels; this is my new life of service and caring, please stay with me on my journey, and take care of everyone at home for me."

She made a quick call home on the landline at the bottom of the stairs, apologising for not making a call last night because it would have been too late, and they would have been in their beds. Mary wanted to know what the house was like — was it clean, was her bed comfortable? How near was the house to the university and hospital? Had she eaten and was there any food in the house?

"Mammie, it's all lovely," she replied, "Claire will be splendid company, I'm going out to eat now, and I will find the shops and bring back some food. Tell Dad that I found his bible in the corner of my suitcase and I have my rosary and my amethyst crystal under my pillow; I will be fine and safe, and you mustn't worry."

Finishing the conversation as quickly as she could without causing offence, Robina pulled on her new green duffle coat and brown ankle boots and shut the door behind her.

Despite only being the third week in September, some of the leaves were already falling from the trees that uniformly lined the row of elderly terraced houses. The sky above was a dull blanket of grey, with only a watery sun offering any warmth. Robina was surprised by the noise of the traffic, and the sheer volume of cars and lorries that rushed by so closely. Although she was keeping to the pavement, it was narrow, and she found herself nervously skimming closely to the front garden walls. The dismal greyness and dampness of the city air didn't lower her spirit, despite her usual hypersensitivity to her environment. She was energised with hope and wrapped in the love and security that home had always provided. Her heart was full of the light of kindness and compassion, and she purposely breathed in deeply and slowly as she walked, to calm her excitement and nerves. As she neared the university and turned the corner, the tall grey Victorian hospital building came suddenly into sight; she stared upwards in excitement — this was to be where she would spend the next three years of her life.

Before she knew it, the day had rolled on to late afternoon and she was feeling elated and excited after the visit to the university. Busying herself in the kitchen she was startled out of her reverie as the doorbell rang loudly and repeatedly, and Robina dropped the tea towel onto the kitchen floor as she rushed to answer.

"Coming! Oh, it's you, Claire, I wasn't sure what time your shift would finish — do you not have a key?" Robina asked in surprise.

Shaking her wet coat, Claire smiled apologetically. "Thank goodness that you are home, and yes," she answered hurriedly, "but I forgot the blasted thing — oh, something smells nice" and she rushed forward into the kitchen, eagerly following the spicy aroma of fresh coffee. Clapping her frozen hands, she gasped in delight at the sight of the mouth-watering bacon joint bubbling away in a huge saucepan and the heavy round of soda bread cooling on the baking tray.

"Oh, my Lord, am I in my Mammie's kitchen? Can this really be happening?"

Robina laughed, explaining that she had been for a 'rekey' that morning, had a walk around the university and hospital site and on returning home, finding that there wasn't much in the freezer, she had returned to the supermarket and brought back a few things 'just to tide us over'.

The girls sat around the kitchen table and broke the warm soda bread into quarters and covered it with thick butter, cut the bacon joint as best they could because Claire couldn't find the bread knife, and finished the spicy coffee and made more. They spent a pleasant two hours, chatting and giggling; Claire reminiscing about her home and parents and Robina inquisitive about the nursing course and asking countless questions about the medical ward that her new friend would be working on for the next eight weeks.

Finally, it was time to clear the dishes and for Claire to have a short rest before joining 'the crowd' at the pub.

Robina passed the next hour reading through the university prospectus before making a short entry in her diary, a habit that she'd continued from that age of twelve, when her mother had made her a present of her first diary; purple, embellished with silvery butterflies and water nymphs with gossamer wings. She had faithfully written in it every day, recording her hopes and anxieties, her sightings of the 'little people', her strange dreams and the stirrings of her developing womanhood. She'd escaped the sometimes-harsh realities of life by pouring out her anger and pain onto its pages — it gave her comfort and release.

The protection of a loving home hadn't always hidden what went on around her; the slaughtering of livestock, the coarse comments made by the boys at school and the whispers and taunts from other pupils about her 'oddness', her unwillingness to take part in the teasing and bullying of others that 'had little', and finally her slightness and late development of womanly attributes which set her aside.

The diary was her friend. She hadn't shared her experiences with her parents; she hadn't wanted to upset them or cause 'a row'. Her dad was always fiercely protective, and she'd dreaded him finding out what went one on. She always feared that he would create 'bedlam' up at the school.

Right now, the warm kitchen and the effects of the heavy meal, the travelling and change of air made her drowsy. Her head slumped onto her folded arms and she slept peacefully until a loud shriek interrupted her rest.

"Holy Mother!" Jumping up from her seat at the table she knocked the chair over, only to be startled by another wail and the kitchen door flying open. A streak of grey fur jumped up onto the table and snatched a slice of cooked meat off the carving plate before slinking away with its trophy. Recovering her equilibrium, Robina laughed in relief, kneeling beside the table she investigated further. A pair of amber eyes met the turquoise gaze with a challenging stare, and the intruder gripped onto his 'prize' with fierce determination.

"Well, and who have we here? Come on out, puss, I won't hurt you," she coaxed gently. "Come on out, I don't want your meat, come," she invited.

Slowly, still unsure, but eventually responding to Robina's gentle persuasion, the furry visitor crept out from under the table and darted towards the corner of the tiny kitchen where he greedily pulled at the ham and devoured it, all the time keeping his watchful gaze on Robina. Creeping forward, Robina knelt before him; smiling and murmuring reassurance she leant forward and softly stroked his lean body, all the time gazing into his face and continuing to silently communicate her love and promise that she meant him no harm.

There was no doubt that this creature was needing help. She was distressed at his obvious need for food, his coat was patchy and in poor condition and, as he allowed her to gather him up in her arms, she was overwhelmed by a nauseating odour from exudate that had dried in a crust on his tail. Robina huskily hummed and whispered. Her hands tingled with heat as she stroked and poured out her healing energy of compassion and light. She was totally oblivious of the time that passed between the creature's entrance to her world and her linking with spirit to bring comfort in the way that had been instinctive to her for as long as she remembered. Searching on his collar for a name tag, she was not surprised to 'draw a blank', and she finally placed the purring 'patient' onto her coat in the corner, making a mindful commitment to ask Claire about him when she woke.

The calm of the moment was eventually broken by Claire clambering down the stairs and bursting into the kitchen with a yawn and exclamation that she had needed that rest and now she was 'ready for some fun'.

Her rumbustious entrance brought Robina back from her reverie with a sickening jolt. "Are you off to get ready? We'll be meeting the rest in a couple of hours. I bumped into Moses just before I finished 'my early' and it seems that you've made quite an impression on him," she giggled, as she leant over the sink and filled the kettle for tea.

"Yes, I'll go up in a minute," Robina replied hurriedly, "but I need to ask you something first. Just who does this poor creature belong to, Claire, for he's in a dreadful condition and he needs to get to a vet quickly; surely, he's not yours is he?" she asked reproachfully.

Claire turned towards her, puzzled, and then, noticing the sleeping bundle stretched out on the coat under the window, she exclaimed in horror, "How on earth did he get in here? No, he's not my cat, he's been hanging around since the neighbours did a 'moonlight flit' two months ago. I've been putting out saucers of food and milk for him, but I've not been able to catch him. How did you ever manage to coax him to come in?" Claire gasped. "Let alone calm him down enough to sleep."

"Perhaps he crept in this morning when I left the door ajar when I ran back upstairs for my purse. He tore into the kitchen and I nearly had heart failure I can tell you that," laughed Robina. "But seriously, he's in a bad way and we need to help him quickly — do you know if there is a vet's nearby? For I couldn't go out enjoying myself tonight knowing that he was in this sorry state."

"Well, I believe there is a practice just ten minutes away but how are you going to manage him? He won't let me near him, and we haven't a cat's basket or anything," Claire pondered. "Besides which, vet's fees aren't cheap, and I'm broke until I receive my next bursary at the end of the month," she added apologetically.

"Don't worry about that, I have 'some pennies' from my da' and I'll put him in that shopping bag on wheels that is in the cupboard under the stairs. Can you telephone and explain for me, Claire, and I'll quickly change? If I miss tonight then there will be many more," and with that Robina took the stairs two at a time and left Claire staring in wonder.

"I can see that I'm going to have an eventful time with this miss. To give up her first night out for a stray cat, and her knowing that the 'gorgeous Moses' is interested in her too! Can you believe that?" Claire muttered to herself, as she wondered off to find the telephone number for the vet.

Two hours later, Robina found herself alone in the house, apart from her new friend who she had decided to re-name Teddy. Their trip to the practice had been a struggle, with the terrified cat trying to claw himself out from the confines of his 'prison', the tartan bag on wheels, the zipper being closed as a necessity to keep him confined and safe from darting out into the busy road. Robina had certainly made an entrance as she serenely pushed through the automatic door with its 'Welcome to the Practice' sign, seemingly oddly incongruent with the meows and screeching and bumping and banging going on inside her trolley. Smiling, she had struggled to the reception desk and announced to the startled veterinary nurse, "Robina Moran and Teddy — we have an urgent appointment."

'Teddy' was now warm and comfortable in his new 'cat igloo' which Robina had purchased from the vet, along with a beautiful indigo collar with his own shiny identity tag, a course of steroids for his skin condition, a shampoo for his coat and a treatment for fleas and parasites, and, finally, pouches of food and a cat litter tray. Dad's money had very useful, although she wasn't sure if that was what he had intended when he had put the envelope into her hand and whispered, "A little for a rainy day, my love."

Claire had rushed out to meet her friends without a second thought that perhaps leaving her new companion alone on her first evening was maybe a little 'mercenary'. Robina had insisted that she would be fine in the house alone; she was comfortable with her own company and any slight disappointment that she was feeling was more than made up for by Teddy, and besides she wanted to treat him carefully for the next few days at least. She had set up the cat litter tray near the back door and her plan was to try and keep him as a house cat until a trusting relationship with him could be established. She knew that would take a while, at least until he was sure that he would be provided food and shelter and so would not have any need to wander again.

Slightly restless, now that Teddy was sleeping off the effects of the sedation that he'd been given to aid his examination, and the full stomach of food, Robina wandered around the house, peeking out of the back-bedroom windows into neighbouring gardens, and then moving round to the front of the house and looking out onto the busy street.

The September nights had not completely 'drawn in' and it was not yet 'lighting up' time for another hour. She loved the softness of this twilight time; for her it meant that the day and its problems were nearly done — 'the waning of the day' Grannie Boyle had called it! Back home in Ireland she had often slipped outside and wandered in the evening silence; for her it was a magical experience. Quietly, keeping very still, she'd watch the rabbits and other wildlife come out to feed and hunt, hearing the scuttling and giggles and whispers of the elemental beings who were also peeking at her, nervously hiding in the bushes nearby, wondering in excitement whether she would discover them, and if in fact this was the human that could actually 'see them'. For Robina, twilight was a time when the dimensions merged, and as a child she had sometimes been drawn into this fascinating world to the point where she didn't want to leave its beauty.

Sighing, she wandered into her small bedroom and glanced around. A beautiful setting was important to her; she hated ugliness and the newly painted grey emulsion walls lacked warmth. She was reminded of other bleak days when the sky was just a low blanket of steel grey, when there were no clouds or movement of any sort other than an icy cold 'mizzle' that soaked her clothes and dampened her spirit.

Jumping off the bed, Robina decided to make a few changes. She needed to create a space that would represent her belief in positive energy and magic. Feverishly dashing around, she collected a few brown stones from the gravel path in the backyard, she filled a small blue jug with water, arranged her crystals in a circle on her dresser, placed rosemary twigs in the jug, and polished the pebbles until they shone amber and chestnut and grey. Climbing onto a chair, she hung a purple silk head scarf above her bed and sprinkled her favourite patchouli oil on her duvet and rug and finally, lighting a joss stick, she placed it safely on the hearth of the empty fireplace. The finishing touches were her carved figurines of Archangel Raphael and Archangel Michael which she placed on her windowsill. They represented healing and protection and as she smoothed her hands around them, she asked for their help and guidance in her new life and nursing career.

Her spirits raised, she crept into the kitchen and found Teddy stretched out on top of her green duffle coat. Bending to lift him, he raised his head and licked her with his rough tongue; she laughed as his whiskers tickled her cheek. They sat in comfort, only Teddy's purring breaking the silence, until the shrill ring of the doorbell cut into their peace and the startled the cat disappeared back into his new bed.

CHAPTER 9

Out and About

Hurriedly opening the door, Robina was surprised to find a tall, lithe figure leaning inside the porch.

"Moses! I thought that you were meeting Claire at the pub."

"It seemed a shame that you were spending your first night alone. I hope you don't mind, but it didn't feel right and just finishing my late shift I was nearby so, well?" He jerked his head towards his car and laughed, showing the gold in his top side tooth.

Robina dragged her senses back to the reality of everyday life. Gathering her wits, she apologised and asked him inside. "Come on in, please."

Removing his woolly hat, he stood awkwardly, unusually lost for words. He smiled down at the girl who had been on his mind for every minute of the day since he had met her last night. Robina watched as the energy between them sparkled in the darkness. She faintly managed to murmur a whispered, "Thank you, I'll get my coat then shall I — oh no, Teddy has my coat! I'll just fetch my pullover; it's kind of you, Moses, I think that a little company will be fine."

With a final hurried peek at Teddy, she closed the front door behind her into the night.

Laughter and heat poured out onto the street as the heavy door to the bar swung open to meet them. For a second, Robina stood frozen like a rabbit in a headlight. Moses followed just behind and noticed her uncertainty. He smiled in encouragement and urged her forward.

"They're a noisy lot, aren't they — here, grab this table and I'll get us some drinks. What would you like?"

"I'll have a ginger beer please," Robina replied, gazing around the crowded bar in wonder. She sat quietly, waiting for Moses to return, watching his tall figure launch himself through the 'bodies' to get to the bar. A friendly, recognisable shout broke into her thoughts and Claire launched herself down onto the chair besides her. Robina was relieved to be greeted by another familiar face.

Claire welcomed her enthusiastically. "Hey, I'm glad that you made it." Seeing Moses at the bar she called out to him, "Get me a lager please, Mo'."

Claire eagerly snatched a lager from Moses and downed the frothy, brown liquid thirstily. "I'll square up next week when I have my bursary paid into my account."

Moses laughed good-naturedly, and then, glancing at Robina, he placed her glass down carefully in front of her. "And one ginger beer for 'the lady'."

Robina's delicate fingers stretched around the pint glass of ginger beer awkwardly. She drank self-consciously, surprised that the ginger beer could taste so fiery — very different from Mary's 'earthy' homemade brew that was served with Sunday lunch at home. Glancing up, she met Moses's quizzical gaze and she explained hurriedly, "This is fine, really, thank you, it's just a surprise, I mean, it's only 'pop' right?"

"It's alcoholic, Robina, it's ginger beer, not 'pop'!" Claire mocked.

Blushing, embarrassed and feeling stupid, Robina wished that she had stayed at home with Teddy after all.

Annoyed at Claire's insensitivity, Moses reached forward and reassuringly squeezed Robina's hand, his brown eyes meeting the deep blueness of her gaze. Cautioning Claire with a warning glance he apologised. "I should have asked. I assumed you meant beer — would you like a glass of lemonade and ice? Or a coke maybe?"

Flicking her thick auburn mane of hair back off her face, she giggled, "No, beer is fine, it was just a surprise," and she took a large gulp, leaving the froth above her lip like a moustache.

Claire smiled at her friend slyly. "I can see that you'll be an attraction in here, Robina. Those two lads in the corner haven't taken their eyes off you since you walked in."

Moses twisted around and he swallowed hard! Medics! Second year house officers just let loose on the wards and already keen to make use of the student nurses to provide their female entertainment. He had seen it before; two guys from very different social backgrounds, oozing confidence on the ward, and off. He knew they studied and practiced long hours — it was expected of them and he accepted this with grace, but they treated the junior female staff as if they were their personal 'provisions', and from what he'd seen of Robina's trusting nature and learnt from Claire about her friend's protected, rural upbringing, well, he didn't want them 'messing' with her.

Naively unaware of her very physical beauty and the interest that she was creating, she nodded her head politely, smiling shyly at the two young men looking over, for she lived her nature naturally. She followed her feelings as instinctively as did the 'ebb and flow of the tide', she wasn't aware that this could be taken as anything other than being well-mannered.

"Christ," Claire muttered, "don't encourage them over Robina; they caused havoc with two of our student nurses last year — they'll charm you and leave you and before you know it, you'll be behind with your studies, trust me!"

Robina laughed and, dismissing Claire's damning statement, she shook her head. "Oh Claire, you have no need to be protective of me. I have a big heart, yes, but that doesn't mean that I'm going to let anything get in the way of my nursing career. For goodness sake, I had enough of Mam and Dad 'watching' my every turn."

Moses moved his seat nearer in to the girls; maybe they would take the hint that they weren't exactly welcome at this table.

He didn't care about position or authority. He accepted that his position as a member of ancillary staff, a porter at that, meant that he was at everybody's beck and call! It suited him just now — he enjoyed the freedom and absence of responsibility; he had no interest in chasing wealth or status, not just now anyway. He saw these as trappings of a society that he never wanted to be a part of. He was self-assured and held a vague plan that at some future point he would find a profession and make something of himself.

However, despite his air of gentle adaptability and charm, he had a hidden level of determination and drive; to become master of his own career and fate, he just hadn't discovered which path he would follow yet. Abandoned at an early age, the frustration of following the rules and expectations of adults who had dutifully, but not lovingly, shaped his young life, had left Moses with a swirling complex need and ambition.

The 'medics' took note of Moses's territorial move, and despite Claire's alarm that they were about to slope in on her unassuming friend, they were content to enjoy the atmosphere and the music blaring from the jukebox and appreciate the view from afar. They were keen to 'lie low' — last year's stern reprimand about their behaviour not meeting the ethical standards that were expected of someone in their profession was fresh in their minds. They'd noticed the buxom dark-haired, pretty colleen on the wards last year, but this red haired beauty was surely made to create havoc in their world! She was something else! They'd bide their time.

Robina smoothed down the sides of her empty glass. Claire laughed "Would you like another drink?" Robina was hesitant and unsure whether that meant she would have to push through the wall of bodies to the bar.

Moses graced her with a winning smile. "No, my shout, it's your first night out with us. What would you ladies like?"

Robina sneaked a peak to her left to her neighbour's pint of black Guinness. "Well, if I'm going to have alcohol, I would like what he is having please."

"Make that two, please, Moses," Claire assented, with a broad smile.

Savouring the first sip, Robina thanked Moses. "Delicious." Claire nodded in agreement — maybe they would have some fun together after all.

The music was good; the crowd were singing along to the blaring rock and blues and tapping their feet. A few couples were trying to dance amongst the jostle and heat of bodies. Slowly, bit by bit, the crowded room thinned out, and a male voice called out, "Give us a song, Claire!" The request was seconded by loud knocking on the tables, and whistles and shouts of encouragement.

Robina wasn't surprised; it was a frequent occurrence back home that someone would give a song as the night and the effects of alcohol wore on.

Claire made her way over to the bar and was handed a small glass of ruby liquid which she took in one shot and then turned to face her friends.

"Will you start me off then, Willy?" she called out to a stocky fair-haired male, who immediately obliged by joining her and striking a chord on his guitar.

Claire's dark eyes sparkled, her cheeks were a high red with the effects of the rum that she had downed in one and she confidently began in a strong clear voice; the traditional Irish ballads had the effect of quieting the chatter and drawing the attention of everyone in the room.

"Robina, come on over and join me," she called out enthusiastically. For a moment her new house mate hesitated and shifted her feet nervously, but with continued yells from others and feeling more confident she asked Moses, "Shall I go?"

Not waiting for an answer, for the question was aimed mostly at herself, she squeezed past him to free herself, and he found himself looking straight into the piercing blue eyes that had haunted him ever since he'd gazed at her for the first time, last night.

The girls hurriedly consulted together and whispered their choice to the fair-haired guy in the tartan shirt. He then nodded, and began strumming out a rhythm on his guitar to accompany the popular country song. On the last verse, Claire excused herself and rushed off, whispering, "A call of nature," leaving Robina startled, standing alone with the guitarist, facing the many expectant faces. For a moment she was tempted to rush back to the anonymity of her seat but decided against it. They were a jolly crowd and they'd given a friendly welcome to this pretty, delicate young girl, who had materialised in their company tonight. Besides she had always loved joining in the harmonies at family gatherings, and she'd inherited Mary's clear melodious tone; so, with a raised eyebrow and a smile from the guitarist she suggested her choice and he nodded.

He softly picked out the chords and Robina's gentle, haunting rendition silenced the crowd in seconds. The melody flooded Moses's senses with intense emotions of sadness, and fuelled a fire in his belly that shook him to the core.

At her invite her audience joined in the choruses, but not Moses! He was mesmerised — he couldn't take his eyes off her, and his interest was noticed with amusement by those around him.

His pal, Johnny, sidled up to him and smiling slyly he asked, "All right mate?"

"I believe that I have fallen in love with a woman that I've only just met," he laughed quietly.

For once, Johnny was lost for words!

CHAPTER 10

What a Surprise

Robina was roused the next morning by the roughness of a warm tongue and insistent meows. Moaning, she sleepily pulled the covers up over her head.

The cries continued, louder, and glancing over at her small travel clock she was surprised that it was nearing ten a.m. Quickly snatching up the protesting wriggling bundle of grey fur, she rushed downstairs to the kitchen and filled his dishes with food and clean water.

There was no sign of Claire and she assumed that she must be on another late shift or a day off. Making a pot of tea, she leant sleepily on the table top and thought back to last night. She was eighteen and three months, and she was making good use of her freedom already. What would her mam and dad say, she wondered? Returning home last night was a bit of a blur other than remembering that it had been raining, and 'herself and Claire' had been soaking wet after walking home.

It was still drizzling and, staring out of the kitchen window, she was dismayed by the leaden sky. Used to walking in all weathers, a bit of cold and wet didn't distress her but a heavy, low grey blanket of sky always lowered her energies, and she longed for a break in the cloud. She'd always loved her private time, when she'd wandered amongst nature and communed with spirit, and after last night she needed to rebalance the conflict that she'd woken up with.

Her strong desire to devote herself to a cause, to be of service to the sick, had always been a part of her, but this powerful attraction for a man that she had only known for two days had thrown her out of balance. She was sure that she wouldn't allow any strange fancy or person to interfere with her dream, but she was disturbed and honestly couldn't wait to meet him again. Noticing the time, ten fifteen., and panicking that she wasn't even dressed, she quickly washed her few breakfast dishes.

"Right, Teddy, I'm off upstairs to shower and then I'm off to find a park or somewhere quiet where I can clear my head, and more than likely get very wet!"

It was eleven a.m. when she finally closed the front door behind her. The cloud had cleared, and her spirits lifted as the sun shone its warmth down onto the pavements. She lifted her face towards the sky in appreciation and smiled, feeling her mood lift as the last few clouds parted, exposing a powdery, blue sky.

Hands in her pockets, ponytail bobbing and her heavy fringe blowing back from her face in the breeze, she hummed a little childhood tune. Robina made a pretty picture — a slim young woman sauntering along happily, dressed in a bright-yellow sweater and calf-length, blue denims and flat, black, patent leather pumps.

Passers-by smiled as they encountered her wandering down the street as if she didn't have a care in the world. She greeted them with a friendly, "Good Morning," or "Nice now the sun's out," for Robina was raised in a friendly community where everybody greeted each other on passing, whatever the time of the day.

Just before the hospital grounds she came across a small grass clearing surrounded by railings; a sweet haven of nature amongst the noise and traffic fumes. Stretching back on the cast iron bench, she stared up at the sky and breathed in deeply, closed her eyes and allowed her thoughts to drift. Tomorrow would be her first day at university, the beginning of her three-year Nursing Diploma course. Her grey- striped uniforms were hanging neatly from the picture rail in her bedroom, and alongside she had placed two pairs of shiny, flat, black shoes that her dad had lovingly polished before she left home. Eight weeks in the classroom and then she would find herself on her very first placement in the hospital.

Passers-by glanced briefly at the young woman asleep on the bench. Last night's antics had caught up on her; the tall willow and birch trees dulled the sound of the busy road and Robina dozed under their canopy until she was startled awake by laughter and the screech of tyres.

Arriving back home just before 2 p.m. she was greeted by Teddy who was sitting on the bottom stair. The house was otherwise very quiet. Stopping to fuss him, she stroked and petted him until he stretched and purred softly in delight.

Surely Claire would be up and about by now? She peeked into the kitchen and the tiny front room. Maybe I need to check her room, she asked herself and, acting on her question, she took two stairs at a time and knocked on her house mate's bedroom door.

"Claire, are you okay, are you there? Can I come in?"

Soft whispers sounded the other side of the heavy door.

"Are you okay?" she called again, putting her ear to the door.

Why wasn't she answering? She could hear something!

Feeling worried she knocked and opened, and stood, and stared, and then closed the door quickly again, apologising.

Heart thumping, face burning, she 'flew' down the stairs and into the kitchen. Once again, she saw the image of Moses's naked, brown body, his long legs draped around Claire's plump white form, the sheets in a heap on the floor. Stunned, she sat, frozen. "Oh my, what a fool I am, what must they think of me?"

And at that very moment, as she was trying to process her thoughts and reaction, the sound of bumps and hurried movements from the upstairs bedroom filtered down to the kitchen and the telephone rang. It continued, insistently shrill, an unwelcome interruption that jarred her senses and filled her with panic. She ignored the call.

"Oh! Sweet heaven, no!"

It continued to intrude — she wouldn't answer it, not at this minute.

She heard the receiver lift, a low voice answered and then called out, "Robina, it's for you."

Quietly, she took the receiver. Not looking up, she held it closely to her ear, pulling her hair loose to hide her face.

"Yes, Daddy, hello, yes it's me. Who was that? Oh, a friend of Claire's. No, he doesn't live here, he just dropped in to collect some books, that's all. How's Mam and everybody?"

Moses softly closed the door behind him.

Robina continued an unusually stilted conversation with family, and thinking that she was still tired from travelling; they made their brief goodbyes and wished her luck for tomorrow.

Placing the receiver down, she sat herself down on the couch and turned on the TV. Teddy climbed onto her knees and she absentmindedly stroked his patchy fur. Puzzled and shocked, she realised that she had a lot to learn about the ways of men and women after all.

"I thought that he liked me, Teddy," she crooned softly. "How right Grannie was."

"Be careful of men," she had counselled, "for they have their brains in their balls!"

"Well Gran, I'll take heed of your advice," she cried out angrily. "Tomorrow is a new day! I'm here to learn, and to work hard; a lesson well learnt I think, a lesson well learnt."

Despite the unfamiliar surroundings she had slept well. Stretching leisurely as the sun's buttery streaks shone through the faded curtains, her mind drifted back to the events of yesterday afternoon. This was going to be very awkward if she didn't act quickly. Jumping out of bed swiftly, she decided that she needed to apologise. Sharing a house with other than family was a new experience and she would have to adjust quickly to avoid any further embarrassing incidents like yesterday.

Teddy protested loudly as he was so rudely awakened and accidently shaken onto the cold wooden flooring along with the dressing gown that he had taken a liking to.

"When did you sneak up here," Robina giggled.

Her three nursing uniforms hanging proudly on the opposite wall caught her attention, and she checked them once again. Belts, epaulettes, RCN pin, a notebook in each pocket, yes, all in order, although they wouldn't be required until she had completed the first eight weeks of study.

Pulling back the curtains, she pushed hard on the aged window frames and threw the window open as wide as it would allow, looking down onto the yard and the neighbouring gardens on either side. The blue sky above filled her with joy and she breathed in deeply, the morning air fresh and sweet. Teddy brushed himself softly along the back of her bare ankles, meowing his request for breakfast.

In no time she was showered and dressed in smart black trousers and a cream, linen blouse, hair dressed in a single auburn plat draped to one side, complete with Grannie's sapphire studs in both ears to remind her of the family back home. Books at the ready, bedroom tidied, the cat fed and sitting up on the kitchen window ledge, she found that she had plenty of time to spare.

Knocking on Claire's bedroom door softly, she called out, "Are you awake? Can I come on in?" This time she waited for permission to enter!

"Oh! Sure, get yourself in," Claire answered sleepily.

Robina carefully placed the tray down onto the chest of drawers. There was a pot of tea, jug of full-cream milk, ginger biscuits, bananas, soft boiled eggs and a little china vase holding some sprigs of green that she had collected on her visit to the park yesterday afternoon.

Claire sat up and looked on in amazement. Her thick, black curls sticking out at all angles, face crumpled with sleep, she found herself unusually speechless.

"Well, it's a little apology, Claire, I'm so sorry for barging in, it won't happen again. This has been your home for over a year, and you've welcomed me in, introduced me to your friends. It would have been very lonely arriving here an' me not knowing anyone at all," Robina explained.

"I'm sorry too," Claire replied, "It was me that made a Holy show of myself — it didn't mean anything, we are just mates. We'd swallowed copious amounts of alcohol and Moses brought my purse around — can you believe that I'd left it on the table in the pub? I am so ashamed, please don't think badly of me, it's not a regular occurrence, I promise."

"Come on then, eat up. I'll admit that I was a wee bit upset and, in a strange way, jealous too. Odd, for I've only just met Moses! But I was really 'taken with him'."

"He has that effect on almost everybody, especially the females," Claire agreed, whilst hungrily dipping her soldiers of bread and butter into the yellow yolk of her egg.

Finishing breakfast, both girls were a little relieved that they had 'cleared the air', although Robina still had to meet up with Moses and she hadn't any idea how she would 'face him', but for the moment she would try not to worry about this too much. She reminded herself of Dad's advice that he gave when she was going through difficulties. "Hold onto your hat Robina, it will pass — all things pass." Yes, she was sure of that, but it was getting through it until it did; that was the tricky bit.

CHAPTER 11

Missing Home

The lecture room at the university was filled with chatting, excited first year student nurses. Robina sat quietly looking on, content to be taking in the bustle and the view from the windows; the campus was teeming. It appeared that many of the students had already met; there were a few male bodies within the largely female group, and she wondered which field of nursing they had chosen. She recognised a few faces from the pub, and they remembered her too, smiling over cheerfully at one of the two inebriated females that had given them all a song.

Her day quickly passed with form filling, photographs taken for I.D. badges, curriculum programmes, tours of the labs where they would practice their nursing skills, and finally the many classrooms, canteen and student bar. The overpowering cooking smells of fried food and strong coffee and heat assaulted her senses in such a way that she had to excuse herself to find a silent corner outside in the cool air. By the end of the long afternoon she had finally 'settled her nerves', and, keen to begin her learning, she made a final stop at the library, where she wandered amongst the many shelves of books, enjoying the quiet and stillness of study.

Returning home, she took a slow walk through the park and, sitting amongst the company of the trees, she gazed up at the crows and blackbirds as they settled in for the night. The clear song of a robin guided her attention to a shrub close by. Perfectly still, she watched as he hopped up onto the heavy briefcase beside her, already bursting with the weight of books collected from the library. The robin stared at her with his black, unblinking gaze, fluffed out his scarlet breast and tilted his head to one side.

As she was drawn into the intensity of his dark gaze, the physical reality of 'now' melted into a different time and place; she was transported back to Grannie Boyle's bedside, where the lamp filled the room with a dull glow and her mother was sitting at the side of the bed, watching, quietly talking and soothing in a low tone, holding her mother's hand. Robina crept close; she brushed a strand of pure white hair, once as bright a red as her own, from the wrinkled brow. She softly kissed the freckled, aged hand that lay flaccidly over the crucifix. Gran was as pale as a wax candle, her life in this world clearly fading — it broke her heart to find her like this.

She recalled past times when Faith had chased her out of her kitchen, annoyed by her many questions; how she had waved her wooden spoon and pretended to scold. "I can't think straight with all of your pestering — keep out from under my feet and give me some peace, child."

Emerging later, the open kitchen door releasing delicious odours of warm soda bread and oat biscuits, her face rosy from the heat of the oven and hair caught up in a woolly hat to keep it from falling into the food, she had protested, "Mary, your daughter will be the death of me with all her 'questionings'. I've never known such an inquisitive child."

But that had been a very long time ago, for Grannie was now 'well into her eighties'. It was all so very real! She was overwhelmed by the sickly, sweet odour of death.

Grandad's dog, Reilly, whimpered and scratched at Mary's legs. He was aware of Robina's shadow. Mary turned towards him, and the same moment Robina found herself back in Liverpool, sitting on the bench, staring into the robin's dark eyes.

He flew away, his mission complete!

Upset, she made her way home amongst the busy traffic and the workers returning home for the day. Her gran had supported her choice of career and understood her decision to establish her independence, but a half-days travel and a ferry from Liverpool back home had not seemed a worry then; right now she would give anything to be able to 'pop in' to see family when she had a notion, for she knew that Gran wouldn't be around to see her graduate.

As she turned into the path a wave of nausea flooded her body. Rushing into the porch, she quickly unlocked the front door and lifted the receiver and dialled.

"Hello, Ma, it's me, what's wrong with Grannie Faith?" she blurted out hurriedly, leaving no time for 'niceties'.

"Your gran suffered from a mild stroke during the night, and she's had another, just as the doctor had arrived. She isn't expected to recover, but I'm going to keep her at home."

Robina's telephone call hadn't come as a surprise to Mary. Faith had insisted that she shouldn't trouble Robina but after the second stroke when her mother had lost her speech and movement, Mary had asked Michael to make the call. Robina had pre-empted the need.

"I'm going to call off now, pet, the nurse is here, and we need to set up the oxygen and make her comfortable . I'll tell Gran that you've called."

"Of course, Ma, please let me know how she goes on; kiss her for me, and Ma, I was with her in spirit, she'll know that I was there. She will be able to hear you still — give her my love, I'll call you later."

Tears stinging the back of her eyes, she let them run freely down her cheeks and nose until they soaked the collar of her blouse; cold and wet she made no attempt to wipe them away. Unaware of time passing, she sat on the bottom of the stairs until her face was uncomfortably sticky and cold and her blouse damp with tears. Head in hands she drifted back, lost in her recollections of life back in Ireland; back to the first time when she and her dad, Michael, had stayed out in the biting cold darkness and waited, and watched the flashing, dancing colours of green and purple lighting up the heavens. They had returned many times as the evening sun illuminated the rocks to crimson red just off 'Malin Head'. The wonderful, wild coastline of north west Ireland, and the warm verdant green of the south west — they were in her blood, part of her DNA inherited from Michael and Mary, and right now every part of her was aching to be there.

A soft, feathery touch on the side of her cold cheek alerted her to her surroundings, to the coldness; to Teddy pulling at her hair and his weight as he leant against her legs. Closing her eyes, she smiled as a faint tickle moved above her top lip and up to her brow. The comfort of this touch was a reminder that she wasn't alone. She had been aware of this happening from a young child and she believed that it was her guardian angel showing her that he was there with her. Through all her trials he had never deserted her, and he never would. The familiar scent of rose and lilac surrounded her with its comforting bouquet, and she hugged herself, its soft reminder warming her with encouragement and hope.

A sharp rap on the front door and Teddy jumped out of her arms and sped into the kitchen.

"Hello, is anybody in?"

She recognised the deep husky voice. Moses!

She opened the door slowly. His tall, masculine figure filled the entrance, towering over her petite figure and, for a second, she had an impulse to slam the door shut in panic. Instead she stood and gaped up at him, not able to bring any suitable greeting forth from the 'helter-skelter' of emotions and memories that were dancing around her mind.

"Are you leaving me outside?" he questioned softly.

She gestured him to come in and he stood at the bottom of the stairs as she rushed into the kitchen and splashed her face with cold water. Moses waited, hands in pockets, hesitant and awkward until Robina invited him into the kitchen.

"I've just had some news from home, Moses. My gran is ill and not likely to recover, and hearing Mam's voice I was just swamped with loneliness, you know? It's the first time I've been away from family and yet I've had a wonderful first day at the university. Gran's a good age but I was shocked all the same. Sit down, I'm sorry for leaving you 'on the door'," she explained, whilst moving away to fill the kettle with water — an automatic response to gather some normality.

"I'll make some tea, or would you prefer coffee?"

Moses moved towards her. Placing both hands on either side of her face, he gently kissed her brow. He sat her down and silently made a pot of tea. Bringing it over to the table, he poured out two steaming mugs of brown liquid, stirring a heaped spoonful of sugar into each. They sat in companionable silence. He was weary after a gruelling twelve-hour shift and this kitchen was 'home from home' to him, for he and Claire had hit it off from the time that she had presented herself at the 'local' just over a year ago.

There hadn't been any physical attraction, not from his side at least, but he enjoyed her company. She was energetic and enthusiastic; had a natural warmth and he admired her common sense and practicality. She 'gave her all' to the patients that she nursed; being compassionate and committed, she was never in a hurry to finish her shift and could often be found sitting with a lonely patient that didn't have family or visitors. Yes! She could be too direct and sometimes demanding in their friendship, expecting Moses or others to be as driven as she was herself. But somehow, when the melancholy overwhelmed him, for this was a periodical happening since he was abandoned in the orphanage as a young boy, she had offered him an easy and comfortable friendship which he valued.

Never in the past year had this supportive relationship evolved into a sexual liaison, until now. It had happened, and Claire had already laughingly shrugged the incident off, and so would Moses usually, but this time he had been unable to do the same. Robina's shocked expression when she had walked in on them naked, wrapped around each other, had deeply upset him. It was obvious, he knew, that he'd destroyed any chance of developing their new friendship any further.

Lost in his ruminations, he was disturbed by a shabby, grey cat leaping down from the windowsill. Looking up, he met Robina's intense deep-blue gaze.

She smiled tentatively. "It's Teddy — I've adopted him; he was left behind when the 'next-door people' moved away. He looks a bit forlorn, but he'll soon be 'right as rain' with a little care and good food inside him."

He leant forward to stroke Teddy. Moses smelt good, his linen shirt was freshly washed, and he was wearing a beautiful cologne. Robina swallowed; his nearness caused her to take a quick intake of breath. The attraction was powerful, not any less despite finding him with Claire the previous evening. She flushed a deep crimson and Moses took her blushing to be discomfort at his presence.

He couldn't have been farther from the truth!

Claire arrived home just before ten p.m. after completing a twelve-hour shift on the medical ward. Collapsing on the sofa, she regaled Robina with a detailed inventory of the minor tribulations of the day. She proudly showed off her epaulettes that signified that she was now a second-year student nurse. After leaving the hospital, she had collected her books from the library which she needed for the fifteen-hundred-word biology assignment that was to be handed in before the end of October. Finally, feeling ravenous, she had called in at the Chinese takeaway and eaten two spring rolls on the way home and, feeling generous, she had brought some back for Robina and left them in the kitchen, unaware that Teddy was investigating the delicious odour of duck spring rolls at that very moment.

Robina told of her phone call home and of Moses's visit. Claire was not surprised that Moses had called around. It was 'his way' — he often popped in for a bit of company and she was pleased that Robina had sat with him and made him tea, wondering briefly if they had managed to clear the air about the other night. The girls sat chatting until nearly midnight. The telephone in the hallway was silent; Robina knew it wouldn't be long and she had an unsettled night, waiting for and expecting the inevitable news. After comforting her new friend as best as she could, then Claire had eventually taken herself off to bed and had fallen into a deep sleep almost immediately. Relieved that she wasn't on the next day, she hadn't set her alarm clock for the next morning.

The next three weeks rolled on and passed in a haze of activity, Claire continuing with her twelve-hour shifts, whilst at the same time working on her biology essay. Mid-October she would be back in the classroom and would remain there until the Christmas break. At the same time, Robina would then begin her first three-week placement on the medical wards; she couldn't wait to wear her uniform and begin the task in hand.

In the same way that Robina kept up regular communications with family, then every week, Claire also telephoned her mum and dad. Being an only child, her family had high expectations of her. She was the first of the cousins to attend university and, as much as her parents loved her, they had projected certain expectations onto her from early childhood. During her weekly chats she was very careful; they would be anxious and disappointed if she wasn't conforming to the standards of behaviour that they'd insisted on back home. Study was important to her too. Completing the course and obtaining her nursing qualification meant a lot to her too, but she was aware that her visits to the pub, her alcohol use and her 'larking about with men' would be totally unacceptable to the parents who were supporting her financially. She needed their help, for although she had a bursary each month it didn't cover her rent. Up till now she had succeeded in alleviating their concerns, dutifully sending home her excellent academic records and the glowing reports from her practice placements on the wards. She hadn't given them any reason to worry, and most importantly, any reason to visit!

CHAPTER 12

Daddy

Five a.m. 'Was that the doorbell?' Claire slept in the front bedroom and she peeped through the nets down onto the street. A tall, dark-haired man wearing a black overcoat and blue scarf stood on the doorstep. She was the first to clamber down the stairs and she called out crossly, "Who is it? What do you want at this time of the morning?" Easing the door open a few inches, she peered into the cold darkness. Robina came down the stairs a few minutes behind her; she didn't ask who it was, she already knew.

"It's Daddy!" She pushed Claire aside and flung open the door.

"I took the early evening ferry, love, I didn't want you to be alone when your mother rang. I'm sorry that it's such an unearthly hour to call."

Claire forced a weak smile. "Crikey me, this is going to be a pain if her parents just arrive out of the blue like this," she muttered under her breath, as she sleepily pulled herself back up the stairs to bed.

It was a sweet, familiar comfort having Dad stay, although she was aware that Claire wasn't comfortable with the situation. Naturally, Robina understood this visit was an intrusion but Michael soon wore down any resentment from her housemate. He was an elderly, indulgent father and he spoilt both girls equally during his stay.

Although in his early sixties, Michael was still an attractive man. His once coal-black hair, although flecked with grey, was as thick and wavy as ever and his blue eyes hadn't lost any of their sparkle. Claire blossomed under Michael's charm and kindness; it was hard not to like him. He had a way of listening to her, as if she really had something to say. Claire was an only child; her father had been disappointed that he hadn't a son, especially when his sickly wife hadn't been able to produce any more children. She'd always strived to please him, to make him proud, she studied hard to achieve good exam results, took interest in his sport, but she was never the 'daddy's girl' that she so longed to be.

However, her diligence had been rewarded and she'd been ecstatic when she'd been offered a university place. Finally, she hoped that her father would recognise that he'd been wrong to disregard the qualities of his daughter. But 'for all that', she knew that he would never cherish her as Michael did Robina, and this made her sad. She knew she wasn't a beauty, but she was bright, and she would work to get to the top in her career, and one day she would earn her father's respect and love.

Michael didn't have a firm idea how long he would stay. He hadn't thought it through, he'd just simply responded to his need to see where his daughter was living and to prepare her for the situation at home. He remained long enough to see Robina dressed in her nursing uniform, ready for her first day on the ward —

he took photographs. It was a shame that Faith would not likely be around to see them — she would have been so proud.

Here she stood, his daughter, so young. A fledgling nurse, with her hair scraped back in a tight bun, wearing the soft grey dress, the elastic belt with the silver buckle pulling in her tiny waist, thick black tights and heavy lace up shoes and a fob watch pinned on her breast — she melted his heart. The paleness of her complexion and the severe hairstyle set off her delicate features, her deep-blue eyes shone with excitement and anticipation; at last she would be doing what she had come for — caring for the world.

He kissed her cheek and wished her luck and he wondered how his tender, kind-hearted daughter would cope with the many demands and responsibilities that she'd be faced with.

She laughed at the worried frown lines on her dad's early morning face and smiled gently. "Da', don't fret, it makes my heart sing to help others and make people happy."

She set off in the early October morning, walking briskly, feeling the fresh breeze cold on her young face; she marvelled at the clear blue sky, there wasn't a cloud in sight and she whispered her thanks to the heavens above. As she arrived at the hospital, her early morning angsts had melted away, and the 'gabble, gabble' of her busy mind cleared. Pushing open the heavy door to reception, she was welcomed by a strong smell of antiseptic and disinfectant. She took a deep breath!

"This is what I'm going to do with my life, this is where I'm meant to be!"

The office was packed with sleepy bodies waiting to take 'hand over' from the even wearier night staff. Robina was briefly introduced, and a friendly body pushed a mug of tea into her hands.

"You're a first year, aren't you? Here, you'll need this," they smiled.

Sipping nervously, she observed as everyone, heads down, frantically scribbled in their notepads. She frowned, trying hard to concentrate and interpret the nursing terminology that she would need to become familiar with. Transfer of responsibility and information was completed in under twenty minutes. The night staff rushed off to their homes and she joined the auxiliary nurse making the early morning cup of tea for the patients, whilst the qualified nurses checked the medication trolley ready for the 'drug round'. Sister came onto the ward at eight thirty and shook Robina's hand, explaining that she would be allocated a mentor, but she hadn't assigned one yet so would she like to shadow the nursing auxiliary until she "had a minute."

The first two hours passed in a hectic round of toileting, bed baths, emptying night time catheter bags, 'turning' the patients who were unable to move their own bodies, making beds with 'hospital corners', patient breakfasts of cereal and toast or feed bottles for those who had lost their swallowing reflex; another round of making tea and finally she joined the 'second breaks' in the canteen for tea and toast.

The staff were a friendly 'bunch', made up of Eileen, the auxiliary, Maureen, a state-enrolled nurse in green, and Helen, wearing blue, one of the two staff nurses on the morning shift. Twenty minutes and the break was over. They rushed back along the long corridors to begin the toileting again, whilst the drug trolley made a second appearance.

At twelve fifteen the dinner trolley arrived and Robina and Eileen and a male auxiliary, Robin, helped those who were able to get out of bed for their lunch, and fed those who couldn't. Then another round of toileting, washing, changing positions before they were given another short break for lunch. There was little time to chat to the elderly patients, the handover notes in her pocket were a 'godsend' — twenty-eight patients, how would she ever remember?

At one thirty pm the late shift trouped onto the ward and they disappeared into the office with the morning staff nurse for handover. The nurse in green, Maureen, allowed her to observe the dressing of a pressure sore on an elderly lady's hip and then she was asked to join the auxiliary nurses in tidying the linen cupboard and cleaning the sluice. At 3.20 p.m. the early shift went home, and Sister called Robina back to introduce her to her mentor, Hilary, a staff nurse on the late shift. Looking less than thrilled to be given the extra responsibility, she arranged to meet up with Robina the following morning when they'd both be on early shift together.

Walking away from her first shift, Robina realised that she'd spent less than thirty minutes in conversation with the sick and immobile people in her care. As she left, she met up with relatives and visitors passing her in the other direction. She comforted herself with the thought that at least they would be able to sit and offer some much-needed company to their loved ones.

Teddy met her at the door. She knew that he needed to go out; Michael was nowhere to be found and Claire would still be in her class at the university. She quickly showered, ready walk with her furry companion to the little sanctuary of trees and park that she visited daily. Teddy's fur had improved greatly, and he was now a picture of sleek, grey health, apart from a patch near his tail that was slow in healing. He now wore a purple collar with an amethyst crystal attached, along with his name and address tag. Robina carried Teddy in her arms as they made their way to the park — this time of the afternoon the traffic was horrendous.

They made a charming picture, a petite young female with flowing red locks sauntering along the pavements with a large grey cat hanging onto her and looking over her shoulder. As soon as they arrived at the park, Teddy jumped down and dashed over to the trees, scooted up the trunk of a tall beech and clambered along a branch, looking down contentedly at the world below. Robina closed her eyes, enjoying the late afternoon coolness settling on her upturned face, breathing in the sweet mustiness of the falling leaves. She stayed until the air became uncomfortably damp and then she called Teddy. He took his time. He's a cat after all, she mused, with a mind of his own. The hunger in his belly finally prompted him to jump down — she chuckled as he climbed back onto her shoulder and they made their way home.

Arriving back, she was surprised to see Michael painting the front door in a bright-green gloss — Claire sat outside on the step chatting and looking on. They laughed as Robina and Teddy approached.

"You look a strange pair," joked Claire. Teddy shot past her through into the hall and into the kitchen, hoping that he'd find a tasty titbit put out ready for him.

"Doesn't it look more welcoming now, love," Michael beamed, "I've cleared it with the landlord; he was only too pleased to agree. It was your mam's idea — she said that we should paint it green to welcome in the good folk and bring a bit of luck and who am I to argue?" he laughed.

"Oh, Dad, I'm really tired, did you need to do this now? My feet are throbbing and all I want is some food and the telly."

"Well, I'm back home at the weekend so this couldn't wait. You get yourself inside, there is a pan of soup on the stove and Claire's made an apple crumble. This is quick drying, so I'll stay out here for a while and then hang a wet paint sigh up outside."

The girls took Michael at his word and left him to his own devices. Michael was unaware of a midnight-blue Ford Fiesta driving slowly past. Moses wondered who the heck was painting the door. He knew the landlord and he wasn't known to have his properties 'titivated' without good reason; after all, they were only student lodgings. His curiosity wetted, he decided he'd

have to call around and have a catch up with Claire —
he knew she wouldn't be in the pub until her assignment
was finished.

CHAPTER 13

Working the Wards

Robina's first week on the 'continuing care' ward had proved to be physically demanding and at the same time both disappointing and satisfying. Her mentor, Hilary, had clearly been pressured into the role of teacher and confidant and Robina found that she was constantly chasing her for input, or being 'sent off' on escort duty. Once or twice she'd met Moses on her travels and he'd joined her for a quick cup of tea in the canteen. Charmed by her gentleness and lack of guile, he loved hearing of her life back in Ireland. She too remained besotted by this confident, attentive male who made her giggle with his cheeky tales and stared soulfully into her eyes, making her feel as if she were the only women in the world.

"So, how are they treating you Robina? Honestly?" Moses queried, now serious. "For sure, they are all fine," she answered softly, "although Matron and Sister are terrifying; they stare at me as if I've something hanging off the end of my nose."

He howled with laughter at her account of Matron, who had seemingly appeared out of nowhere and screamed at her like a banshee, "Student Nurse Moran, is that how you make a bed?"

Things were far from perfect. Her Mentor continued to send her off on escort duty, so she wouldn't be 'bothered' with her; she understood but was saddened. Most of the elderly patients were in the later stages of their illness and would never recover from their ailments and few of them could hold a conversation. Robina knew they welcomed having someone to sit by their side and hold their hand. As a student nurse she'd hoped to have more time to spend with them.

On the third day of her placement, one of the female patients had a cardiac arrest and she'd watched from a distance whilst medics and nursing staff performed interventions, without success. They'd briskly swished the curtains around and 'nurse in charge' called the relatives; their wife, mother, grandmother, had taken a turn for the worse. Sister brought out the best china and had tea with the family, whilst breaking the news that, "It was too late, she'd passed away peacefully." Sobbing, they were taken behind the curtain whilst staff discreetly carried on with their duties, leaving them to say goodbye and pay their respects.

Robina stayed at a discreet distance and was shocked to hear raised female voices. "Who was to have Mam's wedding ring and jewellery?" The junior doctor who'd been involved in the 'call out', charged in amongst them and ushered them all to the nearest side room off the ward. Robina recognised him as one of the medics who had been in the pub that first night when she and Claire had sung together.

He remembered her too and gave her a cautious nod. Noticing her shocked expression, he smiled kindly.

"This isn't so unusual, I'm afraid. They barely visited her during her time with us; Sister used to call them when there was a need but other than that she was forgotten. Don't worry now, she was well cared for during her time here — she's been with us since her stroke three months ago when she lost her speech and movement. She'll be at peace now anyway, free from that lot," he added. "She wasn't for resuscitation, but we did our best to ensure that death wasn't too distressing."

Robina nodded.

Within the next half hour all the curtains were closed around the remaining twenty-seven beds on the ward and Robina joined the auxiliary nurse to 'see to the patient'. She'd seen death in animals, but this was a first! She was asked to open the window next to the bed. The nurse talked respectfully to the corpse; it was surreal — only two hours ago she'd been sitting up in bed eating her breakfast. The 'Last Offices' complete, they tied a tag with the name and hospital number around the toe and pulled the white sheet up and over the waxy, cold face.

The porters were asked to 'remove a parcel'! The deceased patient was placed into a large metal box on wheels and taken off the ward. Then they rushed around and opened all the curtains — 'Business as usual'.

Just as it was time for the early shift to finish, Sister summoned them both into her office and poured them tea. Neither spoke; as usual, Sister's desk was covered under patients notes and papers — the stillness was uncomfortable. Robina broke the silence.

"Why did you ask me to open the window?"

"It's so the soul can fly out," Eileen answered.

Claire was back from uni' when Robina arrived home. Michael had taken a walk to the supermarket, and Teddy was curled up on her bed. Not waiting to shower and change out of her uniform, Robina called home; it seemed an age before they answered.

"No, Faith was still 'hanging on', she wasn't in pain, your Grandad is reluctant to leave her for even a minute," Mary explained. "We've flowers in her room and she's very peaceful; I've dressed her in her best nightie and the perfume that you gave her before you left. Doctor said that she could last days like this, even without taking food, although we have a drip set up." Mary insisted that Robina "shouldn't come home, Grannie wouldn't want it and she wouldn't know anyway!" She asked how her day had been and Robina chose not to tell of the patient passing — it seemed disrespectful somehow. Finally, Robina made her excuses, apologising that her 'feet were on fire' and that she must take a shower. It all seemed so unfair; she couldn't help comparing how the lady had passed today, lonely, and probably frightened, and her own Gran was being lovingly cared for in her own home.

When Michael returned, he was carrying groceries and bunches of flowers.

"Dad," Robina protested, "Did you walk all the way carrying that lot?"

"Well, you'll never believe it, I was making my way back and one of the blasted bags broke. I was rescued by a friend of yours — luckily he was just passing, can you believe that?" Michael asked incredulously. "Come on in, lad."

Michael heaved the heavy shopping bags into the small kitchen and Moses followed suit. Claire whispered fiercely to Robina, "For the love of God, if my father hears that I have males in the house I'm done for."

"Shush, Da won't think any more about it, although I'm sure that he will have been 'checking him out' on the way back," Robina replied with a smirk.

Moses hung back awkwardly, filling the kitchen doorway with his solid physical bulk and colourful presence. Robina reluctantly swung her tired legs off the sofa and Moses squashed in beside her. She flinched as the warmth of his thigh pressed onto hers and she shifted sideways.

Claire glared at him. "Moses, you're as sharp as a beachball, this is Robina's Da, what are you thinking of?"

Moses laughed, ignoring her annoyance and Robina's obvious discomfort. "Just being a good Samaritan," he answered mischievously.

"Will you have a drink lad — tea?" Michael called, as he put the shopping away, oblivious of the dynamics in the front room.

"Don't you dare!" Claire hissed.

"Umm, yes please, that would be nice, if it's not too much trouble," he answered, a wide grin almost splitting his face.

Teddy flicked his tail and stretched out his soft body across Robina, possessively.

Michael carried the heavy tea tray and placed it down on the coffee table amongst the seating. "Here we are, a pot of strong tea to revive us and some chocolate digestives."

"'Bang on," Moses added happily.

The two men chatted as if they had known each other for years. Moses had a way of putting others at their ease and once he realised that Michael had worked the liners, he was genuinely very interested in hearing of the many places that he and Mary had visited. Although he was content for a while with his work at the hospital, he explained that it was only a stop gap; Michael nodded. Meanwhile, Robina had drifted off into her own space, stroking and fondling Teddy's ears, humming a quiet song and occasionally murmuring her interest as Moses elaborated his future plans. Claire sipped her tea and flicked through her text book, lifting her head occasionally to interject.

Robina wondered when he'd leave, her head was in a spin with an overload of sensory input. Pulse racing each time Moses moved or leant near, she was acutely mindful of the heat that rose up through her body like a roaring furnace and the more she became aware that it was probably noticeable, the darker the flush became. Moses was appreciative of the proximity between them both, and he was enjoying it. Her perfume filled his being with a sensuous pleasure and he responded to the musical, softness of her conversation with delight.

It was a strange experience for the naïve, young female — sitting in the familiarity of her father's company and at the same time being 'assaulted' with an overpowering awareness of an awakening, sexual response to the male sitting beside her. Eventually, Claire dropped her book and, taking an advantage of a natural lull in conversation between the two men, she enquired of Robina, "So, how was your day on Ward Seven?"

Careful that she protected the identity, she described the sudden passing of the elderly female patient, of her dismay when the relatives began squabbling and arguing and "her not being gone more than an hour or two before." Michael listened quietly, noticing for the first time his daughter's flushed complexion. He took this to be a sign that she was still upset by the afternoon's unpleasantness.

"Do you know, pet, I think that you'll be needing an early night after all," he comforted, as he stood and swiftly collected the dishes onto the tray. Following the obvious but kindly hint, Moses took his leave, thanking the company for their kind hospitality. Teddy too, decided to make a move; stretching, he padded after Michael to investigate the delicious smell that was wafting in from the back room — it was past seven in the evening and his stomach was growling.

His meal finished; Teddy lay contentedly on Robina's lap as she gently massaged coconut oil into his paws. Claire had disappeared upstairs to her bedroom to study and Michael was lounging in the only armchair, browsing through the sports page of his newspaper.

"Claire's studying hard, isn't she love?" he enquired suddenly.

"Yes, Da', she's a 'Student Rep' too, always volunteering for anything that will promote her profile. She is so keen to make her parents proud; she wants to prove that a female can achieve status and climb the ladder as quickly the male nurses seem to do. It's different for me though. I'll be happy to focus on care and just blend in — this is all I've ever wanted — to bring comfort and a little peace into the world. It's what I was born for, I know that, and you and Mammie have made this all possible for me. I won't let you down."

"I know that too; all we want is for you to be happy. It was a hard thing for us when you decided to take your training in England, but now I've visited I will be a little more settled. I'm sorry that I sprung myself on you like this," he apologised, leaning forward to kiss her gently on top of her red gold top knot.

Michael left early the next morning to catch the ferry, leaving a note under the tea pot in the kitchen. Robina read it hastily before rushing off to her last shift of the week. Inside he had enclosed two twenty-pound notes,

"My mother always kept the hearth warm and food on the table — do the same and you'll not go far wrong. I'll call you when I arrive home. Love you, Dad."

CHAPTER 14

A Passing

Friday evening and Claire, her friends and work colleagues, were relaxing at their 'local'. For some reason, Robina couldn't settle. Her first week on the medical ward had been exhausting; she'd survived, scraped through 'by the seat of her pants' with little support from her nursing mentor. She hadn't joined them — she needed to be on her own. The dark nights were 'drawing in', the house was a warm and cosy and she was content to be in her own company for a while.

The radio was still playing in Claire's room upstairs and the soft music and DJ conversation provided a little company; Teddy was about somewhere. She made a hot chocolate and, munching on a biscuit, she decided to pull the back door to — the sun had gone down and she was chilled. As if responding to her thoughts, a huge blast of wind blew it open with a force that terrified the sleeping cat and scattered Claire's revision papers about the kitchen. The bulb in the ceiling light flashed and dimmed. Trembling, she stooped to snatch Teddy up into her arms — she knew!

"It's Grannie Faith, Teddy, passing through to say goodbye."

The hands of the kitchen clock moved around: unaware of the present, she sat, eyes closed, picturing home. Gran's cottage, Grandad Eamon on his knees at his wife's side, Mary treading softly, reaching up and opening the window, the curtains flapping in the night breeze. Mammie brushing Faith's hair, its thick whiteness still long and wavy, sponging her coldness with lavender water. Placing the rosary beads on the crisp, white, linen pillow, folding her hands together and tucking a sprig of rosemary in her stiff fingers. Grandad Eamon bending over and kissing Faith's forehead, tears flowing unashamedly down his lined cheeks and finally Mary pulling the sheet up and over her mother's face.

Robina didn't notice the coldness creeping along the smallness of her back and into her shoulders. She wasn't aware that she was shivering, or that her colour had drained away, leaving her face as white as an alabaster mask. The shrill ring of the telephone continued unanswered; the clock ticked loudly.

The cat watched, immobile, his eyes closing and opening sleepily; his mistress sat like a stone. He waited for some movement, a flicker of consciousness or communication. This was a bad day for his human, he would stay by her side and keep vigil!

They tumbled through the door, laughing, into the darkened hall; the cold from the open back door had filled the house. The silence was palpable.

"Robina?" Claire shouted, "Oh, Christ, whatever's happened," she asked, turning to Moses in alarm.

The telephone rang again, cutting in, loud and insistent. Robina didn't make any move to explain and Claire hurried off to take the call. Moses took one look at Robina, sitting and gazing into nothing as if in a trance, and quickly wrapped his jacket around her shoulders. Fastening the back door, he shut out the blackness, searched for a new light bulb and then methodically made a pot of tea, whilst every now and then glancing back at her. He could hear Claire's calm voice quietly murmuring, "Sorry, yes, I'll take care of her" and then the sound of the receiver being placed down heavily. Claire, practical in nature and with an innate ability to manage a crisis, briskly took charge of the situation.

"Moses, get a blanket, she's in shock! Here, Robina, sip this slowly," holding the cup to the girl's frozen lips with one hand and taking her pulse with the other. "Just how long have you sat here? You're shaking! Come on, let's get you up to your bed."

Robina tried to stand but her legs didn't respond, and she collapsed into a heap. Wrapping the blanket around her, Moses lifted her up and, holding her close, he carried her up the stairs, lay her gently onto her bed and sat down beside her whilst Claire comforted with quiet words of support and commiseration.

"Your Dad's home safe, Gran passed peacefully, and would you give them a call when you are up to it, or your Mam will try again in the morning."

"How did she know?" Moses whispered. "You took the call."

"You'll get to know her Moses, she's Fey!"

"She's what?" he asked incredulously.

Claire sighed. "Second sight, 'you big lump'! It's a gift, and a curse too if you ask me. Talk to her about it later, she'll explain, but for now I'm tired and off to my own bed. Are you staying?"

"I'll sleep in this armchair if that's okay; we shouldn't leave her alone like this. I've never seen anything like it, I thought she was dead!"

"Please yourself then, I'm off to get some 'shut eye'; get yourself a cover of some sort, it gets cold in here in the night. These windows are just about ready to 'give up the ghost'."

Robina slept fitfully. Moses dozed — he wanted to be near her and he was shocked at her reaction to the loss. He'd never had the opportunity to become truly attached to family. Other than his brother, he'd never known how it was to be loved and cared for and nurtured. But his heart was open and kind; the stability of his childhood in the orphanage, although restrictive, was not unduly harsh and, as Mother Nature had been generous with his physical attributes, he was never short of female company.

She woke and smiled at finding a slumbering Moses next to her, his strength gave her comfort and she welcomed his presence. At last, awake and alert, she glanced over at her alarm clock. Four a.m. and the sky had already lost its blackness. She could hear the beginning of the morning bird song.

Moses breathed evenly and softly, his long legs sprawled out at an angle in front of him and nearby his tan boots and leather jacket and a plate of last night's pizza lay on the floor. Smiling to herself she 'drank in' his handsome face, gazed on the curl of his eyelashes and his blue-black hair falling over his brow, at his generous lips; how she longed to kiss their softness. She remembered the warmth of him and the scent of his body as he'd held her to him and lifted her.

He stirred, she shivered and wondered if he was warm enough; the draught from the window was fiercely chilling. She reached over and felt his hand — it was freezing. Waking at her touch, he found her looking straight at him; the blueness of her eyes melted into his soft brownness.

"Moses, you're cold, come and lay next to me, here," and she pulled aside the bed covers and welcomed him into her bed.

He hesitated, not wanting to take advantage of her vulnerability.

"It's fine, I'm all right now, I've been awake for a long while thinking things through. I want you to hold me — I like you. Please, come and comfort me."

Michael stood alone, anxiously scanning the disembarking passengers, waiting for his daughter to emerge from the early morning ferry. At last he caught sight of a slim, petite person struggling with a large suitcase and he waved frantically to catch her attention. Following closely behind her was another figure that he recognised. It was Claire, and she spotted Michael before Robina herself noticed him. He saw her nudge his daughter and next minute they both called out happily, relieved to see that they would not have to wait around in the fresh morning air.

Michael swiftly moved the girls along, loaded their luggage into the boot of his Range Rover and then suggested that they all have a breakfast in the corner café. He ordered three 'full English' and was taken aback when Robina added hurriedly, "Vegetarian for me please, I'm not eating meat now dad," and she glanced at her father with a challenging stare, waiting for a response. Michael shrugged; he wasn't going to discuss this now; he would have a talk to her mother later.

The girls climbed in the back together. The long drive home was a sad, quiet affair, Claire slept for much of the way. Robina stared out of the open passenger window in ecstasy, breathing in the damp greenness, the dense, musky undergrowth of shrubs and slanting, wind-torn trees; soaking in the verdant emerald green and the freedom of the vast, limitless skies. Its wheels turning relentlessly, the Range Rover pushed on solidly over the roughening tracks, lulling them into a heavy silence until Claire's request broke into their thoughts. "I'll need to stop, Mr Moran, here will do well enough," she added hastily.

Both back passenger doors flew open and Claire scurried off, disappearing into the dense undergrowth, followed by a giggling Robina. Stretching herself tall, she pulled off her pink trainers and twirled, her arms outstretched, spinning, barefoot on the wet grass.

"Whatever are you doing?" Claire laughed.

"She's spinning, always did it as a little girl!" Michael sighed.

"Come on, Claire, join me," she cried, "It's heaven, come on!"

Quickly giving Michael an apologetic glance; she yanked off her ankle boots, ran over to her friend, spread out her arms and joined in. Shrieking with laughter they eventually fell in a tangled heap. Michael called out in exasperation, "Come on now, we've a good way to go yet, get your backsides in this car before I lose my patience!"

The morning of the funeral was wet, not the familiar drizzle, but a rain that came down in hard, sharp, angry sheets, flattening the hollyhocks and crimson peonies growing in the church grounds. The mourners pushed open the gate and the water ran down in rivers, flooding the rough, stone path and drenching their legs and feet.

Faith Boyle was buried under the shade of an ancient yew tree, next to the graves of the three daughters that she had lost before they even became adults — Susan, Bernadette and Margaret. Mary held the funeral breakfast at her own home, the mourners were plentiful, and Eamon soon found it all too much for himself and disappeared. Eventually he was found at the bottom of an old bath tub, fast asleep, and clutching a bottle of his favourite malt next to his ample belly.

The following days after the funeral passed quickly to Mary; she enjoyed having her daughter home. Michael took a trip into town, returning with a heavy, gold crucifix in a blue satin box for his daughter and with two enormous boxes of quality chocolates, one for Robina and one for Claire.

"Just a little something for them both to enjoy when they are back in Liverpool," he explained to the protesting Mary.

Robina was pleased with the beautiful cross and chain and she immediately fastened it around her slender neck; Michael smiled approvingly. Hugging her father, she suddenly paused and turned to her mother. "What happens now Mammie? How will Grandad manage, he'll be hopeless without Grannie Faith."

"He'll have your uncle Daniel at home with him, and the truth is he will either get through it or turn to the drink, it's his choice; he's lucky my Mam stuck by him as she did, and he has me, the old goat! Meanwhile, you must go back now, and get on with your studies, Robina. But before we finish here, I've something here for you that your Gran wanted me to give you."

Mary handed over a mauve tissue paper and she opened it carefully — Gran's delicate, pearl rosary beads tumbled into her hand.

"Oh, it's her rosary from Lourdes," she gasped. "I'll treasure them, oh, thank you, Gran, I'll keep them forever."

Now back in Liverpool, Sister called her into her office on her first day back on the ward, listened politely, and then briskly added that Robina would have a lot to catch up on and that being busy would be a good therapy — it would stop her 'moping'. Robina found the advice harsh and seemingly dismissive, for on her return to the city she had felt completely alone. But she acted on the advice and found the words of wisdom to be true; focusing on the caring role meant that she was able to come to an acceptance that deep down she already knew.

It was Gran's time and she'd been ready to go; she knew in her heart that her gran's spirit had survived and that she would meet with her again someday. Each night before she slept, she took up the rosary beads and prayed for release and blessings for Faith, and on the second week home her gran came to her in her dreams.

As she came towards her, she was smiling, but her eyes held a gentle warning. "You have a gift, you are very precious, stay free from attachments, concentrate on your vocation, for a man will demand all of you and he will not be ready to commit!"

CHAPTER 15

A Loving Pair

For the next two weeks she saw nothing of Moses; she had expected him at the very least to come around for a visit on her return, and his cheerful presence had also been missing around the hospital. Claire had brushed off her concern and, sensing an awkwardness, Robina hadn't pushed for any more information. She'd given freely of herself that night, and she hadn't expected any commitment from him. Moses had been so gentle with her. He'd held her in his arms and stroked her hair and he'd waited, until she had urged him on, whispering, "Please Moses, I am fine, I'm ready."

Afterwards they had talked in low voices of her plans to travel home for the funeral and Moses promised to keep her in his thoughts.

In the early hours he had climbed out of her bed and Claire had been 'none the wiser'. He had set off for his morning shift at the hospital before she was out of her bed and downstairs and the same day, she and Claire had packed for home and caught the morning ferry the day after. Holding the tender memory in her breast, it had comforted her during the unhappy time of Gran's burial and mourning.

Her intention had been clear — to share of herself with someone who was generous and kind and she hadn't any expectations to further the relationship other than to be good friends, but his complete absence and lack of contact since she'd returned left her with a hollowness inside. She was uneasy. Grannie's words echoed in her ears!

She was woken out of a restless, confused sleep by a loud metallic, 'rat a tat' on the front door. She waited, not sure if the sound was from her door or from further down the street. Sitting bolt upright she listened. No! It was someone knocking on the door downstairs.

"Who is it?" she shouted, as she made her way cautiously down the stairs. On seeing the tall shadow behind the frosted glass, she opened the door, leaving the security chain in place. Moses stood, his silhouette outlined against the dark, early morning sky; she was both relieved and embarrassed. Relieved because this wasn't a random stranger hammering on the door, and embarrassed because she had dashed down in her dad's old tartan dressing gown.

It was now weeks since her return from Ireland. She bit back the angry words at the forefront of her mind. She was hurt, he knew of her loss and he hadn't been near.

She felt herself stiffen, her confused thoughts rushed around in her mind and she made no movement to ask him in, and then, impatient with her naivety and in an attempt to clear her mind she shook down her hair and took the chain off. " Why should I fret, he's not my friend, he used me that's all."

He made a striking figure as he waited; his tall broad shoulders filled the space and his jet-black hair fell to the side, heavy and lustrous. His dark, flashing eyes locked with hers and she softened as he pleaded, "I'm sorry, let me explain, please."

"You've nothing to explain!"

"Please Robbie," he begged softly.

She moved back, and he stepped in, opened his arms wide and she went to him. He held her fiercely, and the familiar scent of his skin enveloped her. Finally loosening his grip, he looked down into her face, and kissed her, softly.

"I thought we were friends. I lost my gran and you didn't come and see me, that's all I wanted," she explained, with a catch in her voice.

He shrugged, "I'm sorry, I was locked up!"

Sitting on the bottom step, she listened. Moses told of his involvement in the poll tax protests that had been happening whilst she was away at the funeral. Following the riots in London, the establishment came down heavy on their smaller demonstration. Intent on setting a precedent and in an attempt to prevent any further looting or violence, they had determined that any hotheads would be suitably punished.

With the passion and energy of indignation and righteousness; he waved his arms about excitedly as he elaborated on an injustice that surely penalised the poorer element of society. Pushing a lock of jet hair away from his eyes he explained how the protest was meant to be peaceful, but the situation had quickly become inflamed; people had panicked, and the police had lain in heavy.

"The 'coppers' were free and easy with their truncheons. I stepped in when I saw my mate curled up on the floor under a pair of heavy boots. They started on me, smacked me around the head, pushed me about, twisted my arm up my back, dragged me along by my hair and threw me into the van. I was thrown in the cells and charged with common assault, but I was released on self-defence; it was more than obvious that I had been hammered. I did have to pay a year's poll tax of £280 though. My face was a mess and I took time off to get myself sorted out. Oh Robbie, I'm so sorry that I didn't come around, here, look, I took a kick from the heel of a boot right here — I've lost my tooth," he added ruefully.

Robina was silent, engulfed with a sadness that often overwhelmed her when she saw or heard of cruelty or injustice.

"I'm not a trouble-maker, Robbie, but I'm not ashamed of being working class. This is big; we have to stand together against this bill, I refuse to be processed," he added angrily.

She didn't need to hear any more, her heart was unlocked with his key of honesty, and she reached up towards him and threw her arms around his neck. Tenderly kissing his brow, she told him that he looked like a pirate with his missing tooth; her eyes shining with the fire of love and mischief. Laughing, she clutched his hand and pulled him behind her, taking two stairs at a time. Pushing the bedroom door open, he threw her onto the bed. They kissed each other frantically, dragging off each other's clothes. They made noisy love to each other, and in their rush, and forgetting Claire was sleeping in the room on the other side of the landing they were stopped in their tracks by Claire's boot banging on her bedroom wall.

"Will the both of you 'stop acting the maggot'," she howled in frustration, pulling the covers over her head.

"Sorry, Claire," they shouted in unison.

Laying side by side, they swore that they would take care of each other, that they would treat each other kindly and always be truthful with each other, not making demands and agreeing that when or if either of them found someone else they wanted to be with? Then they would finish this relationship before either of them made a move, and they would remain friends!

"I've never known any woman quite like you, Robbie," Moses whispered, as he stroked along the softness of her breast.

"I don't see love as a trade," she answered, "But I do see it as a sharing between us. I give myself freely and take of you gratefully. For now, I do not have any expectations other than to hold you to my heart and offer my love and friendship in return."

Robina didn't consider a future together, other than time would prove one way or another if their strong fascination and need for each other would last. She had her dream to follow — the nursing career was everything to her, and Moses, well, he was a free spirit; she was aware of that.

Claire was concerned, and at the first opportunity, she had a heart-to-heart with Robina. Not waiting for her to finish brushing her teeth she pushed her way into the bathroom and set too.

"Now listen, we've both of us worked hard to get our places in university. Look, I mean, Moses is a 'fine man', he has a kind nature, but he is known as a 'bit of a chancer'. Don't let him break your heart, and don't set your stall out just for him. We come from a very different world you and I, we've an opportunity that our grandmothers never had and I don't want you to spoil things, for you or for me either".

Robina appreciated her honesty but shrugged it off. Rinsing her mouth, she turned and gave Claire a quick hug. "Oh! I'll be fine, Claire, I do know how it is, and I know how it was for the women in my family. I want my independence too, but I don't intend to close myself off to loving relationships either. I want both!"

"Do you think that is realistic? Or even possible!" Claire huffed, "I remember Grannie telling me how she learnt to survive. Grandpa earned a good wage for most of the time but he always kept her short. She used to sit at his side, patiently watching and waiting until he had fallen asleep in a drunken stupor after a night on the ale, and then she would sneak into the scullery and shake out his trouser pockets and scramble for the loose change. In the morning he would swear that he was robbed by the little people on his way home — he never was any the wiser," she giggled.

"My little gran, Elizabeth, that's my dad's mum, used to wag her crooked finger at me. "Once they put a ring on your finger, they own your very soul! I don't ever want marriage!" Robina joined in.

"Well then, look at you! Remember that you stepped off that ferry as a homegrown Irish virgin; it won't hurt for both sets of parents to still believe this is so. The last thing that I want is my father discovering that my new housemate has her boyfriend over to stay. I feel responsible in a way — I introduced you to Moses after all. Whatever happens, don't get yourself pregnant, and don't leave it to him. Get yourself on the pill."

Teddy, now used to a routine and tired of waiting for his empty dish to be filled with his usual tasty morsels, decided to take action. Leaping onto the kitchen table, he misjudged the distance and clawing at the tablecloth he upset the teapot, and even worse knocked the milk jug into Robina's lap. He meowed piercingly, his hunger making him irritable.

"See what I mean," Claire sighed, "Males have a way of turning everything upside down."

"I hope that wasn't a sign," Robina answered, distracted by Teddy's behaviour.

"Yes, it's a sign that overfed cat of yours wants his food. He rules the house. Now I must crack on and don't forget — Moses may look like a golden god, but — ah, well you know, I'm not your ma."

PART 3

CHAPTER 16

A Bit of a Shock

"Mary, are you ready no?" Michael called out for the third time, "It's a long way to the ferry; we really need to be going," he shouted back over his shoulder.

They stretched out on their bed in the cabin, listening to the chug of the engines. The first year had passed quickly for Robina, not so for Michael and Mary. Mary especially missed her daughter's company now that her mother, Faith, had passed over. She regretted the lost years and yearned for the special friendship between mother and daughter, realising the time she'd spent working on the cruise ships may have been harder on her mother than she'd understood at that time. She swallowed the hard lump in her throat, agonising on her own 'young selfishness'. Her mother had lost three of her daughters as children and she'd left, never giving her a thought.

"I'm sorry, Mammie, I didn't realise how it was for you, forgive me," she whispered quietly into the darkness, her tears trickling down onto Michael's chest.

The ferry docked at Liverpool in the early hours of a damp September morning. Robina was expecting them later in the day, but Mary had been impatient, so they'd caught an earlier ferry. The little café that Michael knew of hadn't opened its shutters yet, so they walked to the taxi rank and waited for a cab. They didn't have to wait long. Mary didn't give a thought to the inconvenience of the early hour; she was excited and keen to reach Robina, eager to hug her and to hear her news. Michael had a key that Robina had given him on his last visit, so they hoped to let themselves in quietly and have a cup of tea and wait until the girls woke up.

Mary chatted away as the taxi made its way through the empty streets. "It will be a lovely surprise for them both. I've brought a few things for Claire too — her mother is not well as you know, Michael, I hope they'll like them." She poked around excitedly amongst the parcels and hand luggage.

Michael abruptly leant forward and wiping the wet off the inside glass, he shouted, "It's here I believe, you're about to go past it."

The black cab screeched to a halt.

"Sorry, lad, me glasses are all steamed up," the driver apologised.

"Aye, it's a bad night, or morning, should I say," laughed Michael.

Mary eagerly fumbled with the key in the front door as Michael paid the driver and struggled with the many packages that his wife had insisted on bringing. Teddy sat on the top stair, still, watching as the two humans let themselves into his house. He remembered the tall man wearing the checked cap, but he hadn't met the woman before. He decided that caution would be best, and he hid himself away under the bed in Claire's bedroom. For some reason, his mistress had closed her door and he'd been unable to climb onto her bed as he usually did.

Michael heaved a sigh and dropped the heavy parcels onto the sofa in the front room and Mary pottered around quietly in the kitchen, looking for the tea and tutting at the unwashed dishes left in the sink.

Waiting for the kettle to boil, they sat in companionable silence, Mary browsing through a local paper and Michael staring at the fading darkness outside as the sun slowly showed itself in the dawn sky.

Three cups of tea later, Mary could no longer wait.

"I'm going to wake her up, Michael," and she ran out of the kitchen and up the stairs before he could pull himself together and caution her to wait a while.

At the top of the landing, the first door on the left had a purple butterfly painted on it. "Well, will you look at that," she exclaimed, "This has to be Robina's." Throwing the door open, she launched onto the bed.

"Surprise!".

"Sweet Jesus! And who is this?" she screamed.

In the next room, Claire woke with a start!

"For the love of God! What time is it?" She pulled her blanket around her and stumbled into a scene of carnage next door.

Hearing Mary's howls of protest, Michael had run up the stairs at a rate that belied his sixty-four years of age, and on finding Moses in his daughter's bed, he had pulled him out by his long legs, leaving him in a dazed heap on the bedroom floor. As Moses attempted to stand Michael pushed him down again, strong in his rage —

he had the younger man at a disadvantage. Mary was dancing around the pair of them in disbelief.

"Who the hell is this?" she yelled, as Claire looked on from what she hoped was a safe distance.

"I know who this is, Mary, it's Moses. What are you doing in my daughter's bed — where's Robina?" Michael demanded in a cold, menacing tone.

Moses pulled himself up off the floor, "Man, oh man, please, Mr Moran, let me explain."

Claire jumped to his defence. "Robina's working a night shift on agency, Moses came back with me and I let him sleep in her bed — I'm sorry. We weren't expecting you here until ten a.m. — Robina will be finishing her shift at any moment."

"And who is Moses?" Mary demanded. "Do you make a habit of sleeping in my daughter's bed? Why couldn't you sleep on the sofa?"

"Oh, Mrs Moran, he's just a friend, it was late, and it means nothing, really!" Claire answered uncertainly.

Turning quickly, Mary noticed the discomfort in Claire's flaming face. "What would your mother say? In the name of heaven, something's not right here," and she opened her daughter's wardrobe.

"Oh, please God, just shoot me," Claire muttered.

Moses's jackets and jeans were hanging there, his tan boots were stood just inside. A guitar leant on the wall next to the window.

"You'll have to do better than that!" Michael sighed and took his wife's arm.

"Mary, enough now, leave the girl alone, we need to talk to our daughter. Meanwhile, Moses and I need to have a chat; I think it's obvious what's going on here."

"Hello, it's me, I managed to finish early. You'll need to get up; Mammie and Daddy will be here in a couple of hours," Robina called up the stairs.

Michael met his daughter in the hall.

"We took the early ferry; your mam was unable to wait. She's in the kitchen. Your man, Moses! Well, we've had a chat and he's off to work right now. You put Claire in an impossible position, Robina — she's upset with you, and quite rightly too," he gently admonished.

"Oh! Dad, I was going to tell you, I'm sorry that you had to find out this way, but we love each other, we really do."

Robina threw off her coat and rushed into the kitchen where she found Mary apologising to Claire, who looked the worse for wear with her tear-stained face and dishevelled hair. Throwing herself into her mother's arms, she glanced over at her friend.

"I'm sorry, Claire, I was going to tell them. There's no need for her parents to know about this, is there Dad?" she pleaded.

"Yeah, and I'm the pope," Claire answered angrily.

"In the name of heaven, why didn't you talk to me? Your happiness is more important to me than any pretentious moralising, Robina, but you've such a lot to learn about life yet. It's only a year gone since your Gran died, you're starting out in a new life, and well into your

149

nursing career. Couldn't you wait? Or at least talk to me? In heavens name," Mary shrieked, "you are only nineteen years old — he's most likely years ahead of you in life experience."

"If you love someone, and they return your love, then it's not wrong, Mammie, and I was going to talk to you, really I was. He truly cares for me. He has nobody, no family, only a brother who is away in the army and he's never in touch with him; he needs me!" Robina cried out in justification. "You knew when you met Daddy that you wanted him — it's the same for me."

"Great 'thunder in heaven', Robina, I was older — twenty-five — and a deal more level-headed," Mary reasoned.

"Yes, I'm nineteen but a woman all the same. I want my career and I want him; I want both," Robina's eyes blazed in defiance. "I won't live in fear as they did in the past, Mammie; I choose love, I choose Moses, and he's only three years older than me! And another thing. Before you start, I don't want marriage — this is the twentieth century and it's different here, it's not like it is back home."

Claire's jaw dropped. "I'd never have the balls to take my parents on like that," she muttered. "Such a wee thing, but she has the courage of a lion!" Mary and Robina both laughing at Claire's exclamation were suddenly stopped in their tracks by Michael shouting down the telephone in the hall.

"Now don't mess with me son! You'll come around here this evening and we'll get things on a steady foot one way or another. Aye, that's right then," and he banged the receiver down, his face purple with agitation.

At this point, Teddy decided to venture out from under Claire's bed and present himself amongst the humans. Disgruntled that his dish was empty, he tore around their ankles in a fit of rage, flicking his tail and screeching his protest until Robina scooped him up and wandered off, gently calming him with her soft murmurings until he purred with delight.

"And when did you get the cat?" Mary asked, distracted, "Where did you find him?"

"He found me, Mammie, he was a present from Grandma. She knew that I'd be lonely," her daughter called from the kitchen.

Michael stared in bewilderment, Claire giggled, and Mary decided 'enough is enough', she needed a rest.

"Come on now, Michael, we'll need to have a lay down; this is not good for your blood pressure, it'll be sky high," and she urged him in front of her and up the stairs.

"This will be sorted out tonight, Robina," she called back down the stairs, "We'll resolve this one way or another to be sure, or I'm not Mary Boyle, my father's daughter!"

"Mary Moran!" Michael exclaimed.

"Shut up, husband, it's all the same!"

"Tell me, Moses, tell me about your family." Mary smiled.

Robina, sensing his anxiety, squeezed his hand tightly, it was clammy. She moved closer to him, offering encouragement.

"My father's name was Samson, my mother's name is Alannah, I have a younger brother Samuel — he's in the army. My father's dead. I've never seen my mother since she put Samuel and myself into the children's home when we were both toddlers. Dad died in an accident at the docks." Moses swallowed the knot of anxiety that burned in his throat and stumbled on. "She had no money and had to work. She promised to fetch us home as soon as she could. She never came back — she left us!"

The wrench of desolation tore through him; it was never far away. "All that I have are a few photographs and some of her letters."

"Where are your folks from, Moses?" Michael enquired, carefully.

"Well, I wasn't told much but I do have some photographs, as I said, and letters. Dad was given his British citizenship along with others who came from the commonwealth countries. He came to England in 1960. He was born in Jamaica, but his roots go back to a group of escaped slaves called the Maroons. It's said they ran away from a Spanish-owned plantation when the British took the island of Jamaica way back in the seventeenth century. It's important to me, I like to remember that. Mother wrote in her letter that my 'da' was very proud to be one of their descendants. My ma' was Irish. She had no family either, other than my dad. She was brought up by nuns in Southern Ireland, that's all I know, other than she came to Liverpool when she was eighteen."

"Can I have a wee look at your photographs, son?"

Mary gazed at the photograph of Samson and Alannah. Samson was black and handsome and had a wide smile; Alannah, beautiful, with a heart shaped face and blue eyes and long, curly, pale-coloured hair. They were staring out of the photograph, a young couple deeply in love, black and white! A taboo that had still been powerful in the sixties and, even now, still was to some. Mary passed the photographs to Michael with a warning look that said, "Be careful what you say."

"I can see that you take your father's looks with his wide smile and beautiful brown eyes, and you have your father's straight glossy hair too" Mary smiled, "but you have a look of your mother also. What part of Ireland did she come from, Moses? Have you ever tried to trace her?"

"How can you tell that, Mammie. His dad's wearing a cap in every photograph," Robina giggled.

Mary gave her daughter an incredulous stare!

Moses hung his head, miserable, wringing his hands together. He answered softly, "No!" he swallowed the pain, "She left us there, forgot us — it was easier to cast off her two mixed-race children and start a new life," he answered bitterly.

Robina took a deep breath. She hurt inside at her image of a young, lonely Moses, staring out of the orphanage window night after night until he finally gave up, and learnt to hide behind a veneer of carelessness and charm.

"Moses, sometimes these places keep secrets, they play God and decide that the children are best kept in ignorance. Perhaps your mother did try and get you both back," Michael advised, "It's not unknown; you read it in the papers all the time!"

"She didn't try hard enough then! I've thought about tracing my father's family, you know, back home in Jamaica, and will do one day. My brother, Samuel, isn't interested, but I have a hankering to do it sometime or other," he smiled, apologetic for his angry outburst.

There was a short silence.

"Right, let's cut to the thrust, lad," announced Michael. "If you plan to be a couple, and I can see that you do, I want things done properly. Robina has insisted that she doesn't want marriage and that she plans to continue with her nursing career."

Robina flushed. "We don't need to make civil vows in front of a priest or a civil servant; we love each other, that's enough."

Michael raised his hand in an attempt to placate Robina. "I can't see why this will be a problem if you are both careful not to bring a family into the equation, at least not until you've both achieved some stability. My daughter needs to complete another two years at university, and you've told me, Moses, that you're hoping to travel, once you've found work with better prospects.

Moses stared down at his feet.

"Now, don't write yourself off, lad, you've had a bad start in life that's all; I can see that you're bright, and you have a way with you. " Mary and I had fifteen years travelling the world together before we were ready to settle and have family."

Turning to his daughter, he added, "Heed my words Robina, I can see that you are both very much in love, but you can't live forever in a dream world. Children cost money and are a huge responsibility; just listen to Samson and Alannah's story. Wait, and live your lives before having a brood."

Robina reddened and turned to Moses for a second. Then, looking down at her hands, she replied shyly, "Da', I'm taking a birth control pill, but Daddy, will you help us with the bond for our flat? I think Claire wants us out now so that she can find another lodger; one that doesn't involve a couple!" she laughed.

"Aye, it's Daddy when she wants something, Mary!" Michael answered in resignation.

"And Daddy, I don't think that I ever want children anyway, there's enough in the world to be cared for. No — no children!"

CHAPTER 17

Filled with Hope

"Say it again, Robbie."

She hesitated, then, "I'm pregnant."

Moses lay his brown hand on her white belly, tenderly stroking, pondering on the contrast between them.

"Our baby, yours and mine Robbie, same as Samson's and Alannah's, black and white!"

She stretched up from the bed and curled her arm around his neck. "No, coffee and cream; we are having a golden child, a child of hope, Moses, the world is changing!"

He scooped her naked body up into his arms and carried her over to the window, looking out at the moonlit sky.

"My own child, my blood and your blood; never will I feel alone again. Thank you, sweet lord." and he whooped out in sheer joy, calling out 'halleluiahs' to the heavens.

"Moses, put me down, I'm naked and all the world can see me."

Bending his head down towards her, he kissed her open lips, and ever so softly he lay her back down on the bed.

At the age of twenty years, just two years after moving to England and meeting the love of her life, Moses, Robina gave birth to their first child, a daughter. Moses, being respectful of his Father's pride in his ancestral tribal African origins, named his daughter Adamma, meaning 'child of beauty'. Two years later they had a second daughter and they named her Kamaria, meaning 'moonlight', and four years afterwards, Robina gave birth to a son. She named him Finn, because, well, it was a name that she'd always liked, then Moses, after his father, and finally Michael, after her father, of course. In the space of six years, Moses and Robina had a family of three children. By this time, Robina was twenty-six and Moses twenty-nine.

What happened to the birth pill? She couldn't take to it!

The early years were happy and busy. The couple created their own social network with friends who embraced social reform and who were free thinking like themselves. With Robina's encouragement, Moses joined a gospel choir at the Baptist church and, to his surprise, he embraced it with gusto; he was able to lose himself in the joy of it, and he discovered that the music calmed the restlessness inside him that never seemed to settle. The warmth and fellowship and the uplifting energetic music gave him a taste of his heritage and greatly helped his mood. Robina took yoga classes and joined a local healing group whilst managing her family and nursing career. She embraced the freedom that she found in the Liverpool community; she was no longer regarded as strange because of her views, or watched with suspicion as she had been when living back home.

Fortunately, the nursing course offered some flexibility, and she was able to continue with her nurse training until a short time before Adamma's birth, and then take a further gap year when she gave birth to Kamaria two years later. Finally, she was able to complete her third year at university before her son was born.

Her parents travelled over from Ireland with Grandad Eamon and they'd proudly taken their place, with Moses, at Robina's graduation ceremony at Liverpool University. Claire was happy to take care of the two girls, who she adored. She had been doubtful whether this day would ever arrive — her two friends never ceased to amaze her.

When young Finn was born, they'd all expected that Robina would have to give up on her career but, between them, Robina and Moses managed their working life and childcare with dexterity and humour. They resisted any attempts from family back home in Ireland to persuade them to marry, particularly from Michael's mother, Elizabeth, who was very concerned for the children.

Robina worked four days a week whilst Moses continued with his night shifts and slept down on the sofa for a few hours each day in between the children's naps. It was hard, but this way they managed to save money on their childcare. Moses found relaxation with his ciggies and Friday night 'bevies', whilst Robina occasionally met up with Claire, who, despite their many differences, remained friendly, their Irish heritage and upbringing being the common denominator.

Claire remained totally focused on her career, and she was already proving to be successful in her aims of 'climbing the ladder' of responsibility quickly. Robina was content, and had found her niche nursing in palliative care; with her strong belief in the continuation of spirit after physical death she found that she was able to bring comfort to the terminally ill and their families.

Moses continued to charm his way through life, but he never managed to collect his scattered ambitions together enough to begin any specific training. Maturity suited him, he drew female attention as a moth to a flame, and many were hopelessly attracted to his warmth and charm and strikingly handsome beauty. He played up to them, there was no doubt of this, but he remained faithful, although Claire thought that he came 'near to the mark' on some of the Friday evenings that they shared at their local.

Claire wasn't without sympathy for Moses. Theirs was a friendship that made no demands and she sometimes felt that Robina's happiness was taken at the expense of Moses's dreams and plans that had never materialised. She didn't rock the boat — she was loyal to the guy who shared his hurts and fears with her and had stoically listened to her on the occasions that she had spilled out the loneliness of her own childhood. She assuaged any guilt about not telling of his flirtations with the thoughts that, "It would serve no purpose other than hurting the family, and besides which, she wouldn't have listened. Robina was totally lost to him; he had captured her wholly."

As the family grew, their tiny terraced home was noisy and full of laughter and reflected the couple's interests of nature and music. The children were, as Robina had predicted, "golden children." Adamma grew tall and had the same proud baring and confidence as her father, whilst Kamaria was petite like her mother and a bundle of energy and joy. Finn was a serious, content baby, but it was noticeable to Robina that Moses didn't seem to bond with his son in the way that he had with the girls. This third child carried the Moran genes — he had a look of his grandfather, Michael. His eyes were a deep-sea blue and everyone around gasped at his beauty. But he was still clearly Moses's son, with his golden complexion and bush of coal-black hair. On the few occasions when Moses did take his son in his arms, there was none of the tenderness that he had shown his daughters when they were babies. Robina was disappointed and a little puzzled — surely every father wanted a son?

True, he was a quiet child, less demanding of attention than his sisters had been at his age, and Robina noticed more and more that unless any of them made a move to engage with him he would spend his time in his own little world, chattering to the rays of sunshine that spilled onto the walls, or babbling to Teddy, who although showing signs of age, was still a member of the family. Teddy was carefully protective of the boy. They were often together; the long, grey cat would stretch out at the baby's feet and Finn would stroke his chubby hand down the length of him, giggling and smoothing his face on the softness of his fur.

On their last visit to Ireland, home, Robina had shared her concerns with her mother about Moses's seeming lack of interest in their son, but Mary was unable to sense anything other than Moses appearing to be a little remote and tired.

"What do you want from him, Robina?" Turning from the dishes she'd dried her hands and shaken her head in frustration, "For heaven's sake, the man's worn out, he's working long hours and doing his best. You expect too much of him; a few days here walking by the sea in the clean air will do wonders for you all."

Hurt, Robina let the matter drop. She put her fears down to her over-sensitivity and gave her husband some much needed space to wander the countryside alone whilst she enjoyed the company of family and her old haunts. The children loved the farm, especially her son who 'lit up' when his grandad took him to meet the horses.

At the end of the week, Moses appeared to have regained his joy of life, and they made a happy picture of family, as they all bundled onto the ferry back home. Robina was hopeful that her mother had been right; he'd just needed a rest that's all. Of course, everything was still well in her world — she was sadly unaware of Moses's increasing dread, and the agitation that was building up inside him as they neared home. If only he'd been able to share his feelings with her, his fear of the inevitable sickening 'day to day' tedium that he knew was returning to; but they were both caught up in the daily grind of routine and family and had stopped really sharing their thoughts and cares.

As they neared the port of Liverpool, he glanced at his sleeping family, acutely aware that he 'owed' his partner and children. Over the last year he had desperately tried to shake off the resentment, he knew that it was wrong, especially now that he was unable to bond with his son.

Leaving them sleeping in the cabin, he climbed the stairs to the deck. The need to escape was strong, he wanted to run.

Sometimes he would call around to see Claire. They always had a good laugh and they would recall their drunken escapades with fondness, Moses often reluctant to return home at these times.

"How did it all move so fast?" he often mused, "Life had been so easy then, yes, I'd been lonely some days, but I was never short of company if I needed it."

In an effort to recover some sort of equilibrium he joined the darts team and started to call in at the pub whenever he had the chance. Making excuses to Robina that they had a match on, became a habit; the deceit no longer bothered him. He 'popped in' to the bookies, spending money that they couldn't afford. Although Robina was earning a decent wage, it got to a point where Moses was gambling and drinking away a good half of his hospital salary and his increasing absences and over-spending started to put the couple under a massive strain. They were finding it difficult to cover the bills, they quarrelled. Robina was always tired now from working extra hours, and the children became fractious, sensing the changing dynamics in their home.

Unable to cope, she retreated into herself; she was unable to express her hurt and confusion. She turned her back and Moses was resentful, she saw the passion ebbing away, leaving a heaviness between them. It pulled on them like wet sand. Moses was in conflict, feeling both trapped, but at the same time unable to cope with the rejection that he had created.

Robina was 'lost' — her beautiful man had lost his 'joy'!

Over the following weeks and months, Moses's mood became increasingly dark, his changeability was distracting, and the children became more and more unsettled. Their father was always angry and their mother was sad — nothing was the same.

Robina knew that her family was in trouble but she found it difficult to share her worries, even with Claire; she couldn't explain her hurt or insecurities easily.

When she did try to rebuild the lost intimacy between them and to ease the growing tension, he resisted her gentle searching — he didn't want to be 'pinned down' to long discussions, it frightened him; he didn't yet want to speak his thoughts out loud, he couldn't quite admit what was in his heart — that if he didn't take himself away soon, then part of him would die.

And Robina?

Her parents were over the sea, she couldn't share with workmates or Claire, she knew that he was bored and restless, and when she tried to stop him splurging money on 'the dogs' or at the 'bookies' he strongly resisted, accusing her of putting limits on his choices, and dictating to him how he spent his time and his own money.

"I earn it, for pity's sake, I work hard, stop trying to chop my balls off."

At these times she was fearful — any further tentative attempts that she made to comfort or reason with him were countered with a glare and an angry protest.

"I'm tired, that's all, I've told you to leave me alone."

And she did, more and more, until they shared a house but very rarely a bed.

When he was in 'one of his moods' she became nervous. It wasn't exactly physical aggression, but it was the way he pushed his plate towards her and would suddenly jump up; the way he would grab the tea cloth after he spilt his mug of tea, the forceful way he would snatch the towel and roughly dry himself down, the way he would snatch his dish of food out of her hands. She would find herself shrinking into herself.

"I can't do this!"

But her thoughts were her secret, still her own, she wouldn't voice them. A thick silence would descend in the room and the all too familiar 'high pitched' ringing would begin. She would open her book and retreat into the corner of the armchair. Once again, she would surround herself with a protective veneer, and each time this happened she found it more and more difficult to break through the shell of deadness that she was creating.

Robina had finally written home. She couldn't bring herself to speak over the phone, she knew that she would break down and cry and she didn't want the children to hear her; it was easier to put it down on paper — her life in the UK was hell, the children were not happy.

"Mother, today I'm crying inside with the bloody hopelessness of it all. Everything is twisted. Keep the lines of communication open? I've tried, I tried last night, but how do you meet someone in the middle when they will not take the first few steps to join you? It has come to the point where I have started to doubt my own reasoning, to question my feelings. What do you do when there is no movement, just a macabre sort of dance? One stood block still and the other repeatedly moving forward and then retreating backwards? And it always ends; not even in stalemate, but in total retreat on my part. And him? Resisting what he perceives as any attempts to restrict his freedom.

So, I go along with it, numbness and small chat take over. Our home is empty, the children are unhappy.

"Today, and every day, I'm crying inside."

Mary read the impassioned letter and passed it to Michael. He fiddled with his broken spectacles, adjusting the tape holding the bridge together. He said nothing for a long time; she knew what was going on in his mind, they didn't have to talk, they understood each other. Finally, Michael stood, wringing his hands together.

"It's as I thought; they were too young and it's clear that Moses is not able to handle his responsibilities. Oh, this is a bad 'carry on', Mary. I know that judging the lad and being harsh with them will not help, but heaven help me I could clout them both for their naivety and selfishness in bringing three children into the world before they hardly knew each other. It sounds like our daughter is at the end of her tether. I need to get over there and work with them. I just hope that I can convince them that family is everything, family is what keeps you safe. They don't have to love each other at this moment, but it's family that watch your back, help you keep a roof over your head. Mary, we need to protect the children — they are the vulnerable ones and so help me those two can tough it out for a while. They owe 'them babies' that. Our Robina needs to turn her mind to practical things; it's the only thing that will keep her sane for a while. If she should lose her focus, then I dared not think what will happen to those children!"

Mary didn't answer immediately. She sat, and blinked, then proceeded to pack two bags. Michael flung the door open and turned. "We'll need the credit cards, Mary."

Michael and Mary arrived in England two days later. They counselled the young couple with love and kindness and firmness; they cleared their debts and cuddled their three grandchildren. They encouraged the two of them to face forward and not to lose heart, Michael acknowledging "that the human condition was 'a tough one for sure'," but warned that if they failed as parents now then, in later years, the consequences from any impulsive actions could cause immeasurable heartache to them all.

On the last evening before their return home, Michael sat with Moses through the night. It seemed that Michael was talking and talking, searching for a solution, whilst Moses sat stubbornly quiet. In frustration, Michael took hold of the young man's shoulders. "Look, you and 'my crazy daughter' created this situation, I don't have all of the answers, Moses. I know that Robina is hurting and that maybe you are trapped, well for now, but you'll find comfort in sticking around and facing up to your responsibilities to the children. If you leave now, you will be haunted by regret in older life, I can promise you that. The lesson is yours, so fathom it out; I'm their grandfather and I'll always be here for them, and so will Mary and the rest of the family. But you and my daughter brought them into the world — be a father, Moses, be a good one."

As they left to take their drive to the ferry for home, Mary took Robina to one side. Mary was a strong mother, she'd been reared by no nonsense parents who had always set solid boundaries for their children, she'd inherited Faith's inner strength and she was acutely aware of the idealistic, tender-hearted nature of her only daughter. She softly admonished her daughter, aware that if she was too harsh, she would only provoke a storm of some kind and that was the last thing that she wanted. Crossing her fingers, she promised that life would get easier when the children were older, reminding her that having a family so quickly was a strain on any relationship. Hugging her son-in-law, she glanced over his shoulder — it broke her heart to think of the family breaking up. Robina was so dreadfully thin, but she had brought some of this on herself with her choices and naivety. She begged her daughter to stay strong and to stand firm for the sake of her three children.

With a sad heart Mary turned and climbed into the front seat, clasping a small card that the children had scribbled on. Michael put the key in the ignition, the engine roared into being and she waved and nodded to them all, hoping and praying to God that they would be good parents and that her daughter would be able to hang onto her man and pull the family through. In her family line it was always the women that held the household together; she hoped her daughter was 'up to it'.

Moses deserted his family one dark January morning when they were all sleeping. He walked away from the job which he had begun to hate, he walked away from the dreaded night shifts where it seemed that the spirits of the dead were pulling on him, beckoning. He walked away from the continual nightmares, where he dreamt that he lay inside the cold, tin coffin that the porters used to collect the dead bodies from the wards. The elderly had always seemed to 'pass away' in the early hours of the morning, between three a.m. and four a.m., and how he had dreaded the call from staff, "Moses, we have a parcel to collect!"

He had picked up his one suitcase, pushed some photos of the children into his jacket pocket and left the house without looking back.

Robina looked around in bewilderment. Why was the room so uncomfortably cold? He'd always lit the gas fire and had the children's porridge ready on the stove after his night shift. It was such a rush getting the three children washed and dressed and fed, and then off to nursery and school so that she could be at work for eight a.m. She clamped her hand over her mouth. "No." Her mind refused to accept what every nerve in her body was trying to tell her. A wave of fear rushed through her body and she rushed back up the stairs and threw open his wardrobe door and drawers. Empty! He'd read her diary, it was open at her last entry,

"Our life together is falling apart!"

"No, Moses, I didn't mean it" she screamed.

Downstairs, she frantically looked around, not sure what she was searching for but she knew there was something. She shook the newspapers, lifted the cushions, looked underneath the clock on the mantlepiece, tipped out the waste paper bin. Finally! There it was, a crumpled-up paper with Moses's untidy writing scrawled across it in the children's red crayon. It read, "I guess it's in my blood, like mother like son. Robbie, I'm sorry, forget me!"

It was getting light outside when she finally hauled herself up from the floor.

She had no more tears.

Robina cuddled baby Finn close to her for comfort. "Go, Moses, I can't watch you burn yourself up any more, go with my blessing, darling, I set you free!"

Walking quickly, he comforted himself with the thought that he was leaving to make some space between them so that he could honestly evaluate their situation. Maybe they had a chance! But as each day begun, he came to the realisation that it was all over; he knew in his soul there would be little comfort for them all if he returned.

In the quiet of his new bedsit, eventually his frantic anxiety and guilt began to wane, and he came to the conclusion, that it served no purpose to continue tormenting himself with questions. Recovering his energy from the routine of sleeping in a bed at night and being awake to welcome the eastern sky dawning and shining a welcome into his day he slowly began to consider his future options. The photographs were tucked away in the back of his wallet. "Don't be a soft lad, it's over!"

CHAPTER 18

Alone

Robina found herself a single parent, with baby Finn just barely walking, Kamaria five years, and Adamma seven years.

Acting decisively, she telephoned work and arranged leave, explaining that there was a family emergency and she needed to return home to Ireland for a short while. Her parents welcomed them all and took them into their hearts, and the young children blossomed from the stability and loving care of their grandparents. Baby Finn especially responded to the laughter in the house and the male attention from his grandad. In a short time, he developed a strong affinity with the two horses in the stable who, sensing the need in the quiet, withdrawn toddler, returned his clumsy, tentative reaching out with patience and gentleness.

As the weeks passed, Mary was hopeful that her daughter would stay and perhaps take up her nursing at home; she was more than willing to help raise her grandchildren.

Their mother too was finding that some days a faint hope was rekindling in her heart and she was beginning to consider her options. There were few reminders of her old life right here; it would all be so easy. Her daddy was wonderful with Finn, the nearest hospital was a thirty minute bus ride away, and then Michael had promised her the use of one of the cars. Her grandparents, Eamon and Brendon and Elizabeth, would not be around for much longer, she'd already lost Grannie Faith, it would be lovely to spend more time with them after all. And at times when it seemed that the sunshine had declined forever in her life then Mary would step in. Her mother was a Godsend, she had a way of comforting the girls that she didn't seem to have, especially Adamma, who was missing her father more than any of her children.

Robina kept her crying for bedtime, unaware that her sobs escaped the confines of the pillows and the thin plaster walls.

For many nights, Mary lay in her bed, haunted by the low moan of the wind outside and her daughter weeping in the next room. The two girls and Finn were so worn out from the fresh air and long walks that they slumbered the happy sleep of childhood, undisturbed by Michael's snoring and their mother's anguish.

Mary thanked God when the sobbing eventually stopped, and her daughter began to show some interest in the life going on around her. She didn't push her — she knew it was just a matter of time and she'd share her thoughts when she was ready.

Robina had always found it easier to talk to her father; knowing this Mary asked Michael to try and have a word with her. The next morning, he took his daughter on a trip into town, left the young ones with Mary, played the local radio station, took a leisurely drive, and waited.

"Daddy, I've had time to think about it all. I'm sure that Moses has never stopped loving me; he just needed to get away, that's all. He never looked at other women, you know Daddy? I think that he'll come back to us, I'm sure of it. I think that I may stay here with the children after all; that's if you and ma' are all right with that — for a while anyway. Nellie has the cat; I'll send her some more money and I'm certain he'll be fine with her, she adores him. Ma' says the rent is covered for another two months. Thank you so much, Daddy, I will pay you both back when I'm working again; I don't want to waste my training."

Michael wasn't so sure that Robina's interpretation of Moses's character and imminent return was entirely correct, but he was relieved that she was staying for a while longer. She obviously found some comfort in her belief — he'd tell Mary when they got back.

"Aye, well, it's good to see some colour in your cheeks again — your mam will be pleased that you are staying."

"Yes, Daddy, I'm a wee bit more settled now, thank you."

Supper was over, the children were in bed, and the adults were enjoying some hard earned peace and quiet; Mary and Robina were browsing through some old photographs at the kitchen table when there was a loud knock on the door. Michael had been in a sound sleep but the loudness brought him out of his slumbers and he jumped up like a drunken man and stumbled over to answer.

"Why, come in, won't you"?

Standing in the doorway, shifting on one foot then the other, was Claire's father.

"I've come to speak to 'your Robina', if that's all right with you?"

Robina came in from the kitchen and nodded, puzzled.

"Well, it's like this." He sat himself down heavily, rubbing his perspiring face with a large maroon handkerchief. "Our Claire has left her post at the hospital. I was trying to catch her on the phone at her lodgings and someone answered and told me that she had packed up and gone. Her mother's not been too well, and I need her at home."

Robina frowned, unable to throw any light on her friend's absence.

" Oh! I've an idea," she smiled, "I have a number for her — she's just got herself one of those new mobile phones — give me a minute and I'll get it for you."

She ran upstairs and searched for her diary. Finding the number that she needed, she decided that it might be prudent to warn Claire of her father's presence before she gave him the number. She picked up the receiver and dialled.

"Claire, it's me, Robbie. I have your Dad here with me — he wants to know where you are and why you left the hospital. Are you okay?"

There was a short silence, then muffled voices. She couldn't make out what they were saying.

"Claire?"

"Well, you might as well know before anyone else tells you. I thought that you would know by now, but I suppose being in Ireland explains it."

"Explains what?"

"He's with me!"

Robina's knees buckled underneath her and she held onto the bannister to steady herself. Unable to find words, she listened as Claire continued defiantly.

"You bloody drained him, you took his essence away with your high ideals and dreams, 'watching' over' everyone like a Mother Theresa or the queen of the fairies. We care for each other in a different way — I'm good for him Robina, he doesn't need Quorn and veggie food, he wants pie and chips," and she laughed.

"Can I speak to him?"

"Robina, have you that number?" Mary shouted up the stairs, stopping in her tracks as she bumped into her daughter with the phone already pressed to her ear. Noting the pallor and shock on her daughter's face, she feared an accident or worse.

"Mammie, leave me," Robina pleaded, with tears flooding down her face. Trembling, she listened to his rich deep voice.

"Robbie, I'm sorry, none of this was planned — we want different things. I know that you have family to go to and the children will be happier over there. I don't know what to say," he whispered, and his voice tailed off.

"He needs me; we are going far away," Claire screamed, "to another life, to start again."

"And you can tell my dad to 'go to hell'!"

Robina couldn't settle at home after that. Hiding away from her life and friends in the UK would be a step back, it wasn't the answer and she wanted her children to live in a world where they were free of religious dogma or the stigma of having an unmarried mother or mixed-race parents. Life in the city was busy and sometimes harsh, but it was also vibrant and exciting, and she missed her friends and work at the hospital. Pleading hard with her parents they had regretfully agreed with her decision. Michael had arranged to take his daughter and his three grandchildren back to the UK, with the proviso that the grandchildren would stay with the family back in Ireland during school holidays. He was doubtful that his daughter would manage three children on her own whilst holding down her nursing post, but there was little that he could do, she seemed determined.

Robina and her young family returned to Liverpool three weeks later. She found a bigger property in the same area. She didn't want to change their school or take them away from their friends. With a full-time nursery place for Finn and with the two girls at school, she was able to take on extra hours at the hospital — she needed to make up for the loss of their father's pay. Neighbours were good; they helped with the children when she worked late shifts and Nellie kept Teddy. Her parents visited when they could leave the farm and, as promised, the children stayed in Ireland during the school holidays. Finn became very attached to his grandad, but she refused Mary's offer to leave him with them back home.

She didn't want to split the children up; there was an age gap already between Finn and his sisters.

Moses didn't make contact and Robina didn't try and find him. She learnt from friends that he'd joined the Merchant Navy for a short while. Samuel made a visit when Finn was four years old and he didn't bring good news. Moses and Claire had emigrated to America.

Samuel was tall and handsome, but any resemblance to his brother stopped there. He was serious and quietly spoken. Not having a family of his own, he adored his two nieces and nephew. Samuel had never put down roots and he was delighted and surprised to be welcomed and invited to stay — this wonderfully compassionate lady and her children were now his family.

Robina had matured into a beautiful woman. Her hair was still a deep red and her busy workload and the three children ensured that she kept her slim figure. Samuel could fully understand how his brother had been taken with Robina's winsome charm and delicate beauty. If things had been different, he would have made a move himself.

He spent two happy months with them, but eventually he had to move on. This was Moses's family first and foremost and he was happy to be an uncle, not their surrogate father. When Finn called him Daddy, he knew that it was time to leave. Samuel left a little money with Robina; he promised the children that he would be back but just now he was going to find their daddy in America.

One by one he stooped and shook the children's hands, and when Kamaria tugged at his sleeve he promised to write to them all as soon as he was settled. Adamma turned away; she didn't want him too to see her tears — she was angry, her daddy had left her and now so was he!

Turning to Robina, he took her by her shoulders and very formally apologised for his brother's lack of responsibility and desertion of his family. She hugged him, reassuring him that she was able to support the children with her steady salary, and with the love and help from her parents.

"Please, Samuel, the children will never go short. Give Moses my blessing; we were very young and I'm thankful for our children."

Kamaria and Finn waved goodbye and ran back into the kitchen to open the present that he's left for them. Adamma hid in her wardrobe.

It had been a long day; the children were in bed and it was good to have some time to herself. She would miss Samuel and she wondered, had she done the right thing bringing them all back to Liverpool — was she selfish?

Her decision to move from her home in Ireland to Liverpool to take up her nursing career again had meant an enormous upheaval, especially with three young children, but she'd been determined to take every opportunity that had presented itself. It seemed that she had inherited a little of her parents' restlessness after all. Hadn't her folks travelled the world before settling down, why, they had worked on the cruise ships for nearly fifteen years. She too had needed to strike out and find her own way in the world. At just eighteen years of age she had trusted, naïvely maybe, in the career that she was about to take up; she'd known that she was venturing away from the protection and discipline of family to begin her adult life as a stranger in a city in the UK. "How very different could it be?" she had reasoned.

Now she was nearing thirty and once again venturing into unknown territory, this time as a single parent with three children, once again leaving her family back in Ireland, but this time with a hell of a lot more to worry about.

Was she being fair to the children? Adamma was distraught when Samuel left this morning, and she knew how Finn thrived in her father's company; Kamaria? she lived in her books — she didn't thirst for attention as her elder sister did.

So? Her plan was simple. She'd focus on her children and work hard at the job that she adored, surround herself with good friends and ensure that Adamma, Kamaria and Finn had a home where they were secure and loved. She was determined they wouldn't be disadvantaged in any way by their father's absence.

His photos were still scattered around the home, she didn't want to remove all trace of him, and when they asked about him, she talked of him lovingly. Moses lived on in her heart, she was never bitter, she didn't believe in such, the darkness of blame was seductive, and she chose light.

CHAPTER 19

Mary, He's Gone

They gathered together around the tree, Adamma and Kamaria kneeling and Finn, now a strong boy of five years, standing close into the side of his beloved Grandfather Michael.

Mary's father, Eamon, wearing a Santa hat and his new red pullover, was getting edgy; he was missing his nap and he motioned his daughter impatiently, "Switch the lights on Mary."

"We haven't put the Christmas angel on top yet, Father."

Bending over, she smoothed the back of his hand; his breath was sour and stale from cigarettes.

'How frail he's become'. She shivered. 'This may be Dad's last Christmas'.

"Gran, let me, let me put the fairy on," cried Robina's eldest excitedly, "I'm tall enough, I can reach."

Turning to Robina, she pleaded, "Mummy, can I? Please?"

Adamma was now a leggy eleven-year-old and her head already reached the height of her petite mother's shoulders.

Mary nodded her agreement.

Climbing nimbly onto the stool, she reached up and placed the family Christmas angel in pride of place.

Perched high on the dark green branches, the golden angel gazed down onto the family. Robina stood in silence, gazing upwards at its delicate wings and the halo that she and Grannie Faith had made with foiled chocolate paper many years ago.

Mary flicked the switch and the lights poured out their silvery magic. The girls cheered and clapped, young Finn blinked in alarm and then, overwhelmed, he threw his arms around his grandad's legs, almost unbalancing him. Laughing, Michael reached down and hoisted his grandson onto his shoulders.

Eamon watched intently, mouth dropping open, his wizened face illuminated against the shadows dancing in the darkness behind him. Memories of Christmases long ago flooded his mind, thoughts of his family, his wife, his shame. Sighing, he clenched his hands and shifted himself back onto the cushions; he knew that he could and should have been a better husband.

Finn stared at the old man with undisguised fear. Without realising Eamon was voicing his tormented thoughts and the twisted expression on his lined face was shadowed by the flickering tree lights. "I ought to have 'kept my temper under control, I shouldn't have hit Faith'. But I'm a simple man with little education and losing my daughters as children was very hard to bear. I was unable to share my grief and talk as women do — the whiskey had been my only solace. I have so many regrets," he whispered. "Lord grant me this one last Christmas with my daughter, Mary, and her family. Then I'll meet you willingly."

He knew his time was short, was aware of the fluid building up slowly in his body and that at some point it would drown his organs entirely. Sometimes his ankles and feet were so badly swollen he couldn't pull his shoes on. Mary laughed at her father's habit of wearing his wellington boots on warm days — she had no idea. Being a proud man, he didn't wish to be a burden or to have the medics interfering with nature. He acknowledged that his symptoms were the natural progression of the aging process. The big heavy boots hid the swelling and when Mary worried about his difficulty in walking, he was able to shush her, explaining that it was down to the damp climate and lots of rain. "Just an old man's rheumy joints."

But how his old body ached today. The children were just too much for him at this moment and he was struggling to smother his irritation. Unfortunately for him Kamaria had noticed his discomfort and sadness and decided to cheer him.

"Robina," he roared fiercely, as Kamaria suddenly leapt onto his lap. Although smaller and much lighter than her older sister, the unexpected movement and weight had frightened him. "Can't you control your offspring?"

"Ah! It's Christmas, Grandad." They're so happy and excited. Kamaria Moran, get off your great grandad's lap. What are you trying to do?" Robina scolded.

Kamaria tugged off his woollen hat and kissed Eamon's wispy baldness before jumping down.

Mary glanced over at her daughter and Robina took the hint.

"Come on then, you lot, let's put on our coats and boots and take a lovely walk outside; the air is beautiful. It's a clear night and we will see all the stars shining out God's glory."

The door slammed noisily behind Robina and her brood. Relieved, Eamon heaved himself up from the comfort of his sagging chair.

"An' another thing — where did she get those children's names from, our Mary? What's wrong with good Irish names like Maria or Bernadette?" he asked irritably.

"Now Da', we've had this out before. Moses named the girls — it was an attempt to link with his heritage."

"Well, he was born in Liverpool, and his ma' was Irish — a lot of ole trollop if you ask me."

Mary ignored his complaining. It was a well-repeated grumble and she didn't choose to reason over it any more.

Michael rolled a cigarette. "Did you need to 'bawl' out like that, Eamon? She's only a wee thing."

"Aye, but she's solid for all that and she caught me in 'my clackers'. I'm off to my bed, Mary, goodnight now to both of you."

The following morning, Eamon was unable to climb out of his bed. It was the beginning of his final collapse. His heart was old and tough and unable to pump efficiently. The family doctor confirmed chronic heart failure and prescribed medication and restriction of fluids. Eamon was not in agreement of any such dietary control and he insisted on having his usual tot of whiskey and copious mugs of lethally strong tea.

Despite his earlier irritation, now that he was resting in his old bed, he discovered that the wee girls could be good company, in small bursts that is. They eased his gathering melancholy, sitting on the end of his bed, singing, demanding he tell their favourite 'scary' stories, "You know, 'Grampy', the one about being lost in the great wood."

Robina made him soups and his favourite cheese scones — despite his illness he still relished his food. She stayed with him while he ate his food and sometimes played her flute for him until he slipped into a light sleep, for he dozed on and off now for most of the day.

Young Finn was still wary of the old man and spent every minute that he could with Michael, grooming and petting the horses or singing and trying to find tunes on his grandad's guitar; even at his young age his fingers were nimble and strong;

"The music is in him Mary," Michael would call out, excitedly, "Let's make a song, Finn, one of our own." The pair delighted in singing and creating music together; they bonded in the way that only grandson and grandad could.

The three weeks of the Christmas holiday were filled with childish laughter and presents, wholesome plain food, carols and church, meandering walks through the dark woods or collecting treasures from the empty beaches.

Eamon's spirits rallied a little. Despite his constant tiredness, he was now enjoying the life and energy that

Robina and her young family brought into the house, and Mary prayed from the bottom of her heart that her father would stay with her a little longer. Robina, even though her experience as a nurse should have warned her that he was very poorly, left for the ferry believing that her grandad, Eamon, 'had a few years left in him yet.'

She was never comfortable living with the hard facts of logic!

The priest was summoned two days after Robina and her young family arrived back in Liverpool. During their stay, Eamon had regained some of his strength but it had been determination and sheer will that had kept him going for their visit. Once they had said their goodbyes he immediately weakened; making no effort to dress or eat. On his last morning on earth he lay back on his bed, content to gaze out of his opened window as the indigo sky lessened and glimmered its pink and yellow welcome to the day. He watched until his sight faded and his whole being submerged into the wonderful heavens, and he breathed his last earthly breath with a sigh of contentment.

Mary found him laying back on his bed, propped up on the pure-white, linen pillows, his head tilted towards one side, his smile frozen, his skin drained of colour.

"Daddy, don't leave me."

Michael rushed into the bedroom on hearing Mary's shrill scream and he touched the old man's forehead; it was cold, his eyes dull, sightless.

"Mary, darling, he's away, he's gone."

For three full days Eamon's body was laid out in the front of the house and immediate family, extended family, friends and neighbours payed their respects. A generation of Boyles now gone — Faith, then her husband Eamon.

Elizabeth and Brendon Moran still struggled on. Michael now wondered how his younger brother would cope when they passed away; James had little success with the opposite sex and was still firmly ensconced in his parent's home and the old life that they'd all had as children. The elderly Moran's made their apologies for not attending Eamon's funeral, the travelling didn't suit them these days, but James made the effort and got 'two sheets to the wind', much to the amusement of his sister-in-law, Mary, who had 'never before' seen anything like the commotion that he'd caused with his version of an Irish jig. The 'wee snifter' that he'd been given, followed on by a glass or two of porter; had set free the wildness that was normally checked by his shy persona. Michael had laughingly intervened and pushed his brother up the stairs where he left him collapsed on the bed, singing a raucous version of a song that should never be sang in the company of lady.

The whiskey and beer 'ran freely' at the wake, fiddles and guitar and flute played through the night and until noon the next day. The door and windows were opened onto the night air and Mary cried buckets. She prayed that her parents were together in heaven and hoped for 'a sign'. She knew that she'd given her father 'a good send-off'; as for heaven —?

"I'll just have to wait and see."

Back in Liverpool, Robina took a little time away from her duties; the hospital was dealing with an influenza outbreak and were in crisis. On the day of the funeral, she sent the children to school as usual, and took time alone in the house, praying for his soul and looking through old photographs of Faith and Eamon when they were younger.

She collected her brood from school and bought flowers. She helped the children fill the vases with white daisies and sunny, yellow roses and cornflower-blue irises. They polished the framed photographs of Faith and Eamon and they placed them amid the flowers. Their fragrance filled their home.

That same night, young Finn woke her as he climbed into her bed. "Mummy, Great Grandad Eamon keeps waking me up, singing his song."

She turned to him; she didn't doubt him. "Which song is that pet?"

"Rosalee," he answered sleepily, tucking himself down under her covers.

The two girls slept soundly. It was clear that Finn was the child to inherit her sensitivity. Kissing his thick mop of black hair, she cuddled him close into her. "You're my precious son and as long as I live, I will always keep you safe, away from the bullies and the ignorance in this world. Sleep now my darling, may angels watch over you until morning light appears."

She lay back in her bed, closing her eyes; she smiled as Eamon's rendition of Rosalee echoed through the sleeping house.

"I hear you, Grandad, I hear you."

CHAPTER 20

Time Passing

Whenever she had some quiet time, just for her, alone, then she would 're-group', align her energy centres, breath in the beauty and images of the invisible realms and rid herself of the impossible, aching tension that cramped her belly and made her shoulders as stiff as a rheumatic spinster's.

Given the opportunity, Robina could find magic in even the smallest happening, just as she had as a small child.

Laying back into the perfumed silkiness, she closed her eyes and squeezed the natural sea sponge, trickling the droplets of warmth over her upturned face and neck and breasts.

"Oh, thank God," she sighed, the sharpness in her now dissolving into the bubbles and the steam. The thousand tentacles that wrapped around her in their vice-like hold, slowly slithered into the water, dissolving their grip.

Muted screams and shouts interrupted her peace; she smiled indulgently. Adamma's strong commands, Kamaria's high-pitched giggles and Finn's gentle humming carried up the stairs and their voices warmed her heart with a gentle flood that brought her comfort and thanks.

Never, not for even one second's breath, had she regretted her children, or the time that she'd shared with their father. Moses remained with her in spirit, he joined her in her dreams and they chatted and caressed and still, even now, when she woke and found him gone, she would cry for the need of him.

Despite her difficulties she held her life together and carried on; Robina was raised by a family who held family unity and loyalty high. The characters of the women were shaped by hardship and strong family commitment. The struggle that the grandmothers had both had with the birthing and rearing of their children had created and passed down a powerful feminine energy. Mary's choice to travel and defy the convention of 'settling down with family' had been witness to this strength, and Robina's wilfulness and determination to work in the UK and to refuse conventionality, had been understood by the older women as a sign of change, and viewed by the menfolk as 'but a step to far'.

Grannie Elizabeth Moran was now the only surviving grandparent. She had survived her husband and reached the magnificent age of a century plus two years. Frail in body, she was still a power to be reckoned with. Robina received letters from her at intervals; the once flowing handwriting was now spidery and the content of her news from home was brief, but according to her son, James, her mind was as clear and precise as it ever was.

She was proud of her many years and she lived vicariously through the achievements of her daughter-in-law Mary and her granddaughter Robina. James was still living at home; they were company for each other. She had her bed downstairs, they had a family friend come in twice a day and when James needed to be away then Michael and Mary would collect her and take her back with them, but after a few days she would always become restless and demand to be taken home. Michael would fret, and she'd tap his hand. "Please, don't you be takin' offence now, son, it's my hope that when I pass it will be in my sleep in my own bed — the bed I shared with my old man, and it's not here, so get me home."

The concept of a care home or involving strangers was never an option. It was not the Moran or Boyle way to 'shovel out' their own, when they were aged or in ill health.

Stretching out, Robina read through the latest note from Elizabeth. Putting the crumpled paper to her nose, she breathed in the scent of violets that was her grannie's signature. Topping up the hot water, she pondered the likeness between Elizabeth and Kamaria — she had 'a way of her great grannie', with her petite grace and delicate features, although she'd inherited none of the shyness that Elizabeth had struggled with at her age.

Where had the years gone? Robina had been in her late twenties when Moses split from the responsibilities of his family and life in Liverpool. She was now crowding thirty and was planning to have a small family party for her fortieth birthday next month.

Michael and Mary were coming over from Ireland and bringing Grannie Elizabeth whilst she was still able to travel. Uncle James was planning to come along too.

All the arrangements had been made to take care of the land and livestock; James had a fancy to explore Liverpool and to see the sights. Grannie wrote that he was as excited as a jumping jack — he'd never really ventured far from home.

What would he think of them all, her 'brood'?

Adamma, a tall, striking twenty-year-old with the arrogance and the beauty of her father; Kamaria, small and petite at eighteen, a vivacious livewire who planned to go into medicine, and Finn, just fourteen, handsome and gentle and following his grandfather Michael with his love of music and animals. Finn, who, unlike his two sisters, was still unclear about his future or ambitions. Robina worried about her son, he didn't thrive in this busy, abrasive city of Liverpool where he'd been born and raised. He only came into his own when he was 'back home', as he called it, on his grandfather's farm on the north west coast of Ireland.

How she longed to see her daddy, now in his early eighty's and still strong and in good health; her mother, close behind in age and 'keeping fine' too. How Grannie would manage the crossing she really didn't know, and Uncle James was 'no spring chicken' either to be caring for her.

"Mum, how much longer are you going to be? I need to get ready, for heaven's sake!"

It was Adamma, eldest child, standing in the now open doorway, bringing in a draught of cold air and disapproval.

Her beauty was striking! Tall and slim, she had jet-black, curly hair which she'd plaited to manage its wildness. She had her father's warm, chestnut-brown eyes, thick, curling eyelashes and fine, soft, straight eyebrows which framed her wide-set eyes perfectly. Her very straight nose, wide sensuous mouth and gleaming, white, perfectly straight teeth were set into a pale coffee-colour complexion. Adamma moved with lithe and grace and she held an air of confidence and authority that belied her years.

She was 'a handful'. With her powerful intelligence and high moral principles, she had struggled with the fact of her father's desertion and her parent's not marrying, and so she'd been driven to prove herself and achieve a position in the top of her field. To accomplish her aims she'd studied hard, worked long hours and ignored relationships with the opposite sex. She was determined to make money and gain a position of power and she let nothing, and no-one get in her way.

As a teenager, Adamma had been livid with her parents. She viewed her mother as weak and feckless and she'd never lost the sense of not being good enough for her father to stay with them. She was critical of his abandonment of his young family, and of her mother; she could never understand why Robina had three children with him without insisting on marriage. At least that would have given them their father's name "for God's sake". When things weren't going her way, she could be controlling and manipulative, and she managed her moments of self-doubt by attacking those around her with sharp criticism and blame.

Leaning on the doorway she tapped her foot in irritation. "I have this assignment and I need to prepare myself, Mum." She made no apology for bursting in and disturbing her mother's privacy.

Robina slipped down under the water and, hooking her toe in the chain, she pulled out the plug and waited as the water gurgled and drained away. Adamma threw her a robe and she clambered out — Robina's still thick mane of long hair dripped over the floor and at her daughter's feet.

"Such a drama queen, Adamma," she laughed.

Adamma gave her mother a push and slammed the door behind her. "Mum, you are the most irritating person alive; you've been in there for hours. This is important. If I get this assignment then I'll be off to Paris next week, can you believe that? This is a big agency — I've got to polish myself from head to toe, practice my French, and don't make me any food — I can't go to them looking like an elephant, can I?"

Robina sat on the end of her bed, towelling her still-auburn hair dry. "I'm not sure that you are doing the right thing, Adamma. Why give up your business studies for modelling, for goodness sake?"

"Because I want to make money, mother! I want to be successful and have nice things; I don't want to be handcuffed to a man and children like you were. We've been over this before, and besides — business studies? Really?"

"There were no handcuffs, Adamma. You'll realise one day if you are ever lucky enough to really find what love is."

"A love so wonderful that he cleared off and left us; great Mummy, great!"

Softly treading into Adamma's room, Robina agonised over her daughter's accusations. Absent-mindedly, she took in the chaos that had been created. The dressing table hidden under an array of lipsticks, blushers, perfumes, hair adornments, nail varnishes, ear rings, bracelets, all indicative of the change in her career direction. Expensive clothes arranged on hangers, hooked carelessly on picture rails, a heap of assorted shoes and boots thrown into a pile in the corner, the wardrobe door now hanging on its hinges.

Slumping on the bed, she drew her hands through her hair in anguish; as usual the verbal missiles had found their target and their sharpness cut deep into her soul. Why couldn't Adamma focus on everything that she had, all that she'd been given, or at least try and appreciate that, as a single mother, she had worked hard to provide and protect her family? Why must she be so angry? Always so judgemental and disappointed in those around her and in the world that she had grew up in? Adamma's intelligence and drive had once given Robina and her parents cause to be proud, sure that she would carve out a career that would sustain her and feed her interest and provide a secure income and living. They'd always offered encouragement and support, financially and otherwise, but now their granddaughter rejected their ideas and what she viewed as a 'hopelessly provincial' lifestyle. It worried them greatly, and Robina too, who feared that her daughter was 'hell bent' on following a very different life path; a path that was so alien to her mother, who was struggling to understand or even like her.

Celebrity magazines and posters of sports cars and 'high end' properties were pinned to the walls. She sighed at her daughter's preoccupation with getting backstage at gigs, the countless interviews and meetings with modelling agencies. They argued about her group of acquaintances that, even for Robina's naivety and new age outlook, were seemingly either outlandish or superficial in the extreme. Robina knew these now reflected Adamma's choices, her goals and ideals.

Groaning, she gazed around the once orderly bedroom and across to the window. The moon was full, she loved a full moon and as usual it shone its silver brightness over the shadows on the walls and into her soul. The window and curtains were wide open — staring down into the yard, she watched as 'Teddy the Second' slowly stretched himself and pawed at the back door for entrance. He was nothing like their first cat who had been long and grey and sly, but they'd insisted on naming him Teddy the Second because he too was a stray who'd invited himself into their home. The door opened and she watched Finn bend and gather the ginger 'tom' into his arms, nuzzling into his fur and humming a tune as he carried his pet inside into the warm.

Why couldn't she and her first born have the closeness that she and Finn shared. Her love was equally full and strong for all three of her children; different, yes, but just as powerful and true. Why must Adamma always accuse, hurt, judge? The anger would appear like a black thundercloud and then fade away quickly, it never lasted. Most of the time she would wake the following day and revert into the honest, loyal, protective daughter that she also could be, but the hurt lingered.

Robina couldn't answer her own question, she had no answer, but she knew that she couldn't survive these continued outbursts. Miserable and fretful, she was unable to move past the upset caused by these eruptions, which flowed over her as a burning lava, suffocating and filling her being with a heavy sadness and guilt.

"Oh, Moses, what were we thinking of," she sighed, straightening the voile curtains. She crept back down the stairs into the tiny kitchen, not ready to join in with the lively commotion that the younger two were creating with their musical attempts, or the imminent, inquisitive questioning from Kamaria.

Too late!

"Mam, can we? Mam? Your eyes are all red! Are they sore?" Kamaria raised a fine brow.

"No! You've been crying — are you crying Mam? Why? Ah! What's wrong?" And she rushed forward, throwing her slender arms around her mother, head tilted, her young face scrunched in concern.

"I'm fine, pet, just a wee bit tired from too many night shifts." Robina smiled and shrugged.

"It's that bitch again isn't it? Mam? And Kamaria charged off, blue eyes dark, reflecting the storm of protective emotion raging inside her.

Finn, eyes closed and now gently strumming his guitar, listened intently. Hearing the eruption of shouting and screaming, he glanced up at the ceiling before throwing down his beloved Gibson in a panic.

He found Robina sitting at the kitchen table, her hands tightly pressed over her ears, unwilling or perhaps unable to challenge. For a long moment, he was frozen to the spot. He stood, a vein bulging in his neck, concerned and worried, not about the rumpus above him, for this was not an uncommon occurrence, at least not lately. No, he was frightened that his mam would be unable to keep going as she did.

It used to be such a happy home but lately there had been too many 'rows' between his two sisters. Kamaria, small and vivacious and easy to please, who at one time avoided arguments and conflict at any cost, usually her own cost, had tired of keeping the peace, for she had finally realised that she was allowing Adamma to manipulate her, 'cover up', lie. Well, not anymore!

Finn was unable to cope with the ever-increasing conflicts in the household. His 'darling home' that was once glowing with light and music and laughter and togetherness, was being torn apart by Adamma's strange moods and his mam's inability to manage such behaviour.

He stood in the doorway. His complexion blanched as he heard something tumble and smash in the hall; he gritted his teeth, unsure, frozen like a rabbit in the headlights. Robina took his shaking hand and gently pulled him to her, forcing a smile she attempted to reassure.

"Oh, Finn, don't worry son, they're like a pair of banshees when they get started. Come on, let's leave them to it. Make us some hot chocolate? Then we'll have a wee slice of that gooey cream cake each."

At fourteen years of age, he towered above his mother's slight figure. She gazed up at her son, her heart full of tenderness and gratitude. He was so handsome, growing as tall or even taller than his father, broad of shoulder with Moses's dark complexion, his coal-black, wavy hair slicked back in a band — every inch of him shouted out the musician that he aspired to be. He had his grandfather Michael's intense blue gaze, flecked with a gold which sparkled and flashed when he was happy or playing his guitar, but at this moment his eyes were as dark as a night sky, reflecting the storm inside him.

She knew that Moses would have been so proud of his shy sensitive son — he would have helped him, given him confidence, she saw that. A kind, generous boy, he lacked the tenacity and strength that enabled his sisters to navigate their world. Fortunately, he had a very close relationship with his grandad Michael and at every opportunity he would take his holidays in Ireland where he would thrive and blossom, but back here in Liverpool it was becoming increasingly clear that something would have to be done to help him. His friends were few, and apart from his music and love of 'Teddy the Second', his social activity outside of the home was non-existent.

Yes, she'd talk to Daddy when he came over.

Finn and Kamaria didn't remember their father; all they had were the many photographs displayed around their home. Adamma had vague memories of her dad — she alone felt his rejection, keenly.

Robina remembered the first occasion, many years ago, when it became clear that her daughter was troubled. She'd been sleeping off a night shift on the couch and Adamma had slammed into the house, sobbing. Rejecting any comfort from her mother, her angry gaze had scanned the front room until it had settled on a photograph in a silver frame. She'd pounced, snatching the treasured picture of Moses cradling her as his firstborn in his arms — she'd held it to her breast.

Robina had moved quickly to offer comfort; her daughter's eyes widening, lower lip quivering, she'd turned in a sudden rage and smashed it, glass splintering on the hearth.

"I stayed behind to help. I was given a merit for my maths. Mr Thomas told them that if they worked only half as hard as me then they may just get through the exam. They waited outside and chased me through the streets. They called me a skinny half-breed! Said I was so ugly that my da' left. But it's not my fault, is it? It's yours — you drove him away, didn't you. Didn't you?"

She'd screamed and cried in rage. Robina had wept.

Her daughter wasn't the same after that. She grew cold and almost dispassionate, she transmuted her young anger into a determination to succeed, earn money, prove her worth. She stayed behind at school, spent her weekends in the library, shrugged away her mother's concern, and her encouragement to "go out and have some fun."

Her bedroom was a show of neatness; the only one allowed into her orderly space was Mary, when she visited. She listened to her grandmother, she respected her and loved her, and was fond of her grandad. "He was a business man, handsome, cool." She barely tolerated her mother, who bore the brunt of giving Adamma, what she saw as her unfortunate genetics and circumstances. Robina had held out some hope that their relationship would improve, and was so proud when Adamma became The 'Head Girl 'and finished school with glowing reports and excellent examination results .Adamma's future seemed to be all mapped out when she enrolled in a Business studies course at college.

But nature and genes had transformed the tall, leggy girl into a stunning young woman and the metamorphosis was not unnoticed. With the beginning of obvious and persistent male attention, Adamma had deliberated that there may be an easier way. Strong-willed and enjoying the power that her beauty gave her; she altered her perspective. She decided that she was willing to do whatever it would take to make things go her way, to make things happen, and she was very aware that the only people who were able to manage her with a firm hand, Grannie Mary and Grandad Michael, were across the sea in Ireland.

The chaos she was creating and the fights between the two girls were becoming intolerable.

At last — silence! Kamaria waited at the bottom of the stairs. She'd fled, retreated from the cat fight with scratches down the side of her pretty face; she was no match for the temper and strength of her sister.

Adamma's full, deeply-curved lips were skilfully painted in a rich, plum rose. She set them in a hard line, stuck her perfectly straight nose in the air and pushed past her sibling. Slamming the door behind her, she left an empty void, the only evidence of her presence being the heady, exotic scent that permeated her clothes, bed linen and personal belongings.

Despairing, Robina pulled Kamaria and Finn into her arms, giving comfort and receiving comfort. How she longed for the strength and wisdom of her parents and grandparents. What would they have done? Placing all her bets on the coming visit, she decided that she would encourage them to stay a while after her fortieth birthday celebrations, and yes, this would be the time to have a few words with her family about her headstrong eldest.

The thought of their visit brightened her mood. Cheered, she briskly scrubbed the top of their heads, Kamaria protesting that Adamma had pulled her hair, making her head sore.

Robina forced a cheery, "Come on then, Mammie has three whole days off work; let's plan a few sightseeing trips. We're in Liverpool, aren't we? You're born Liverpudlians. So, we'll be like the tourists. Art gallery? Museum? You name it."

Kamaria pouted. "Oh, Mam, I want some fun. Can we go to 'The Cavern'?"

Young Finn nodded eagerly. He smiled and all traces of his anxiety vanished, his blue eyes twinkling,

"Can we get some good 'scran' Mam? Maybe a Chinese?"

She could never refuse him.

"Right, the Beatles and The Cavern it is, and then a takeaway. I wish you wouldn't say that, our Finn, it's called food."

Robina smiled. Some light relief, that's what they all needed, just till Mammie and Daddy arrive. "They'll put things right."

CHAPTER 21

A Welcome Visit

"It's strange that our girl has never found herself another fella."

Mary gazed heavenward.

"Come on now, Michael, it's her fortieth birthday party; it's not the time for that old thing again."

Kamaria pushed forward, squeezing herself down on the sofa between her adored grandparents. Petite and full of laughter, her long, heavy, brown hair a satin cascade down to her waist, she smiled her pretty smile and hugged them both in turn. With her bright spirit and sense of humour, she always put them at ease. Michael battled his tiredness as she 'chatted on' excitedly about her ambitions to go to medical school, or maybe teaching, or maybe she could even take up languages and work for the EU.

"What do you think, Grandad?"

Struggling to keep abreast of his middle granddaughter's excited nattering, Mary, noticing the blankness in her husband's countenance, jumped into the conversation.

"Are you still dancing? How's your Irish dancing?"

"Of course, Grannie, I sing with the school choir and I've kept my dancing up — here, I'll give you a show later on." Her blue eyes shone with eagerness and joy at seeing her beloved grandparents again. "But here, Gran, come into the yard and I'll give you a quick show."

Michael took a deep breath, sat back in his seat and smiled apologetically to no one in particular, glad of the opportunity to 'get his second wind'.

How different his daughter's life could have been, he sighed. The choices which she and Moses had made were either incredibly brave or naively ignorant.

He knew that the experiences of the black and Irish community in post-war Britain, and still in the seventies and eighties, were often humiliating and disturbing.

Moses's Irish mother, Alannah, and his West Indian father, Samson, were part of that social history; a young couple who'd fallen in love, who'd trusted their love would be enough to face whatever prejudice was aimed at them.

But Samson had been the resilient one. Once he'd been taken away from Alannah, she had crumbled; she hadn't the strength or the support from family which would have enabled her at least to provide food and clothes for her boys. Her experiences and her choices left an indelible mark on her sons; both had learned to manage this in very different ways.

Samuel, the younger brother, found security in replicating his orphanage life and the institutional family by joining the armed forces, whilst Moses, hiding his confusion and rejection under a façade of easy-going carelessness, had defied any attempts to subjugate him. His turmoiled soul was hidden under a veneer of charm, but it was there, always.

And his daughter — beautiful, unworldly — she had tried to love him, heal his hurts, give him the family that he'd never had and, just for a while, Michael had believed that maybe she was right. But the damage had been too deep, and now the anger was carrying on in Adamma.

"When will it end?" he mumbled. God, how I'm tired of all of this carry on."

The fierce cold coming in from outside announced the return of his wife.

"What's that you are saying, Michael?"

"I'm no longer a mere stripling, Mary, the bark on my trunk is well defined," he complained to his wife mournfully, "I'm less inclined to take this long car journey and rough crossing on the ferry these days."

"You're what? Are you giving up already, Michael? The night's young."

"I'm feelin' my age, Wife, I'm banjaxed, I'm thinking, but I'll hold on for a while. I might 'get me second wind', if our daughter brings me a shot of whiskey or two."

Mary smiled at her husband tenderly. They were both now in their early eighties, but their minds were as lively, she was sure of it.

"But age will have its way," she sighed, sadly thinking over their time together.

Where had all their years together gone? Brendon now long passed and buried in the grounds of the church where he'd been married — one of the many elder folks taken in a winter epidemic of influenza , and Elizabeth outliving her husband. Frail, but her spirit still strong, and dear James in the family home.

Was that when Michael's hair faded from shining jet-black to this crinkly salt and pepper? And her own flaming, russet locks which he'd always adored were now a snowy silver cloud that trailed over her pillows in cottony strands.

She caught her reflection in the oval mirror on the opposite wall; it was as if time had crept up and aged her overnight.

Could that really be me? Her mouth dropped open in surprise. I don't have much time for 'titivating' back home — up just after dawn and out in all weathers, the both of us — but Michael had aged well and kept his wiry frame and ease of movement, whilst the image that reflected back was that of an elderly female, plump, with an undefined, heavy bosom, wearing a long, fine braid of 'wispy white' over her shoulder. She had never thought to have her hair cut; it just hadn't occurred to her. When she was younger, she'd considered fifty as old; she was eighty for heaven's sake. They'd both weathered well, considering.

"It seems just a 'blink of an eye' since we married."

They'd waited a goodly time before their lust for adventure and travel was satisfied — already in her late thirties when she'd become pregnant with Robina, and Michael already in his forties. How very different was their daughter, who gave birth to her first child at the age of twenty and followed on with another two in the space of six years.

Kamaria plonked herself down at her grandad's feet; she adored him, and she was 'sticking like glue'.

"Where's that big sister of yours? Are you as clever as her?" Michael teased, revived a little now that he had a warm toddy of whiskey and ginger in his hand.

"Ah, not really Grandad, but I think that I'll do fine," she laughed good-naturedly.

Kamaria's school life had been easier than Adamma's, whose intense personality had often kept friendships at bay. Her younger sister's popularity had been a source of a jealousy that still permeated their relationship today. In contrast, Kamaria had enjoyed being the centre of attention, and she had dated casually for fun; Adamma hadn't allowed anyone to 'get in the way' of her studies at that age.

"Well, where is our Adamma? Robina?" Uncle James persisted, his gentle way and quiet charm reminding her of young Finn. "Surely, she's here for your shindig; all the trouble you've taken too, you've done a grand job, the food is wonderful, and you've worked hard. I'm keen to catch up with her — I've plans for me and my two great-nieces and great-nephew to take a tour around the Royal Albert Dock. I would like to visit The Maritime Museum and take in The Slavery Museum too whilst I'm here. With my mother deciding to stay at home, I'm going to make the most of my visit."

James had a generous nature and he was incredibly kind to his family and friends — not having children of his own, he was keen to spoil his great-nieces and nephew; he'd been anticipating this trip for a while, and he was holding out hopes of having a walk around on one of 'The Tall ships' — he'd heard they were here on one of their annual visits.

"You could spend a couple of days there, Uncle James, and still not see it all," Robina added. "The dock is still open to small vessels and pleasure boats; it's a nice place to walk around — a bit breezy but you can get good fish and chips."

"Well, I'm sure that 'me ole' legs will get me around if your young ones keep an easy pace. Well, where the 'divil' is she then, our Adamma?"

Young Finn, sensitive to his mother's discomfort, his face reddened, looked from one to the other. "I'm afraid she's hardly ever here, Uncle James, she's working hard to establish her modelling career, don't you know." Robina smiled, attempting to hide her disappointment that her eldest daughter wasn't with them.

"Aye, I've heard," added James. "We'll be having a few words with her when we catch up with her."

He wandered over to take a look at the table, laden with food; a huge topside of beef gracing the centre, a dish of mussels steamed in cider, corned beef and cabbage rolls, potato cakes with smoked salmon, oat and treacle soda bread, green stuffed peppers and 'banger' rolls, veggie skewers and dips and a huge bowl of roasted potatoes and a golden-brown Yorkshire pudding curling over the sides of a large roasting tin.

He winked at young Finn as he pushed a hot potato into his mouth. "Is there no cake, our Mary?" he asked, as he tried to cool the potato by rolling it from one side of his mouth to the other, hastily brushing the falling crumbs down the front his shirt.

"Yes, I've made a Green Velvet Cake with a whiskey cream sauce; I see you've lived too long without your own woman, brother-in-law," she laughed.

"Well, maybe so; Mam and me never share a table — excuse the manners of a lonely old man, Robina, but your eldest should be here at her Mammie's party, what's more important than that? All you've done for her, Robina, it's not good enough really, not good enough, at all!"

Michael took a plate from the table. "Are you going to eat any of this, daughter, or are you still only munching on those 'ole' vegetables?"

"I am that Da'; I can't eat meat, but I do cook it for the family and there's plenty of dishes for myself — Mammie brought enough food over to feed and army. But, come on everybody, help yourself, I've more in the kitchen. Kamaria, Finn, bring your friends over to the table and introduce them, don't leave them standing in the corner as if they don't belong."

James sat himself down by his brother. Precariously balancing a plate of beef and a pile of 'tatties,' he eyed the young friends with Kamaria as they jostled and chatted and filled their plates with food; Finn hung back shyly, grabbed a salmon potato cake for Teddy and wandered back outside.

"Where's our Finn's pals? And what's going on with Adamma? I thought she was planning on getting a university place, all set for taking a business degree or something like that. What's the crack?"

Michael paused for a moment. "The lad is very gentle and he has never found it easy to make friends; he's happy enough with his music and he helps out at the donkey sanctuary and a local stable's every Saturday and Sunday. He's mad keen about horses still; I'm thinking that he would be happier living back home in Ireland when he's old enough, but for now he's holding his head above water with his studies. He's taking music, art and design and biology don't you know? He's a lot like his mother, he worships her. As for 'that madam', well, you don't know the half of it, brother. 'Jaysus', it would make you 'jump up and never come down', if you did."

Robina hadn't wanted a wild night on the town. It wasn't and had never been her style; she was happy to celebrate her fortieth birthday with family. Her social life was limited to chats in the canteen with the colleagues that she had worked with since she began her nursing career and a few like-minded people who shared her interest in crystals and healing. After Claire's betrayal, she had never allowed herself to become too close to anyone outside of the immediate family.

Nursing was her vocation — that, and her children. Her life wasn't narrow in the way that some of her work colleagues or neighbours surmised. At the end of a working day she was content to relax at home with her family, read her books, potter about in the small greenhouse that stood in the corner of the yard, or take long walks with the children if they would join her. The local animal charity shop benefited from her help when she could spare the time and she held home circles for prayer once a month. Life was good, she was fulfilled and she was hopeful that Adamma's behaviour would improve now that her parents 'were over'. She comforted herself that she'd been through worse times than this, yes, they would weather the storm; her daughter was a good girl, she was just 'finding her way'.

Mary, noticing that everybody had lost interest in the food and taking advantage of the lull in conversation, began to clear some of the dishes. Deciding that it was time to liven up the evening, she called over to her daughter,

"Don't sit in the corner like a lost soul, Robina. Kamaria! Michael! Finn! James — lets be havin' you. Let's have a bit of music, this is all too quiet for a Boyle and Moran celebration — why, there was more life at my old da's funeral. Let's liven things up, gather your friends around and we'll have our own 'jam', and while we are at it, we'll have a toast to my brother, Daniel, God rest his soul, wherever he may be."

Michael filled the glasses and passed them around, even to his youngest grandson who was 'wide eyed' at his grandfather's decision to pour him a whiskey at the tender age of fourteen.

They played well into the early hours of the morning, fast and lively, Uncle James on his tin whistle, Grandad Michael on the flute, Finn on his Gibson guitar, Mary's fingers still nimble on the fiddle, whilst Kamaria and her friends did their best to keep up with their own version of Celtic dancing, jigging and twirling and spinning; the house was again full of laughter, the family cat having long since retired to the safety of the little greenhouse in the back yard.

The young ones danced the dance of the young, the heat in the house was palpable, the window glass shook with the stomping and twirling, the floorboards creaked and moved under their feet. The fiddle played faster, the strings responding to Mary's nimble fingers, her brain forgetting her age in the thrall of the music. The sweat trickled down Michael's forehead and onto his spectacles, and his grandson was transported into a haven of family and safety and beauty, until James brought his tin whistle to a screaming crescendo at which point the bulb popped out of its socket and broke the spell.

Mary wiped a strand of hair from her cheek; she was hot, and Michael was reminded of the time when they'd first met — her face was as flushed as when he'd caught her glance across the crowded pub at the wedding party. On impulse he caught his wife's hand and winked at Robina. "This one is for your ma."

He turned to Mary. "Our tune sweetheart, just a wee dream away, one for our youth. Finn, let me have your Gibson for a wee while", and he sang, and the years slipped away.

"The stars are all shining, shining for you.

"Can you see it, shining on you"

Mary locked into the intenseness of his dark-blue, hooded eyes, into the deepness that she knew so well, soul met soul as her aged lover strummed his guitar, softly, tenderly, and she was transported back through the years.

The owl calling, she'd taken its presence as a sign; the two of them stood under the vastness of the midnight sky, the taste of his first kiss. Oh, how he'd adored my full breasts and then loosened my auburn hair and taken me, wholly, in the warmth of the barn, and she'd known no shame. And he was looking at her now in the same way that he did back then; she smiled tenderly as he sang their song and she began to hum softly.

Old Nellie from four doors down was mesmerised by the show of love from a generation that rarely showed their feelings in public; conversation came to a halt; the listeners were captivated. James had seen it all before but even he was caught up in their moment tonight.

Robina looked on and remembered too, when Moses had looked on her as her father was gazing at her mother now. She sighed, remembering how he'd loved her when she told him that she was carrying his first child, and as always, at this very moment her heart ached for him, and for what they had once shared.

Kamaria laughed off the show of emotion between her grandparents; although secretly touched, she was embarrassed in front of her friends and so she led her young followers into the kitchen with a bottle of Uncle James's whiskey hidden under her jumper; they closed the door behind them, and they could be heard singing and laughing and telling their Liverpudlian jokes. Robina was fine with it; they could come to no harm whilst they were under her roof and at least they weren't wondering the streets, but she was mindful of their youth and sneaked the bottle of whiskey away whilst nipping in and out of the kitchen on the pretence of replenishing the already groaning table.

The generations of family and guests celebrated in their own way until the sun came up, and one by one they began to tire. Kamaria's friends eventually 'crashed out' in her bedroom, three of the boys sprawled out on the floor covered in an old duvet, two of the girls collapsed on the bed, and one of the lads had curled up inside the shower cubicle with a pillow. The family party that they thought would be a drag had turned out to be the best laugh they'd had for ages. They would enjoy sharing their antics back at school and Kamaria, already a favourite, well, her popularity would know no bounds.

Downstairs it was also now quiet. Uncle James was sitting in the corner playing cards with Jacob, the elderly Polish neighbour from two doors away; Finn was strumming quietly on his guitar, and Robina was sleepy, wondering when it would be polite to put an end to the party without being rude. Mary being an 'old hand' at this sort of occasion, disappeared into the kitchen and, after ten minutes, appeared with a tray of tea and coffee whilst urging her daughter to fetch in the birthday cake, already sliced and wrapped for the guests to take home.

Uncle James was 'put out', because he was finally in a good position to win this last game but Jacob's wife Aneta was quick to catch hold of her husband, who was as reluctant to finish, as was his opponent.

"Come on, old man, I need my bed." She thanked all for a wonderful evening, took some cake and kissed Robina on each cheek; Jacob followed, still protesting quietly, Nellie shuffled after them and Mary softly closed the door behind them.

Kamaria had disappeared into her mam's bedroom, Finn and his grandad were softly chatting and strumming, intent on finishing a tune they were composing, and James decided that the armchair was a comfortable option for a bed. He was suddenly very weary now that the adrenaline rush of the card game had worn off and he couldn't face the climb up those steep, old stairs.

Eventually the need for sleep overcame Finn's enthusiasm and interest in the song that they were writing, and he made his goodnights.

Robina turned to her parents. "Shall I pull the settee down for you both now? It's very late and you look 'bushed' Da".

"Aye, but one moment, we have something for you," and Michael fumbled in his pocket pulling out a small blue velvet box.

"Open it now, don't just stand there, open it."

She did, staring down at a gold band. She took it out carefully and examined its beauty; it was stunning and in its centre were two hands holding a crowned heart.

"Oh, it's beautiful Daddy, but —?"

"It was my mother's, your grannie Elizabeth's — she wants you to have it. It's eighteen cwt gold — it was bought with the help of the old squire, at that, but your grandmother chose it all the same."

"Try it on, your mother is sure that it will fit your finger. My mother is as tiny as you are now."

Robina placed the ring on the third finger of her left hand, explaining, "I'll wear it on my left hand, on this finger that represents love. Do you know that people say that there is a vein that travels right to the heart from this third finger? I'll never marry — I'm married to my work and my responsibilities are to my children; another man would only bring jealousy into my home. Grannie Elizabeth warned me many years ago, it's as if she knew that the man I would fall in love with would never totally commit — strange isn't it?"

"Are you sure about that, our Robina? I mean, it just doesn't seem right to wear it on that hand," worried Mary.

"No — friendship, love and loyalty, that's what the symbols mean, it can only bring me good luck as it will still hold Grannie Elizabeth's good energy. It's perfect, thank you," and she slipped it onto the third finger of her left hand.

Grandad Michael's fry up! That's what greeted them all as they woke with headaches and stiffness from last night's antics and the discomfort of foreign beds.

Bacon and sausages, white and black pudding, free range eggs and potato bread, all fried in butter, fresh tomatoes and mushrooms and brown soda bread, strong Irish tea, and toast and marmalade — a veritable feast welcomed by some but a queasy nightmare to Robina who usually started the day with oatmeal or fruit.

Squashing Kamaria's friends into her small Vauxhall, Robina delivered them all safely home. Mary took the opportunity to telephone her wayward granddaughter whilst Robina was out of earshot; being unsuccessful, she reluctantly settled for leaving a text message.

"Adamma, darling, please make contact because 'myself,' and your grandad Michael and Uncle James would love to see you before we leave for home. James will only be here for another couple of days, loving you always, Grannie Mary."

She could only wait and see.

After breakfast was cleared away James kept to his word and left for Liverpool docks with Kamaria and Finn whilst Robina relaxed with her folks, enjoying the closeness and unconditional support that only her loving parents could give her.

They advised their worried daughter to be careful, not to push Adamma too hard as to do so would only bring conflict and defiance, and may cause Adamma to stay away altogether. Robina explained that she was too tired to battle anymore; her daughter's behaviour was making her feel very low, and unsettling the other two young people in the house.

"Daddy, I'm frightened that she's using drugs — she's no weight on her. I understand that, as a model, she needs to be very slim, but something doesn't add up; she eats like a horse when she is at home, and she is so moody!"

"Just be there for her as much as you can, don't stand too much nonsense, and pray to God that she'll come out of this phase before she comes to any harm," he sighed. "Do you know, Mary, it's at times like these I miss me da', although he's long passed; if the 'oul fella' was here now he would, 'eat the head off her."

"Aye, and 'box her ears too'; I know that, but that sort of thing doesn't happen now as you well know. No, we do it our way, Michael, in a loving way; times have changed, and young ones don't live in fear of their parents any more, and that's not such a bad thing."

It was the middle of the following week when Adamma returned home bearing presents for her mother, waking the whole house by knocking loudly at the front door and throwing stones at the bedroom window, calling to be let in because she had forgotten her key.

Young Finn was the first down the stairs to open the door, to meet his older sister falling over cases and parcels and laughing wildly.

"Oh, my baby brother, how sweet you are, getting out of your bed whilst the 'old farts' are still snoring."

"There's no chance of that young lady," Mary called down as she struggled to get into her dressing gown.

"Gran, how wonderful to see you, I'm sorry," she giggled. "By the way, did you know that our Finn is 'not the full shilling'?"

Finn crept into the kitchen.

Mary couldn't believe what she was seeing. She caught hold of her granddaughter as she swayed into her; she shouted for her husband. Robina was ahead of her father, keen to spare him the sight of Adamma, obviously worse for wear and reeking of alcohol.

"Halloo! Mammie, why, you have a face like a bag of spanners, go off to bed, you'll turn the milk sour! I want to talk to my beautiful grannie, not you, you 'gobshite'!"

Michael almost threw himself down the stairs.

"Get her in the kitchen, Mary, here, I'll give you a hand. Robina, pet, off to bed, me and your grandma will sort this out."

"Oh Adamma," said Mary softly," this isn't the way my lovely, it breaks my heart to see you wasting your life like this, and your poor mother, whatever has she done that you talk to her in this way."

"She kept us here, when Dad left we could have had a home with the both of you and the rest of the family back in Ireland, but she chose to keep us here, in this 'feckin' city; we may have been sheltered at home, but school was hard, being mixed race was hard, look at the state of my brother for fecks sake, an' we didn't even have a mobile between us, I had to use the computer in the school library for my studies until Grandad bought me one for my A levels. What was she trying to prove, Gran? Tell me, I'm listening, I'm all 'feckin' ears!"

"It seems that the other two have survived, Adamma. Life isn't meant to be a bed of roses, your mam has a good heart, she gave whatever she had to you all — her only crime was falling in love, and she believed that you would all be open to the many opportunities that a city could offer."

"Oh, don't preach to me, please spare me the hearts and flowers, Gran, she still lives in the seventies, in the grips of flower power and San Francisco. My generation? Well, we're different. She loved Dad, and he loved her you say, really? Really?" she screamed. "He cleared off! Do you think that he ever thinks of us? Has he ever written? He's a buffoon! He left me nothing, apart from his good looks, oh 'yeh', he passed on those genes to me! Well, I'm all grown up now, I know what men want, and I'll make my own way, my eyes are open believe me!"

Michael stepped forward. "How has a young person like you become so bitter? Listen to me, I'm your grandad, I only want the best for you. You have your education, your life in front of you — come, it's just the drink talking."

"Yes, Grandad, I'm well educated, she did see to that, and I am now well equipped to grasp the good things in life, I'm no Irish bumpkin. It's my right to choose my life, isn't it? Fine, she birthed me and raised me — that doesn't give her the right to spoil things for me. And it's not just the drink talking as you would have it! So! I get high sometimes, it's my escape from this bloody ugly world that promises everything if you only work hard, but that's not the case is it? We all know that only happens to the few, or if it ever did, then it would take me years to achieve it."

Robina, ashen, stood quietly listening in. "It doesn't have to be like this, Adamma, the beauty is all around you, you just have to search for it sometimes."

"Oh, Christ, here she goes again. Mam! I despise you! I don't believe in the things that you do; give me a good reason why I should stay. I'm just twenty years old and while I have my face and body, I'll market it. You talk of love, Mam, it's lust, lust not love that men feel for me, and when I grow old and fat then I'll maybe settle for a balding man with a paunch that worships the ground that I walk on, a man that would stay with me! But until then I will have the luxury that I want and can earn for myself."

"Enough, stop her, Mary, before I do something that I regret. You need your family, Adamma — one day you will deeply regret the way that you are living your life."

"Give me one good reason why I should stay."

James, finally woken by the commotion, stormed into the melee, seized his grand-niece by her shoulders and, with ice in his voice, shoved her down onto the sofa.

"I'll give you a reason, you little eejit, and I thought you were the brainy one! Because we are your family, and one day, God willing, you will wake up and see the truth; you are not the only child to be raised without their father. Yes, you've found his absence painful, and you're clearly struggling. But, despite making choices that are clearly breaking your mam's heart, she will never give up on you, and neither will we. Now, get that muck washed off your face and get yourself to bed before I carry you there, and take that smirk off your face — aye, I'm an old man but I've still got my strength when I've 'got my gander up'. Now, go, get! Quick! Before I change my mind. And don't ever let me hear you say that about your young brother again; you should be standing by him, and helping him through his shyness. Now go, I'm ashamed of you!"

James stayed for another week. He could stay no longer; he was needed back home for his mam and the land, and the truth was he'd spent enough time enjoying the sights of 'old Liverpool City'; he longed for the lush green hills, the soft comfort of his own bed and the quiet banter between him and his pals over a game of darts and a Guinness or two. Michael and Mary decided to stay a few more days after making a quick call back home to their farm helpers to ensure that all was well, aware they needed to be here to keep the balance until all settled. Robina was glad to have her parents around her for a little while longer.

Adamma skulked around the house, making little effort to socialise with her grandparents, although Michael had managed to entice her out with him for a game of pool down at the local pub, hoping to find a way to break down the barrier that she'd created. There were glimpses of vulnerability, but she continued to knock back his attempts to reason with her; her sarcasm brought out a side of him that he didn't want her to see, and Mary too, on their shopping trips together, found her granddaughter defiantly unresponsive.

Together they had little success and it seemed that they would be returning home as weary and disappointed as their daughter was at this point. The three of them had been hopeful that Adamma would respond in a positive way to the family party and to the visit from her grandparents, who she'd once doted on.

It seemed that Adamma delighted in hurting them all. She 'threw their love back in their faces' and continued as she had before, uncaring of the pain that she was causing to those around her by her indifference and spiteful outbursts. They silently watched as she left the house at odd times during the night, sometimes not returning until late the next day; the few times they ate together they were careful not to fire too many questions at her. Softly, softly, Mary advised, keep the status quo for now, whilst she earnestly prayed on her knees every morning and night for help from God, and Mother Mary, and Jesus, and all the saints that she could ever think of, begging for help with her wayward granddaughter.

Meanwhile, Finn embraced the comfort and familiarity of the older generation. He'd wept and pleaded to go back on the ferry with his great uncle, but it was decided that he needed to carry on with his school work for 'the now', and he was guaranteed that he could travel over to Ireland for the Christmas holidays if he kept his head down and studied hard. It hurt Mary to see how frantic he was when James left. Holding back her tears, she'd held his hand and carefully explained her decision; she and her husband were always mindful of her grandson's demeaner; he was a 'delicate' boy.

Robina was also painfully aware that his gentle way of being and his sensitivity to his surroundings made him retreat into himself and shy away from the vibrancy and the raw, noisy, school environment. It hurt her that he'd been unable to form many friendships. She knew other pupils found his shyness 'off putting.' Finn made them feel awkward and uncomfortable, so they mostly gave him a wide berth.

Mary worried about his difficulty in coping with the outside world — yes — Robina had been similar but young Finn, well, "he was a step further, that was for sure."

However, at this moment they were concentrating their love on Adamma, although they were becoming to realise that unless they could persuade her to return home with them there would be little they could do; she was determined to pursue her goal of becoming rich or famous, hell bent on 'hacking out' a successful modelling career and treating those close to her with disdain or open hostility when challenged.

The last night in Liverpool they all had a meal together at one of the expensive restaurants down at the docks — it was time to return home, and Mary was ready. Robina had made her choices after all, and Michael was looking weary; this trip had 'knocked the stuffing' out of him.

They had woken early whilst it was still dark. The rain came down hard, the gusts of wind driving it down onto the window panes; it splattered from the divide in the guttering in a torrent that splashed down onto the front door below. Robina and Kamaria and Finn had insisted on accompanying them to the ferry, the eldest grandchild was still cocooned in her bed — ignoring the noises of the awakening house, she pulled the duvet over her head. Robina's attempts to stir her brought on angry protests. "For God's sake, Mother, I'm tired, leave me alone," and lastly, they'd heard a muffled "Bye, all", as the front door closed behind them.

The taxi screeched to a halt on the wet road; the rain ceased and they shivered together as they waited in the thick wetness of the steel-grey morning, until they couldn't put off their departure any longer. It was time to say their goodbyes.

The slamming of a car door and a high-pitched squeal stopped them in their tracks; Mary turned, laughing with relief as Adamma, all arms and long legs, threw herself into her gran's embrace. Mary took her into her arms and held her tight. "We love you, remember that, no matter what you do, you will always have our support; we are only waiting for you to cross back into the threshold of our family. But remember, out there you will be held accountable for your actions, be careful, think first, and listen to your heart, Adamma. Now go, God Bless you and keep you, take care of your mammie; she loves you more than you'll ever know, she is part of you, and me; think on, and be careful who you trust, darling, please, for me? If something doesn't feel right then it probably won't be — believe in yourself! Now, go and give your grandad a kiss, quick."

CHAPTER 22

The Letter

With the promise of a trip to Ireland ahead of him, Finn put his mind to his studies; making a good start and achieving excellent grades in his mock exams, it was looking hopeful for his finals the following year. Although school life was difficult, his quiet charm and gentleness were winning him a few friendships outside the educational environment. His voluntary work with animals, and his kindness to the elderly neighbours in the street brought him some comfort and in return they welcomed him into their homes and they couldn't do enough for the shy young man who helped them home in the dark and carried their groceries.

As for his future, he had no idea; the responsibility of making his place in the world terrified him. Any questions in that direction sent him into such a panic that he was unable to give a sensible answer. He knew he wasn't clever and Kamaria's academic aspirations and Adamma's supreme confidence terrified him; despite encouragement from the school and his mother, he was certain that he would never match up to their expectations of him.

He couldn't express his worries; he wasn't able to transmute the thoughts from his brain into words and Robina was unaware of his conflict — he was a quiet boy. "What if I'm not able to make it, like my da'? And now the teachers are asking me if I want to take a college course? My work is promising, they said. Did I want to work with animals maybe? Be a vet? Art and design? It's time to start making choices."

Around and around, his head in a spin, fear taking over — a dread of the inevitable demands that he was sure he couldn't meet, and a fear of something more.

He knew from experience that when he panicked the voices would start; he would wrap the pillow tightly around his head, desperately trying to shut out their whispers and taunts, and when that didn't work, he turned the radio up to full volume until Kamaria burst in shouting that she couldn't concentrate on her studies.

She didn't think any more of it and didn't mention it to Mam, why would she? He was just her strange, younger brother obsessed by his music, that's all.

And Adamma? She'd found him sitting in the bathroom, screaming at the top of his voice, "Go away, leave me alone, I'm not stupid, go away, go away!" He'd rammed his fingers into his ears; how they'd laughed and screeched.

There images and voices were clear in his mind, they tormented him to the point of desperation. "He thinks he can get rid of us by putting his fingers in his ears; it won't work. Ahh! The boy is just plain stupid, we are everywhere, outside, inside, inside of your fat, brainless head!"

Adamma had laughed and dismissed it; her brother wasn't as innocent as Mam thought — he'd obviously been trying out something from the street. She'd put him to bed, told him that he was having a bad trip and told him not to take it again.

Robina, often preoccupied with her work, tired from working irregular shifts and keeping the house going, wasn't totally unaware that Finn sometimes struggled, but she had no idea of the extent of his distress. Yes, her son needed to live close to nature; she knew his nervous system couldn't cope with this high-tech age, and that he would never be one with the industrial 'tribes'. She understood and valued his sensitivity; she struggled herself with the ideals and materialism of the Western world. Her son was so unlike his sisters, who embraced every facet.

Robina found comfort and consolation in knowing that very soon he would be finished his studies and he would probably choose to live back home in Ireland, maybe taking up some of the responsibilities on the farm, away from the pressures that threw him out of balance; she was unaware that the roots of her youngest's psychological illness extended far beyond those of a lack of socialization and an environment that didn't suit him.

Finn didn't know how to fight these episodes of darkness; sometimes he dreamed that the evil would swallow him whole; at times he sat in his bedroom for hours on end, locked into his surreal, fear-based world. But he did understand that feeling pressured or worried brought the voices on — the voices that cautioned him, be careful. "Mention us to anyone else and we will certainly 'finish you off', kill you, make your head explode! We can make you hurt someone that you love, make you hurt them badly when they are sleeping."

Finn couldn't let that happen! "No, I won't tell, I won't tell, ever, ever!"

And so, his pain continued. Treading softly by his room and, hearing him muttering or talking in his sleep, Robina would smile, peep around the door, relieved that at least she didn't have to worry about the company that this one was keeping; he was safe at home in his bed. She climbed into hers, oblivious of her son's agony.

His grandparents, happy to be back in Ireland had little idea of their grandson's distress, their main worry and focus was that Adamma would straighten herself out. Cocooned once more in the verdant, green, dampness of home; Liverpool city, UK, seemed to be much farther away than a short car ride and a ferry trip over the Irish sea.

The elderly couple had retired for bed earlier than usual. Nestled in the softness of goose down pillows and crisp white linen, the weary pair were relieved to be in their own bed; outside, the pale, watery sunset faded into dusk and followed swiftly into darkness. The curved branches of the elderly oak tree scraped its welcome on the small square bedroom window, the leaves slapping on the glass like a wet sheet.

"How I like this time of evening; all is 'tucked away', me and my old woman layin' side by side, and knowing that there's nothing else expected of us till daybreak."

Mary turned, placed her head on her husband's shoulder and rubbed the softness of her palm against the stubble on his chin.

The tenseness in his body belied his words.

"What is it Michael?

"I can't help thinkin' our girl is out of her depth with 'that one', Mary. Going back in my mind to my early years, me and my brothers, we never actively sought trouble with my ma and da'. They recognized the way of things too, you know, made the best of what they had. And it was the same with you and yours too, we all pulled together, supported each other. Me and you, we made our own way, yes, but we accepted our own class and our upbringing and heeded our parents, well, mostly. But our granddaughter is a loose cannon, hell bent on what, for heaven's sake? Our Robina is fretting, and for once in my life I am frightened — what the hell is Adamma getting herself into?"

The screech of the owl nearby overshadowed his words. Mary was chilled with a sense of foreboding and, shivering, she buried her face into the grey fuzz on Michael's chest. It seemed that the weather outside echoed her uneasiness as a rumble of thunder and flickers of lightening lit up the darkness outside.

"I don't know either" Mary answered, hesitating before rushing on, "Sweetheart, there's something else."

Michael turned. "And I thought we were going to have a lovely sleep. What is it? Now, come on, what is it? Oh, you're not pregnant, woman, are you?"

Mary laughed. "Oh, you're an old fool, that would be a divine miracle wouldn't it?"

Michael prodded her. "Wifey, are you saying your old man couldn't manage it?"

"No, listen, I'm serious now, you're an old lecher; there was a letter delivered whilst we were away in Liverpool and, God forgive me, Michael, I hid it from you."

"What? Did you keep it? Did you burn it? What was it? Mary, why couldn't you show your own husband?"

Mary pulled the creased envelope from under her pillow and handed it to Michael. Leaning over for his reading glasses, he propped himself up on the pillow and held it under the light. Mary looked on, comforted that she'd at last released the unquiet guilt that had lived inside her for the past months.

"Why! It's from Samuel, Moses's brother! He says that he would like to visit Robina and his nieces and nephew, and could he please have their address; he was told they'd moved, and that Moses only has our address here in Ireland. Mary! There's a very generous cheque enclosed; he wants us to give it to Robina for the children. He's out of the army, he never married, and he wants to make amends for his brother."

Michael dropped the paper onto his lap.

"Oh Mary, this cheque will be out of date now. Well, we must write back, at once, and invite him over here for Christmas to meet them all. Well, this is wonderful news, isn't it?"

"Michael, there's something else, read on, please!"

He continued — didn't look in her direction, only once, thoughtfully — then climbed out of his bed to stare out into the darkness, the sad moaning of the wind outside matching his low tone of reproach as he finally turned to her, forcing himself to stay calm and take it slowly. "How many months have passed and you kept this from me? Oh, how could you think that this was the right thing to do? God in heaven Mary, we may be too late. This is the most welcome and the most miserable piece of news altogether. Within a single sheet of paper our hopes have been both raised and dashed."

"Oh, Michael, how could I tell her? At the very time when she was having all of that trouble with Adamma. She'd have wanted to take him in, care for him, you know that. I am sorry for him, but he chose his course and in 'all these years' he's never once made contact. I've been torn with guilt, I can't carry it any more.

But I did answer his letter immediately and I told him that Robina had made a new life and remarried, that they didn't need his money and I wished him well. I've tried in vain to ease my conscience, to justify that I was right in making the decision to protect my daughter. Michael, she'd have insisted on tending him and nurturing him, and yes, it's a vile, horrible disease. Dear God, now I'm thinking — who am I to stop the children from seeing their father. But then, would they really want to see their father, the father who deserted them, to see him again after 'all these years'? He'll be a shell of a man, a man dying of AIDS!"

His chest swelling, he roared, loud and fierce. "God give me strength, I can't believe you, Mary, whatever possessed you to keep this to yourself. You could have shared it with me, we would have worked it out together. Do I even know you?"

"Michael, stop it, you're frightening me."

"Is there a telephone number on this? We need to put this right, and quickly." Noticing Mary's hands trembling as she scanned the writing he softened. "Oh, Mary, she never really divorced herself from him. I know they didn't marry legally but his name is on the birth certificates of all three of her children and Samuel makes no mention of Claire, did you notice? Robina will be over here on the ferry in five days' time for Christmas. How can we tell her all of this now? How can we tell her this over the phone?"

Mary dragged her hands through her hair in anguish "I feel so wretched. I was like a rabbit caught in a headlight when I opened that letter — I froze, didn't know where to turn or what to do and the truth remains that I really couldn't face any more trouble at that point and yes, for a short while I thought that I had done the right thing."

"Aye, well my own head is in all of a spin just now, I'm exhausted just trying to work this out; this is what comes of having a child later on in life; we both of us don't have the vigour that we once had. Come on now, let's go downstairs to the kitchen, we'll not be getting any more sleep this night."

CHAPTER 23

Christmas

The slope of the low roof cast the corner of the kitchen into shadow whilst at the further end the lights on the tree flickered; their blue and green sparkled in turn over a huge, tumbled array of presents. This year the pile of gaily-coloured boxes and glittering wrappers were higher than ever before in the history of the Moran household.

Smoking his cigarette in the shadow, his lined face lit up only by the flames of the fire, sat Michael, his thin legs stretched out in front of him whilst his slippered feet rested on the old stool that his father, Brendon, had carved out of an oak brought down by a storm.

Christmas Eve, a joyful yet poignant time; a time when he remembered family and friends that had passed over and reminisced on the landmarks in his life — some he would choose to live over again, if only he could, and some he regretted. His parents gone, first Brendon, and now Elizabeth, sleeping with her husband in their plot under the yew tree; Eamon and Faith, Mary's parents, all departed, along with the numerous siblings, either overseas or in heaven with their parents. Only James, his youngest brother, was still here with them in Ireland.

And Michael himself was feeling nearer to his grave than ever before. He was less inclined to take his walks in the countryside as he used to, a weakness in his legs sometimes making them fold underneath him in a suddenness that was embarrassing. Mary insisted that he use a cane to steady himself, a fine, curved stick carved out of a strong ash wood that she'd bought him a few years back. "This is for when you may have a need of it," she had joked.

Well, he was glad of it now.

A log slipped and it spat out and crackled; he brushed the hot sparks off his brown corduroy trousers, already full of tiny, singed holes from his habit of sitting too close to the fire. Despite almost sitting atop the hearth, he couldn't feel the warmth reaching his feet these days.

Pulling himself up slowly, he unlocked and unbolted the heavy door and stared out into the ancient darkness. He breathed the cold and wetness deep into his lungs, considering the plans that he'd made for his burial and the visit with the solicitor who'd arranged his financial affairs. It was important that Mary and 'the others' would be well provided for when his time came.

Tilting his head backwards he stared into the midnight sky, searching in vain for the Christmas star. Tonight, the heavens were blanketed by low cloud. Feeling disappointed, he spoke out into the darkness, "Aye, I've seen first-hand the bitterness and turmoil that follows a person's inability to face up to their own mortality, fearing that making the necessary arrangements would bring them closer to their grave. Twaddle! Well, I've had a grand life, and I'm mostly content to meet my maker whenever he calls me but as for that poor lad, Moses, God help him; that this should befall him, wealthy or no, his will likely be a sorrowful end."

He felt the presence and smelled her familiar perfume even before her outline became distinguishable in the heavy darkness. Returning from midnight Mass, Mary had been fully expecting her husband to be in his usual place, dozing in front of the fire, but instead she found him standing outside in the darkness, the door to the kitchen wide open to the elements; he was chilled to the bone.

The womenfolk had been noisily busy getting everything ready for the festivities and she'd known that Michael would welcome an opportunity for some time alone. Her concerns that someone would need to stay and keep watch over the slow-roasting leg of pork and braising beef and the simmering Christmas puddings, offered him an opportunity to politely excuse himself from their company and attend the midnight service vicariously, through their gossip when they all returned..

Just one sharp glance and she bustled him inside; taking note of his pallor, she heaved a sigh of vexation, but she wouldn't have cross words with him, "well, not the night anyway."

Michael took note. "Aye, I'm an old fool, I was lost in my thoughts you know, Mary; didn't notice how chilled I'd become."

Tutting and fussing around, she settled a blanket over his lower body and busied herself with taking the pork from the oven and rubbing salt into the crackling. "It's nearly there, Michael, it's looking fine."

A yell and faint laughter broke up the silence. They listened as the voices got louder and nearer until the door was flung open and they all fell inside in their eagerness to get into the warm, keen to sample the roasted pork that would be served up in batches with Mary's homemade savoury stuffing — the long walk from the church had given them an appetite.

First was Adamma, stunning in her tight leather trousers and snow-white fake-fur jacket, next Kamaria in her red student duffle coat, then young Finn in his green Christmas jumper with flashing lights — it was a surprise present from his mam — then Robina, wearing a long, purple, velvet dress and an emerald-green, sparkly scarf, then Uncle James, huffing and puffing, and finally the very tall figure of Samuel, last, because he'd respectfully shown the elder of the group inside ahead of him.

It was a merry party, they filled the home with laughter, all except Finn, who had the strangest notion that figures from the past were hiding in the shadows, watching and waiting, but for what or who he didn't know.

Mary was determined that this would be a good day. "Wet the tea, Robina, for its Christmas morning, a blessed day, and more than that, who'd have thought that we'd be sharing our table with Moses's brother? And our Adamma here with us too? After the shenanigans she's put us all through lately I didn't hold out too much hope that she'd join us this year, what with her being away so very much and mixing with that 'brutal crowd' of hers."

Adamma, an unexpected early riser, crept up and touched Mary softly on her shoulder. "Ah, Grannie, you and Ma blathering away as usual, that makes me think that all is right in the world after all. It seems that I couldn't keep away, so I chose to be with me family of 'culchies' instead."

Robina turned — even at this early hour, her daughter's beauty was flawless.

Leggy and very slender, she wore saffron-yellow silk pyjamas and, with her heavy-braided hair scraped back from her young face with a matching ribbon of broad satin, she epitomised sophistication.

"So, 'macushia', here we are, just us three women together; I could never have wished for a better present than my eldest daughter here within the closeness of her family — it means everything to me." Robina, face flushed with hope and love, hugged her daughter and then her mother and, with a tender smile, she took hold of Adamma's hand. "For your uncle Samuel to be with us too, why, it's as if the magic of Ireland and all of its spiritual energies have conspired to give us all a wonderfully happy Christmas."

"And my prayers, maybe they were answered; could be they had a hand in it — this is the Lord's day, Robina."

"No doubt, mother, but this land is sacred too, you know that, and a force for good, wherever it's from, can only be welcomed."

Adamma, unusually attentive and thoughtful, stood rock still, her dark eyes suddenly welling over with tears. "I'm so very sorry; I've been so muddled and I know that I've been nasty. You know, for a while, I was ashamed of you, Ma', but it was the most miserable thing to be ashamed of my home and who I was. And I know that I've hurt Grandad too, hurt all of you. Oh, and Grandpa's looking so very old now, Gran, so old."

A strong male shout coming from the darkened corner of the kitchen put a sudden stop to Adamma's wailing. "Aye, that shook you all, aye, it's me, I've been sitting in 'me' chair since before the sun rose this morning. Couldn't get any sleep, what with this aching in 'me' legs an' all. And, I'm not in 'me' grave yet I'll have you know, and what do you mean old? Why, I've still got all 'me' hair don't you know?"

Michael tipped back in his chair. "It's good that you've altered your ways, now, no more crying you poor thing, and another thing — you call us 'culchies? Well, I can't argue with that young lady, country dwellers we may be but don't you forget that your gran and I did a fair bit of travelling before we both settled down," and he shot from the chair and seized hold of his daughter, then his wife, and lastly his granddaughter, squeezing them all in close to him.

Adamma pretended to struggle. "Ouch, Grandad, you're scraping my cheek with your bristles."

Releasing his grasp, he turned to Mary. "Oh, my lovely wifey, come here, come here me 'ould' flower." She stood back in amazement and so, instead, Michael caught hold of Robina and attempted to waltz her around the kitchen.

Adamma roared with laughter. "Mam, Grandad is 'plastered'."

"Whist, you'll have the whole house awake, Michael. Here, you've been at the whiskey, have you?"

"Just a wee drop and a glass or two of the 'black stuff'; I couldn't sleep and, well, this bottle that Samuel gave me last night is beautiful, so smooth it went down like cream, warmed me up a treat."

Mary, trying to put some severity into her voice and failing miserably, chuckled. "Robina, give me a hand with your da' and Adamma, fetch me some of that strong coffee that you brewed. I think I'll be needing some of it too."

"How are we going to get him up the stairs mam?" Robina cried, "shouldn't we leave him downstairs?"

"No love, he'll be better in his bed. Right ladies — Adamma, you get behind us and push, you're taller than your mam. Come on, Robina, we'll have to pull him up these stairs. I've not seen your da' as 'fluthered' as this, not for 'donkeys' years'; this will be one Christmas that we won't forget in a hurry."

The few days of Christmas had gone wonderfully well, Michael had been none the worse for his bout of alcoholic excess and there had been no more untoward incidents, until now, for they'd been summoned by Michael to get together, there was news. Chattering and pushing, they squeezed around the table, elbow to elbow and Adamma and Kamaria giggled.

Prompted by Mary, Samuel began, then he stopped and then, coughing quietly, he tried again. "I need to have a word or two with all of you. Look, this is difficult, I'm sorry, but I don't know how to start. Robina, well, your ma and da' asked me to wait until the Christmas celebrations were over."

Mary, her eyes shining with tears of sadness, took hold of Samuel's hand and squeezed.

Robina's expectant expression froze." Well?"

Samuel swallowed hard, took a deep breath and, glancing around the kitchen, he brought his gaze back to Robina, struggling to find the words that could possibly break her heart.

"You're frightening me now, Samuel, what is it?"

Mary stroked Robina's hair and nodded to Samuel to continue; he stumbled with the words. "I have news of my brother."

Adamma's smile faded and Kamaria, sitting next to her Grandad, a delicate wisp of a girl, fidgeted; young Finn began biting his nails, his expression guarded.

Mary patted Samuel on his shoulder, gently murmuring encouragement whilst her husband sat rigid, waiting for the expected explosion, and James, bemused, looked from one to the other.

"I finished my service with the army two years ago. Moses had stopped writing, so I went to 'look him up'. I was shocked at the change in him; he was so miserable, but it was a while before he was able to talk to me about his illness — he was ashamed."

Samuel halted, looked at Mary, opened his mouth to speak and faltered again.

Robina's breathing became rapid; she fixed her intense gaze on Samuel, silently compelling him to continue. There was a long pause. "Go on please Samuel."

"He has HIV, he's living a solitary life, almost a recluse, his housekeeper has cleared off and he asked me to come and see you; so, I wrote to your ma a while back, asking for your address, Robbie. Mary, invited me here to spend Christmas."

A heavy silence permeated the room; a harsh clicking sound from Adamma broke the spell. "So, he's down on his luck, is he? And he wants to come back here with us now and he thinks that we'll put out the red carpet. Well, he can kiss my arse! I told you Mam, he's a chancer, was then, and still is now; ill, and he's probably 'brassic', and he's lost his looks and his black charm, has he? Couldn't 'swerve' this one then."

Samuel winced. "My brother has wronged you all, I know, but it's really not like that. Your dad is not what your think and, Adamma, he's not just another penniless guy down on his luck, far from it. He's a wealthy man and he wants to share with you while he can; he's not asking to be cared for, or loved, he merely wants to try and put things right."

Robina, with a chilling command through clenched teeth, pulled Adamma back to her seat. "Sit down now and show some respect for your uncle, and Kamaria, stop your wailing."

James suddenly came to life. "Christ almighty, he's got AIDS; what bloody news is this, our Michael? You knew? You both knew?"

"Damn it, James, it's not that yet; we've not known for too long, and no, Mary!" Recognising that she was near to admitting her guilt in shelving the letter from them all, Michael glared in her direction.

"We invited Samuel over just five days before Christmas, James. We thought it best that we'd have our Christmas, let Robina and the young ones enjoy theirs, and then break the news."

The sound of the door slamming shut upstairs alerted Robina that her son was missing from the company.

"Let him be, Robina, the lad's petrified, we'll see to him later on."

Finn stepped into his old room and he softly skimmed the cold wetness of the window glass with his trembling fingers and smoothed the familiar patchwork quilt on his bed. Then, hand pressed on each side of his face, he rocked backwards and forwards. The murmur of voices from downstairs carried up to him; Adamma's querulous complaining, Mary, steady and firm, and Samuel's thick Liverpool accent, talking to them all, finding that the words came easier now he had started.

"Listen, as I wrote in my letter, it's not full-blown AIDS yet, James. Thank God there are treatments now — there's no cure yet, but they will give him more time. In fact, it's his mental health that disables him more than the physical just now." Turning to Robina, "And my brother is a wealthy man."

"How's that then?" questioned James.

"Robbie, you know that my brother liked to gamble? Well, you know that 'La', above all? He became a professional poker player; he won a lot of money and had a lot of friends."

"So that's it," exploded Adamma.

"Shut up, let him finish," squealed Kamaria.

"No, that's not all of it; he bought himself some land and, yes, he met a wealthy widow."

Robina flushed. "Oh, he married?"

Samuel smiled gently. "No 'La', but this woman, well, she died suddenly — had a riding accident and left him all of her money. They never married; the lady in question was bound by her husband's will, that on the proviso that she never married again, or co-habited, then she would have all his estate. She adored Moses; he made her happy."

"What of Claire?" Mary wondered.

"Claire? She'd long tired of my brother's ways and she settled in New York with a teacher."

"How did he become infected?" queried Kamaria.

"Does it matter how it happened? He had a smash in his car, a head on collision; he found out then and keeps saying that he wished they'd let him die there and then — bleed to death. He's got it fixed in his head that he should have been 'taken out' in the accident, like our old man, Samson, was.

"Now Adamma, honey, I persuaded him to let me come and tell you all about it. I told him that you all had a right to know, he's your father, absent or not, and he wanted you to have money; I insisted that you should have some sort of answers and closure, if that's what you decide on, after you've heard it all, that is."

"He's not expecting a visit. He couldn't face you all but perhaps you could start writing maybe, see how it goes?"

"'Jaysus', our Michael, I understand now why you threw that whiskey down your neck on Christmas Eve. And you've kept the whole shebang quiet until today? It's New Year's Day tomorrow. By God, what a start to a new year!"

James stopped, clamped his lips tight, suddenly aware of Kamaria's pallor and Adamma's pout of displeasure. He glanced at his niece — she was holding herself together, comforting Samuel who was weeping into the sleeve of his jacket.

James sighed heavily. "Come on then, 'niblings', get your coats and take a walk along the lane with your old uncle, and if my ancient body's up to it then we'll carry on alongside the river."

"Finn!" he yelled up the stairs, "come on down, 'you young stud', and join me and your sisters — we're off for some fresh air."

Finn came clattering down and charged through and past them all. Wearing striped boxer shorts, his flashing Christmas jumper and wellington boots, his face covered with an old, black, knitted balaclava once belonging to Eamon, he shot out of the door without a word.

"Dear God in heaven, our Robina, the lad is stranger than you were and I used to think that you were soft in the head," James laughed.

Samuel stared, Mary tittered, Robina giggled, and the girls grinned; they were used to their brother's eccentricities. Samuel tried to stifle his laughter, and this

246

resulted in a snort from him which set them all howling; James hooted until the tears ran down his bearded face. They hooted, with relief, or maybe hysteria, and Kamaria rushed outside to catch up with her brother.

"Well that's that." Michael stretched out the stiffness in his cramped legs; it took him a while to get himself moving in the mornings, and the afternoons, and the evenings! He set down a bottle and four glasses in front of them and, catching Mary's withering glance, smiled what he hoped was a winning smile.

"Now, husband," Mary cautioned.

"Ah, wife,", Michael mocked, "I'm aware that it's early in the day, but there's a need, there is a need, now don't be a scold; it's just a wee dram each, it's New Year's Eve and the lad has a long way to travel to reach his brother for New Year's Day. So, to our Samuel here, a toast for a safe journey and an invite to return and share with us again, for you're one of our family, Samuel, always welcome under my roof; around here — family is all."

CHAPTER 24

Moses

Samuel was half a day's travel into his journey to the Western States of America, arriving at the airport early evening, an eleven-hour flight ahead of him. As he had expected, the terminals were crammed to overfill with heaving, pushing bodies, craning their necks to peruse the flight updates or hoping to find a seat while they waited — children predictably fractious, business men in grey flannel suits, irritated to have their normal routine disrupted by the New Year celebrations.

Already stiff and aching from the long drive, he stretched out his long, booted limbs, much to the annoyance of those passing who were forced to dance around him. He was too weary to be polite, shrugging off their complaints he pulled his holdall onto his lap and closed his eyes.

Samuel didn't intend to drift off. He just needed to rest his eyes, gritty from the dry heat in the terminal. He had a while to wait before he could board his flight. "Can it only be ten days since I left my brother back home?" he pondered, and the Christmas spent with nieces and nephew and his new family already seemed another lifetime away, somehow. The long heart to heart he'd had with his brother before leaving for Ireland played on his mind. He drifted back…

Moses pulled the drawer open, took out the bunch of letters that were clipped together, and handed them to Samuel.

"I didn't have their address. It's been years since I'd heard of them or tried to make contact, or even gave them a thought. It didn't seem right to send these onto her parents; I assumed they'd be long gone. Mary was forty years old when she had Robina, you know! And then, how could I dare to believe that they'd even want to hear from me after the way I left, Sammy? Finn was just past having his first birthday when I cleared off with Claire; as you know she didn't stay around for long — she used me, I was a means to help her escape her da' and her old life. Still, we both know I'd have gone anyway," he sighed.

The brothers had talked long through the night and into the following day, Samuel listening mostly whilst his elder brother told how he'd danced with 'Lady Fortune', of the gambling, taking his chances, moving from city to city, continually searching for the elusive 'more' — that something which was indefinable and always promised to be 'just a rainbow away'. He'd gathered beautiful and powerful women around him; had become greedy and addicted to the highs; what he had thought was respect he now recognised as being other weak-minded people clinging on for the ride. When Samuel attempted to comfort him, Moses was having none of it. "I was a poor minded, sensual creature with ready cash in my pocket; never giving a thought for those back in the UK. I was hell bent on becoming somebody, proving myself, being a success. I took advice and invested my winnings, some anyway, in property and land, and enjoyed the rest."

Eventually, the sophisticated image and life that he had created disgusted and wearied him; he felt jaded, he became restless and the overindulgences and addictions no longer held any attraction. And that's when Isabella, the stunning Latin American beauty, entered his life. In some ways she had reminded him of Mary, Robina's mother, with her strong, handsome beauty and self-assurance. As a wealthy widow, Isabella had been accustomed to having whatever she desired or needed, and she had made it clear that she wanted Moses and wasted no time in winning him.

She'd introduced him to another sort of life out west, a settled, peaceful life, one where he wasn't constricted by the alien unfriendliness of city or the damp, phlegmatic, small Irish community that Robina had been raised in.

Moses thrived in the remote beauty and harshness of the mountains; the wildness of it all with its game — the deer and jack- rabbits, the pheasants and even the rattlesnakes brought excitement and a sense of being alive.

He took to riding out with her; he adored her proud beauty; how dazzling she was, galloping alongside him on her beloved palomino. Sometimes she teased him, her horse galloping way in front, her long, black hair streaming behind her, turning and laughing recklessly as he cautiously trotted along on the chestnut stallion that was capable of so much more.

She introduced him to a freedom that he'd never known, she had beauty and a wildness that replicated the behaviour of the herds of unbroken horses that were scattered over the land. He never tired of her harsh, dark, Latin American beauty, her flashing, dark eyes, almost black, her straight nose, cheekbones as fine as bone china, her wide, sensuous mouth and her impossibly proud bearing. Everything about her was, for him, perfect; her bright-coloured silk shirts and tight, suede riding pants tucked into soft leather boots and her strident, demanding needs that stimulated his senses with a harshness that excited them both.

Poor Moses, he'd been so unprepared for the 'briar patch' that fate flung into his path, taking his love away so suddenly and violently.

Sipping his thick, black coffee, he'd been waiting out on the veranda, peering out into the darkness, feeling it close in and watching the last vestiges of lilac and purple fade into darkness. He loved to sit in the shadow and still emptiness, and melt into the night. Stretched out under a rug he contemplated whether she would come. He didn't know, she was unpredictable, but he hoped.

There's was an honest relationship which in some ways was ruled by the stipulations of her ex-husband's will, but they'd discovered that living independently added a freedom and excitement to their loving and tonight he needed to see her, the desire and anticipation fuelling a slow burning in his loins; he was content to wait for Isabella, to light the fire in his belly.

The trill of the telephone from inside the porch jarred his senses. Throwing down the rug, he wandered inside. "Why is she calling first? That's not usually her way?"

Now, on his hands and knees' he leaned over the basin, the sensation of nausea and fear shivering through his body.

"Isabella!"

The receiver hung down, coiled and resting low on the floor.

"Hello? Hello? Moses? That you? We're coming over." The male voice dragged him back into a hellish reality.

He slumped in a heap, head in hands, struggling to speak.

"Isabella, dead."

When her horse had ridden back without her, they'd gone looking; they had found her laying in a crumpled heap and gently pulled back her spreading cloak of jet-black hair, only to find her neck and jaw fixed at a strange angle, her eyes, devoid of life, staring out into the mountains.

Isabella gone! She'd gifted him everything, he was the only beneficiary to her estate.

Alone now, aside from a twice-weekly visit from his housekeeper, and increasingly morose, he found sleep escaped him. When he did sleep, images of Isabella and his children back home intermingled in a bizarre pantomime of his family life in Liverpool and Ireland and of the mountains and her horses.

Slowly and painfully, during the long empty hours he began to 'take stock' of his life, travel back through time and view 'blow by blow' the chronicle of his selfishness and hedonistic lifestyle. He wanted to meet up with Samuel. He didn't think that, for one minute, the young family that he'd abandoned back in the UK would ever entertain any future connection.

He found himself writing letters to his children, without having any intention of posting them but it helped clear his mind, and he started to plan. Maybe they'd accept his offer of financial assistance, at least. He'd posted a long letter off to Samuel. He'd kept the many postcards that Samuel had sent on to him from his army travels and, to his surprise, his brother had returned his letter immediately. They had relished their renewed contact and shared the possibility that Samuel might stay out west with him eventually; Moses wasn't able to face a trip to the UK or Ireland just then, but perhaps in the future, who knows?

All things pass and he began forcing himself out of bed, taking a day at a time, breaking it up into hours, then a morning, then an afternoon. He took to running and, alone amongst the hills and the endless, clean, blue skies, he was able to stretch his mind, finally arriving home exhausted but filled with a delicious sense of freedom and respite from his over-active imagination.

Yet he was still unable to manage without 'his soother' — the bottle of whiskey which eased him through the darkness. As often happens, the spirit became a tyrant — instead of a liquor-fuelled sleep he became troubled with vivid images. Here was baby Finn curled up on his mother's lap, and Robina's delicate fragility, Kamaria's chuckling playfulness, Adamma's careful watching, and Isabella, laying with her head at a strange angle, eyes wide open. Isabella, reaching up to him from the metal container that he'd collected the bodies in all those years ago, when he was a hospital porter.

Night after night his torment continued. He was haunted by the violence of Isabella's death. The home that he once so loved became a prison to him; the shade of Isabella continually visited, beckoned, pointed and he dreaded the time when the curse of the drink would take hold and finish him.

One night, unable to stay within the walls that were closing in on him, he'd seized his keys and bolted out into blackness. Leaving the house open to the elements, he drove off in a desperate attempt to escape the bourbon-fuelled phantoms that were dancing in his head.

As predicted, those who watched and cautioned that 'it's sure to end in a bad way', were given the macabre satisfaction that their anticipated forecast proved to be a correct one.

"And that's how it finished," he'd told Samuel. "You know the rest; a head on smash, I recovered only to contract this virus and I don't know how long before I develop full-blown AIDS, do I? It could be a year, ten years if I'm lucky."

They'd cried together; Moses had dropped his head down on Samuel's shoulder and sobbed.

"I know why this has come to me, Sammy, I deserve it. I'm sure that Isabella's spirit comes to me because she wants me to contact my children before it's too late. We used to talk of them, you know, she wanted me to invite them over. I still have their photos, the ones I took with me when I left. Robina was just a girl when I met her, a young, Irish girl with strange fancies — she was adorable."

Moses wept hard and loud. "But how can I, Samuel? How can I bring more misery into their lives? I won't do it; my chance has gone forever. They should have left me to die, I'd lost so much blood; if they hadn't found me then it all would have come to you, and you could have sorted the kids out."

And that's how it had ended, almost, for Samuel had persuaded Moses that he should at least get in touch with Michael and Mary, and so, Samuel had written and told them of his brother. The Christmas visit had been difficult and wonderful, and now Samuel was returning to Moses again with news of his family, of the children, so much like their father.

He carried a hope in his heart that he wouldn't be too late, for he feared for his brother.

Samuel walked onto his flight, relieved at last to be boarding the plane. He slumped into a window seat, fastened his seat belt and, whether from exhaustion from the emotional trials of the last few days or from the long drive to the airport he didn't know, but the vivid images of that last visit with Moses eventually faded, and he slipped into a deep, dreamless sleep.

CHAPTER 25

A Year On

Another year passed with a long hard winter, a hot summer, a bountiful mild Autumn; and once again the family were gathering together across the Irish sea. It was late afternoon before Adamma and her sister recovered from their New year celebrations and were able to sit around the 'New Year table' for food.

Robina and her mother laid out a simple spread, helped by young Finn alone, bright and eager, and much taller than your average sixteen-year-old lad, for he'd just turned sixteen the first week in December. Adamma had reached her twenty-second birthday in October the same year and Kamaria was now twenty, three days before her sister's birthday. It had been an expensive time for their grandparents, this Christmas just gone, but they'd enjoyed indulging them. "While we can afford it we will", Mary had reassured her protesting daughter.

Finn, who'd built up an appetite following his ride with his favourite piebald horse, 'Rollo', was tucking into huge slices of soda bread coated with rich, yellow butter and his gran's homemade brawn. Kamaria and Adamma, despite protestations about their delicate condition following last night's revelry, were also doing justice to 'the table'; Robina picked at walnuts and apple with cottage cheese, fully lost in her wanderings and memories of those who no longer sat around the table this New Year's Day.

Mary, noticing her daughter's lack of enthusiasm with her food gave Robina a questioning glance. Robina's bottom lip trembled, "Oh, Mammie, I really thought that my children would at last see their da' sometime, and I was so hopeful when Samuel left us last new year carrying our letters and goodwill. But here we are, another New Year's Day, another year passed, and our Finn turned sixteen, and nothing."

"For fecks sake, Mam," spluttered Adamma through a mouth overfilled with pork pie and potato crisps. "Haven't you left 'all of that' thinking behind yet?"

Mary too, exasperated by her daughter's seeming inability to ever gain some semblance of practicality, banged on the table.

"Enough! I'll not have this language and bickering starting up again, and especially not today."

Her husband, coughing and waving his hands to hide the drift of smoke from his cigarette, and ignoring the tired glance from Mary, shushed and cautioned them all.

"Pipe down now, the lot of ye, I'll not see my women-folk at each other's throats again. Now! That man made no promises to come over here, you all must know that. He has written and put money in a trust for the three of you, half to have when you come of age, and the other half to come to you when you reach the age of thirty; aye, mature enough to make good use of it after you've blown the first half with your fripperies and nonsense."

"Grandad, mine will help me through 'med' school," protested a now studious Kamaria, thick, glossy hair scraped back severely, and rimless spectacles perched on the end of her small nose.

"That might be so," agreed Michael, whilst his glance wondered over to his eldest granddaughter.

Adamma fidgeted in her seat and she stared at him, pouting, defiant.

Michael tucked Adamma playfully underneath her chin. "We'll no be starting that up again, Adamma. Don't fret now, we were all young once," and he leaned forward and kissed her gently on her furrowed brow, tickled a delighted Kamaria, and roughed up young Finn's 'thatch'.

Finn protested loudly. No one could touch his hair, he'd taken to wearing his hair in 'dreads' so that it covered his face and ears, or hid it under a woollen hat; he knew that he was secure in that way!

"You could be taken for a modern pirate, lad, all you need is one of your gran's hooped earrings and you'd be sorted," Michael teased.

"Da', stop, I want to say something. It's important. I'm sorry I wasn't strong enough to hold my family together," and turning to the three young people, Robina continued. "We both failed you all, and I've lived my life ever since trying to make amends and I know that your father will be trying to do the same now, in his own way."

Adamma flicked her hair in annoyance, "I don't agree with all that 'guff' about open relationships. If there is such a thing as true love, Mum, then you should have owned it; both of you. Married when you had your children, 'got legal', you know that; it's what your parents and grandparents did, and then they built their lives around their home and kids and their roots. And don't look at me like that, it's what our Kamaria always wanted too. Why! Look at her, will you? She's screwed up because of you. Hiding her sexuality behind those bloody ugly spectacles and frumpy clothes."

"No! Stop it. Your father loved you all, he adored you especially, his first born. I remember how he always sang to you, soothed you to sleep." Robina's eyes begged for understanding. Sincere and hesitant she gazed at the company. Dreamlike, she continued, the siblings for once altogether quiet. "I was a young, Irish girl, fresh from the country, alone in a city in the UK, out of my depth but with a burning desire to 'put something back into an ugly world. Your father was tall and golden and so, so, handsome, Irish and West Indian blood with a cheeky Liverpudlian charm. You three were born of love, not lust. You were brought into this world on the beam of our hope that one day the colour of skin would make no difference; and we had an absolute trusting need and unconditional love between us. I will never regret any of you or be sorry of my time with your da'. Darlings, please, let's look forward now, we all have each other, it's a new year."

"Nice one, quite a speech, Ma," giggled Kamaria. Turning to her sister she scowled, "and what's wrong with the way I dress? You ole bitch."

Adamma silently glared her answer.

"I'm joking Adamma, 'Sis', stop it. You'll ruin your smooth modelling face."

Adamma conceded and Kamaria rambled out her thoughts with a speedy rate of enthusiasm, "Say, we all know now that if Dad's lucky then he may live for years without that HIV ever developing into full-blown AIDS. I've been reading up on it; he was diagnosed and treated very early on and statistics show that if he takes good care, you know, medication, plenty of exercise and sleep, good food, fresh air and let's face it, he gets plenty of that living where he does surrounded by all of that space and 'them mountains', then he could have a nearly normal lifespan." She took a deep breath and turning to Michael she continued, more slowly, "But if he does come over, then listen grandad, you'd have to cut out that smoking around him."

"'Wheesh'? Me? I only have the one or two, it's a special day."

"It's not good for your circulation, Grandad," Kamari accused.

"Enough, the lot of ye, nagging me! Come on our, Finn, let's get the whistle and guitar; our James will be back soon and you can give us a wee song — my old pipes aren't so good today."

"Why, talk of the Devil," cried Mary, much to her grandson's alarm, as the door flew open.

James stood, larger than life, bringing in the harsh cold and two limp rabbits hanging down at his side.

"You're a bit late for 'first-footing', our James."

"An' he's got no hair," giggled Adamma. "First-footer should have dark hair."

"I put out a dish of bread and milk early this morning," Robina whispered.

"Do you still do that, Ma'?" Kamaria howled.

A lively afternoon passed with much jigging and laughter, a game of draughts or two, a competitive game of Monopoly which James won, as usual, and then more food, even Adamma filling herself as if there was no tomorrow. And when the table was cleared away, they toasted absent friends and Finn and Michael sang and James played the haunting melody to their new composition which they had named 'Maybe'.

Mary opened the door to the outside darkness and Robina lit the candles and they all hushed whilst the men sang and played, and the flames flickered, and the owl called.

"Come with me, you will, or you won't
You do if you do, you don't if you don't,
Take my hand, in the softness of the night,
Lose your fears, can you see the light?
Come with me, won't you come with me.
Now I'm alone, night is closing in,
I knew that I'd lose but I always played to win,
Come with me, won't you come with me."

Adamma, puzzled, "Where did those lyrics come from?"

"Out of my head, where do you think they come from?" Finn scowled. He wasn't going to tell, oh no, he knew better than that.

CHAPTER 26

She Wasn't Ready to Leave Them

Many of Robina's colleagues had known her since her early days in student training; some were irritated by her constant selflessness and her impossibly high ideals and others were secretly in awe of the dedication which drove her on. Whilst respecting the seemingly eternal patience and compassion that she brought to the team, they wondered at her complete disinterest or lack of ambition; apart from short maternity leaves, her nursing career had continued for over twenty years and, despite encouragement, she'd never once applied for promotions.

She had dreams, as any other, and she was achieving one of them already, but it wasn't quite enough; she wanted to travel further afield, to nurse in the less well-developed parts of the world.

And now she could sense that wonderful time growing near. She was now in her early forties and her family were making their own mark on the world, maturing and establishing their careers.

Adamma, at twenty-three, always the beauty, still yearning to see her name in lights and having made some headway in the modelling industry, had joined a theatrical agency and was living in London.

Kamaria, just passed her twenty-first birthday, had made inroads into her five-year medical training and was now set loose on the wards.

And Finn? The youngest, seventeen and with the strongest connection to her by far, had begun a three-year course at the local agricultural college with sure plans to return to Ireland and take over responsibility on his grandparents' farm. Travelling back and forward on the ferry at every opportunity, he was a great help now. Her parents were both a goodly age and Robina was relieved that her son was able to offer them support; despite having reliable farm hands, Robina knew that, 'there was no one like family'.

Finn, affectionate but still very shy, found that his love of the land and animals appeared to override the problems he had with social interactions; he was careful to manage his 'difficulties' in such a way that the elder members of the family were mostly unaware how he weaved and wobbled in and out of everyday reality.

Sipping her fourth mug of strong coffee, she knew that she was more content and hopeful than she'd been for the last few years; at long last everything was positioning into a place where her dream to work abroad would soon be a reality. The troublesome times and the conflicts of Adamma's teenage years had ceased; the future was shining as glaringly as the early sun slanting its rays through the east window of the ward.

Her eyes gritty with need of sleep and suddenly shivering with cold, she gulped down the hot drink, hugging her cardigan around her. She wondered, just for a moment, if it may be possible to restore her relationship with Moses, hoping against hope that perhaps he may still have some feelings for her.

In the soft stillness before the elderly patients started to rouse, the call of an owl echoed from the trees in the fields nearby and she checked her fob watch; her stomach rumbled with hunger; she was never able to tolerate a heavy meal, preferring to push through the eleven-hour night shift on tea, coffee and a few biscuits.

Hearing movement from the side room behind the nursing station she stood to investigate; it was only one hour before the auxiliary nurse took the early morning tea trolley around for the early risers. Knocking softly, she poked her head around the door.

"Is it time for tea yet, nurse?"

"Not quite, there's no need to stir yourself, it's not time yet," she whispered into the dull light of the room. Her senses reeled from the stench of a gangrenous limb, her empty stomach reacted, and she had to move quickly or she'd vomit. She turned to hide any trace of disgust; this poor gentleman was not long for this world — unable to face the rigours of surgery he was being treated with every palliative care that they could offer.

The elderly man pulled his bed covers to one side. "You can join me if you like, Nurse Robina."

The thick, hot air left her gasping for breath. "Now, David," she chided gently.

"Only teasing."

"Can't you sleep, are you in a lot of pain?" Forcing the last vestige of compassion out of her weary body she smoothed his sheets, plumped up the moist pillow under his shiny head and gently stroked his crooked fingers. Waiting until he relaxed, she left him, gently snoring.

At last, her three long consecutive nights were over; the nursing rota listed R/N Moran on A/L for five wonderful days and she'd be able to spend time with Adamma, who was at home for a few days in between her auditions and modelling assignments. Rushing through her notes as quickly as she dared the Handover was completed in record time. Wrapping her heavy cloak around her she stepped out into the half-light.

The rush of cold air invigorating her senses, she drew it inside her in a long, deep breath, welcoming its freshness after the dry heat of the hospital; she listened carefully to the chattering above her, delighting in the morning bird song, it was always a blessing, a symphony to her ears.

"Another glorious morning — thank you, God, for another day."

Just five minutes more and the heavenly quiet dissipated into the shock of the rush hour; the commotion and the leaded fumes were unpleasant and she pulled her hood over and around her head and face. Fumbling in her pocket, she found a packet of mints that Finn had given her as she'd left last night.

"Love 'you' Mam," he'd cried, as she turned and waved. "I'll make your 'fave brekky' in the morning, just how you like it."

Picking up her pace to ward off the cold, she mused, "Such a fine boy, and I have my lovely girls too, and Moses is alive and I have a grand brother-in-law,

Samuel, and Mammie and Da' too, and Uncle James. Oh, and Moses; dear Moses. I've been loving you for so long, I wonder? Oh, life is good, and it's only going to get better."

Robina's heart raced up with a joy that she hadn't felt for such a time.

"Will he need me? Is he coming home at last?"

The sudden coming of the harsh rain took her by surprise, it bounced down hard off her hood, stinging her face with its sharpness; laughingly she pushed out her tongue to catch it and she stepped out.

"Here luv, watch where you're going."

The screech of worn tyres, a sickening thud, someone screamed from a distance.

Too late!

Too late!

The screams vibrated and echoed in her ears and, trembling, she fell onto her knees,

"'Noooo'! oh, dear God, sweet Holy Mother, please, not my mammie."

Clutching tightly onto the uniformed trousers, she pleaded, "Oh, please tell me this is a mistake, it's someone else, you've got it wrong."

This was one part of her job that she would never become used to, the policewomen's hand trembled; in her distress, Adamma caught hold of her tightly; the officer didn't pull away.

"Come now, love, sit yourself down now, can I call somebody? Is there anyone else at home?" She doubted whether anyone else was at home — the young women's screams were loud enough to wake the dead!

Amongst her sobs she managed to point to her handbag and with a broken voice she was able to direct the policewomen towards her mobile. "My gran's telephone number, it's in my mobile, my brother's still in bed and my sister's away at University Hospital in Scotland."

Without warning she jumped to her feet and darted towards the front entrance. "I've got to tell them, tell Grandad, tell Finn."

The accompanying male officer was quick to respond. "Now where are you going, Adamma — is that your name — Adamma?"

Oh, dear Mother in heaven, I don't know what to do, where's my mam? Where is she?" and the shrieks echoed again, whilst upstairs in his bedroom, Finn buried his head in his pillow. These screams weren't inside his head, not this time. No, making a dash to the window he opened the curtains and looked outside — it was raining heavily, it splashed down from the broken guttering in a torrent, the dark heavy clouds joined together in the sky blotting out the light; there was a police car outside!

"What time is it then," he queried. "Mam should be home from her night shift about now, shouldn't she?"

He called downstairs, "What's the time? Who's that screaming?" Not waiting for an answer, he pulled his cap on backwards and bounced down to the kitchen. The portly officer moved towards him. Taking his arm gently, he eased Finn onto a chair,

"Hello lad, now listen carefully, I'm very sorry but I've some bad news for you."

Mary was still unable to accept the news; her mind and heart were struggling to process it. Robina was dead, their only, precious daughter taken, and it should have been them; they were well and truly past their three times twenty years and ten.

The death certificate was signed, her death registered, funeral arrangements complete, and the morning of the burial was now upon them, God help them.

It had been hard to accept that their daughter would be buried in Liverpool but they both understood that it was what she would have wanted; she'd made her life in the UK, met Moses and bore her children in this city, and they knew that her family would find a comfort in tending their mam's grave and having it as a place of refuge when their loss was too painful to bare.

Never in her wildest dreams had Mary anticipated this, her daughter laying still and cold, whilst she and Michael remained. Robina, her wonderfully fey daughter, taken in a flash by the speeding and screeching wheels that had slammed into her body and sent her soul to heaven and kingdom come; hurling her into the oncoming traffic as easily as if she had been one of her rag dolls.

She'd crept off alone, hid herself away for a while, not wanting to break down in front of Michael; she'd called to Faith in heaven, oh how she needed her strength right now. "Oh, Mammie, when we saw her at the mortuary, there was hardly anything left of her beautiful delicate face, her long hair was matted with blood, oh why couldn't it have been me?" She'd stayed on her knees until Michael had come looking for her and finding that she was as cold as a block of ice he'd gently and tenderly coaxed her back inside.

They had taken the children to see her, they'd tentatively kissed her cold cheek and young Finn had horrified Kamaria by leaning forward and snipping a lock of his mam's hair. She'd protested loudly but Mary acknowledged that it was a family tradition, it was Finn's right; she'd herself had taken a lock of Faith's hair when she passed on too.

This morning, Mary's heart was cold and heavy like a lead weight inside her; she listened to her husband wheezing as he shaved at the kitchen mirror. James was standing outside under a large, black umbrella, drawing heavily on his third cigarette. How Michael longed to join him.

Samuel was meeting them at the church and Mary wondered if he'd persuaded Moses to come back with him. The girls were dressing upstairs and young Finn was already fully turned out in a black suit and a crisp white shirt with a narrow, black, silk tie that Adamma had given him.

He sat quietly, refusing all food and comfort, polite but adamant. "Gran, I wish to be left alone."

His grandfather had nodded in agreement and caught her eye. "That's enough, Mary, leave the lad; he's with us, he'll come to no harm, leave him be for a wee while."

The truth was that she herself needed comfort — she couldn't bare it when he shut her out.

The time had come. A smart rap at the door; to Finn it sounded as thunder. Running to his room, he closed the door, pulled the bolt across and turned the key in a panic.

"Finn, Finn," his mam's face spun around in front of him. "Come on now, be a good lad for me, I'm still with you, always will be, now off you go down to the others, they are waiting."

Samuel had called Moses the day after the accident. He'd taken the news with a great sadness, but the many years that had passed since he'd been part of the family acted as a buffer between any strong emotions other than experiencing guilt and his new-found concern for his children; his connection to her death had as much impact as watching a movie.

Samuel failed in his attempt to persuade his brother to fly over with him. He was angry and frustrated with his brother's refusal, and also becoming sickened with Moses's continuing morose mood. They parted on angry terms.

"She gave you a family, the children that you always craved for — they need you. I'm embarrassed by you, your selfishness has no limits, you're still the conceited bonehead that you always were. I'm ashamed of you."

Moses had slammed the door behind him.

Moses attempted to justify his decision; he threw handfuls of clear cold water over his face, he showered, and ate, and paced, and walked. It was all so very long ago, she'd charmed him with her delicate other-worldliness, he'd cared for her and wanted to protect her, for a short while they'd had a need of each other, that was all.

But Isabella — he'd loved her as a man truly loves a woman. They'd excited each other; as lovers they were able to touch each other's souls, physically, intellectually, spiritually; theirs was a love that would carry on for eternity. Samuel just didn't understand. How could he accuse him of being selfish? He was terminally ill and he'd lost the only woman that he had truly ever cared for more than himself. He wanted his family but he dismissed Robina — they were never meant to last.

The day after Robina's burial, Isabella came to Moses in a dream. She galloped towards him on her beloved palomino, dressed in her favourite scarlet, silk shirt, her hair trailing behind her, calling to him, laughing wildly. "Moses," she cried, and the turquoise crystal at her throat sparkled in the sunlight. As she neared her coal-black eyes shone with such tenderness; he had such a need for her and he'd cried softly.

His words came out in breathless whispers. "Take me with you," he'd pleaded.

Jumping down from her horse she held him to her fiercely, whispering endearments and secret words of passion. Regretfully, she pushed him away from her and then warned him, solemnly. "I have been allowed to come to you, please listen to me. If you truly want to make amends, then you need to do more than mope around mourning for your lost youth and health. There will be a time in the future when you are needed back home. I will help you find your strength — I will pray for you."

"Oh Isabella," he cried, "I don't know where to begin. Each day I take a walk down by the river, I talk to the mountain spirits, I've prayed a hundred times. I'm totally alone here and all I want to do is throw myself into that black water; it sings to me, beckons me, it tells me, "Wash your sins away, Moses, come.".

Pulling her hand back she slapped him sharply across his face; he woke with the sting of her words and his cheek smarting. "Fulfil your responsibilities, live up to your duties as a father, before it is too late."

CHAPTER 27

Difficult Decisions

Following Robina's death, the family drifted into a time of darkness, her elderly parents struggled to cope with their loss; the light that Robina carried, her stubborn refusal to acknowledge fear or greed, her gentle kindness — these were the glue that held the family together.

She had only ever seen the best in them all and they'd responded. She'd calmed her father when he'd threatened to 'tear Moses apart', when he'd wanted to lock Adamma in her room. She'd shamed her eldest daughter when her selfishness and arrogance had been 'out of hand'; she had acknowledged the 'strangeness' of her son and loved him more because of it, insisting the girls did the same, and Kamaria? When she worried about her grades, Robina would work extra hours to pay for further tuition, so she could achieve her dream of being a doctor.

She had given them a haven to return to, when the world was cruel and closing in on them and proved, by her own example, that unconditional regard for other humans was possible.

Robina had lived from the heart, and now that she was gone the family were in danger of being scattered and broken.

Grandfather Michael walked in sorrow and his brow held a permanent furrow; Mary, although still quietly supportive, found that her immense stamina and strength had finally been taken away, on the inside and outside. Her once-beautiful hair that, even in old age had been her glory, was now as white as snow.

Mary was unable to summon the willpower to hold them all together — all she wanted was to be in Ireland and to mourn her only daughter; for the first time in her life the responsibilities of the family were a burden to her.

Michael knew they had to get back home. He feared for his wife, she looked so frail; being away took too much out of them now, theirs heart were in the home they'd made for themselves over the years. He knew the time was growing near when they would both be buried amongst the hills that they so loved, it was the way of things, the natural order of life.

It was time to pen a few words; he didn't want to leave this world without writing down what needed to be said.

With this in mind he urged his wife to take herself off to bed. "Go on up now" he urged Mary, "take yourself to bed, I'll join you in a wee while."

She hadn't wanted to leave him; she knew that he'd have the cigarette packet out as soon as she was in her bed.

He'd insisted, "Now, Mary, off you go, you look all in, I need some time to think on my own, we have the young one to sort out."

She was right — he listened for the bed springs lowering and then lit his cigarette, breathed in the smoky comfort and leaned back. The cigarette smoke clarified his worries; he was feared that he would lose her too. The thought of his daughter and his wife leaving him, well it was altogether too much to contemplate.

He watched the shadows from the dying fire slide along the low ceiling above his head.

Two cigarettes on and he was still wondering what to do about the lad.

Hearing footsteps, he called out, "Mary, is that you?"

The soft tread stopped at the door and, moving quickly, he opened it. Young Finn stood, uncertain, still.

"'Wheesh', come on in lad, it's past midnight. Get yourself here in front of the fire, I'll build it up a wee bit."

"Grandad, I can't sleep tonight for worrying. Kamaria's away studying in Scotland, our Adamma is in London, and you and Gran will need to return home soon; it's not fair keeping you both here because of me, I'll be all right."

"I know, lad, but your life has been turned upside down, you're not yet eighteen and we want to make sure things will be as they should be before we leave."

Finn hesitated. "Are you hungry? I'm hungry Grandad?"

Michael poured strong tea from the pot and set a 'mountain' of bacon butties in front of his grandson. It was good that the lad was eating. They strummed their guitars quietly and played cards and eventually Finn took himself back to his bed.

Michael stayed put. He wrapped a blanket around his legs — they were always cold these days.

He needed time to think!

So here it was, the problem and a possible solution. This was the dilemma that was presented after much discussion between them all. Michael wasn't sure that he could rely on these suggestions, even though they were made with the best of intentions he would much prefer the lad to return to Ireland with himself and Mary.

Despite his shyness, their grandson had been very firm. He'd refused to return with them until he'd finished his agricultural course, or at least the biggest part of it. James insisted that they should give the lad a chance, it could work, it was the first time that his great-nephew had ever really been determined about anything.

Adamma swore she would get home and check on Finn every couple of weeks; the Singh family from the corner shop promised that he could have supper with them every evening; the Polish couple, Jacob and Aneta, would share Sunday lunch and help him with the house and any laundry and Kamaria hoped to find time to make a call in between her hospital shifts and study.

Samuel was back in the USA starting up a new business; he would try to visit if all went well in a few months' time, and Moses? Well, he was full of promises in his letters, but he was an uncertainty, as always.

In spite of the empty cigarette packet and the clouds of smoke, the time that he'd spent mulling over all possibilities had not been conclusive. So, reluctantly he 'threw the towel in' and retired to his bed.

The next morning, decisions were made.

Finn's refusal to return with them had to be respected.

"Don't ask me to go back with you Grannie. My mam would want me to finish, I'm nearly eighteen and for the first time in my life I'm doing something that makes me feel happy. This is still Mam's house, she's still here with me; I'm safe here and I've got the neighbours and I'll be busy. Uncle James will come over when he can."

It was finished, a solution at last, one that went against their better judgment, but it was a compromise of sorts. Michael hoped against hope that Finn would manage. The decision did bring with it a sense of relief, so they hugged and acted quickly and decisively. They did a mammoth shop, then Mary busied herself baking and filling the freezer, she gave the little house a 'good bottoming', whilst Michael and Finn took a walk around the docks, then they planned to have a 'takeaway', probably a Chinese — the lad loved it!

The pair of them would be off early the following morning — God help them they couldn't wait — they were both exhausted, they needed to be home. Michael told himself she was no longer here, she was gone, there was no need to hang around; it would serve no purpose. Mary insisted that Robina's sweet perfume hung about the place. He knew this was wishful thinking, didn't he? "It's not real, my darling, she's gone."

Finn stood by as the ferry churned through the dark water. He waved until he knew they wouldn't be able to see him anymore. Pulling his hat down further against the biting cold he turned, pulled up his jacket collar and strode back to the empty house; only to him it wasn't empty, he knew that his mam was still there, she always would be, she'd be waiting for him.

CHAPTER 28

Something's Wrong

Finn woke to the heavy perfume of lavender filling the room. Pushing the bedcovers away he checked his watch; it was time to get moving, he didn't want to be late again.

Soon the rashers of bacon were spitting in the pan; the air was thick with the strong salty aroma and cutting two thick slices of bread, he covered them with grease from the pan, topped them with four rashers and squashed the whole into his lunchbox, throwing a couple of apples in for good measure.

Grabbing his bulky sheepskin jacket, he took a couple of cans and pushed one inside each pocket and slammed the front door behind him; this was the daily routine, it rarely changed.

His days always unfolded in the same lonely way. Out early in the morning, skip breakfast; run for the bus and try to get the same seat, the first single high seat by the window. He didn't like to be hemmed in by a stranger.

Finn knew exactly how many months and weeks had passed since his grandparents had returned home; he marked each day on the kitchen calendar. They called him every Friday evening without fail. The signal was poor because their home was surrounded by hills and so his grandad took a short drive to the pub and rang him from there.

At this time of year, the nights were drawn in. The pearly softness of dusk was a pleasure to Finn, his world took on a dream like quality at this time of day. He stared out of the bus window at the heavy traffic, the rows of cars always moving slowly at these peak times. Stepping off the platform he breathed in the mouth-watering smell of fish and chips from the chippy on the corner. It always drew in a long queue of hungry customers, tonight was the same as always, with much jostling and tapping of their feet in the cold air. This was his home; he'd have a supper with his gentle neighbours and then, as he pushed his key into the door, sometimes, just for a few seconds, he would forget, and in a panic, he'd call out — Mam? Why was the house in darkness? Then, his spirit heavy, he'd remember. He was alone.

Adamma's sporadic visits home had lessened; her singular attention was now focused on her career or, as Mary would see it, this was her selfish nature rising to the fore now they weren't around to prick her conscience. His sister rational was that her brother was almost eighteen, he had neighbours, all his bills and rent were covered by Grandad. Her past life in Liverpool was now a distant illusion. Her mam was dead, that part of her life was gone; the allure of London life, the parties and glamour were her reality now. The echoes of home were easily erased with a few spliffs and a line of white powder.

Well, yes, she'd made a promise that she would most definitely make it home every weekend, and in truth it had been easy to say. And Kamaria? The reliable, diligent, middle child, now bearing the weight of her medical responsibilities and a heavy schedule that left her short-tempered and short on sleep? She too found that the single weekly obligatory calls home became a burden, and Finn's singular presence at the family home and her promise to her grandparents faded from her thoughts.

The grandparents, who were living under the understanding that Finn had the unquestionable support of his siblings, were none the wiser.

Meanwhile, their brother was seemingly unaffected; the solid routine and simplicity of his existence reduced his anxiety and his interest in his college work, the simple love from the animals, suppers with the neighbours, his music, the letters that arrived each month from Mary — they sufficed. The rare visits from Adamma and occasional calls from Kamaria — they'd been icing on the cake; their absence now did little to shake him.

Back in Ireland, Michael was uneasy. His grandson hadn't answered the phone again. He always called at eight in the evening, every Friday on the dot, and even more worrying was that the line to the house was dead.

"What's going on over there, Mary? It's been three weeks since I've spoken to him; somethings wrong, and I've tried to speak to the girls and left messages for our

Kamaria at the doctors' house, and Adamma? Her mobile is flat, so it is."

His face crimson, he wiped the glistening sweat from his forehead with a checked hanky. "How could they, Mary?" Hands trembling, he lit a cigarette. "Please, leave me be, it's just one, I'm worried sick; you know I should never have listened to our James. I should have paid heed to myself. For the love of God, what were we thinkin' of?"

She looked him straight in the eyes, her voice firm. "We trusted them, and we have made a mistake in doing so." Taking his hand gently, she sighed. "I pray from the bottom of my heart that the lad has come to no harm. Oh, Michael, how could they?"

"Aye, and how could we too?" His eyes flashing with anger, he pulled himself up from his chair. Throwing his cigarette into the hearth he raised his head and straightened his shoulders. "Stay here sweetheart, I'm off to drive over to my brother's, we'll sort something out but we'll need to move fast."

Suddenly contrite, he embraced her tenderly. He needed to watch his anger; it wouldn't help her recovery after the 'turn' she'd had after losing their daughter.

She pulled away gently. "Stop worrying about me pet, I'm fine, please, off you go, scat."

He was out of the door within seconds, the engine turned and roared into life and then, just as suddenly, came to a juddering stop. He flung the door open.

"Bless my heart, Michael, whatever now?"

"Mary, pack a bag, just the one, for me, you'll need to stay here and keep an eye."

She smiled and nodded. "Off you go then!"

"To hell with that," she muttered. "Now where's that other bag?"

Within the hour, he'd headed off for the U K with James. They drove speedily through the darkness, caution thrown to the wind, eager to reach the ferry and get across to Liverpool. Michael didn't try to telephone Mary, the service wasn't good at the best of times and besides, he didn't want to get into an argument, he was already het up to the extreme.

Mary stretched out on her grandson's bed; she needed to be close to him. Unable to sleep, she clutched her rosary to her breast and prayed.

Michael had tricked her, he'd not returned for his bag, his request had been a ruse to keep her busy, knowing that she would insist on accompanying him.

"Wily old fox, you, but it's fine, it's important that someone gets themselves over there, and quickly." She knew she would have slowed him down. At these times she turned to her faith, it was always a comfort. She closed her eyes and pleaded for help.

Outside her window the night was black — the new moon gave off little light — the wind was low and the owl shrieked in the distance as the light bringing a vision of Robina poured into her mind.

She heard her daughter's words, pleading with her.

"Mammie, bring them home, bring them both home, P-L-E-A-S-E."

CHAPTER 29

Liverpool

It was dark and cold. The wind cut through them like a knife; at this hour of the morning there was little traffic about and the only light came from the flickering street lamps.

As they turned the corner, James began to run. "Christ, the windows are boarded up."

Michael followed on, breathless, he tried to force the key into the lock, it wouldn't turn.

"The locks have been changed; what the heck's gone on here?"

The men tried to force their way in; the boards made a loud cracking noise as the wood splintered.

Next door, Joseph pulled up the sash window and pushed his head out. Squinting, he was unable to recognise them and he called Aneta to find his glasses. "Wait a minute please. Ah, it's you Michael! It's me, Joseph, wait there, I'm coming down, 'prosze', please, wait". Within minutes, their elderly Polish neighbour was with them. Handing them a chisel, he rubbed his hands together to warm them, the cold was a shock to his aged body, it was only a few moments ago that he'd been cuddled up with his plump old lady.

Michael prized at the boards; one by one he threw them into the kerb. "Aye, quick James, get yourself in, I think I saw a light inside."

He turned to Joseph. "When did this all kick off, Joseph?"

Fidgeting, he sighed, hesitated, he couldn't look Michael in the eye. "Three weeks ago, well about that I think, I saw them hanging around. They slapped my Aneta, pushed me onto the ground, 'keep your mouth shut, old man,' they said, if I called the 'policija' then, they would know, and then come back and put a petrol rag through my letterbox. 'Straszne'y, terrible; they hung around for a few days, strutting and smirking — we were too frightened to leave the house. I haven't seen them since — I thought young Finn would be with you, we've not seen or heard from him."

Joseph hovered, shivering.

"Thank you for your help; I'm sorry to bring out troubles to you Joseph. Get yourself home to Aneta and back into your bed, we'll let you know in a wee bit what's going on."

Joseph flapped his hands, shocked and feeling helpless. He nodded, turned slowly and left them to it.

Michael's heart was pumping violently, he could feel the pulse racing in his neck. "Oh, dear God, it's freezing cold, where can the lad be? Come on, James, we need to get inside, maybe he's in there; I'll give you a leg up, here, put your foot in my hands here, quick."

"I'm no spring chicken either, watch 'me privates'," James hollered.

James tumbled through the window head first, brushing himself down he took a look around, his eyes adjusting to the darkness.

Inside the gloom, a figure huddled in the corner, the face lit by the flickering candles, the only light; they cast their strange shapes on the wall and James shivered. "Oh, 'by Jaysus', it's our Adamma."

She let out a little cry as he bent over her.

"Hush now." He was shocked; she was in a pitiable state. "It's Uncle James." He patted her head — her usually immaculate hair was dishevelled and full of something like grit, she was sitting on a damp mattress, shivering, and there was a strong stench or urine.

Michael yelled out, "What's going on? Here, James, open the door."

She hid her face from him. "Grandad, they took my clothes, they pissed on me, they've took everything I have, it's all gone."

He knelt down beside her and, taking her in his arms, he rocked her gently.

"James, check the electric, see if there is any power."

A triumphant cry from James, and then the house flooded with light.

"I was hiding from them. The landlord had the broken windows boarded up and the lock changed, but he left a small window open into the pantry; I climbed back in and I've been here ever since."

"Who the hell are they, these twisted bastards that torment women and old 'uns'? They threatened Joseph and Aneta too — and where the hell is your young brother? How is he involved in all of this?" Michael demanded. "Adamma, answer me" he roared.

James caught hold of his arm. "Hold on there will you, give her time, she's in a state here," then turning to Adamma, "you're freezing, why didn't you put the heating on then? It's working."

"I don't know," her words poured out in a torrent. "I owed them money, Grandad; they're dealers, they found this address and followed me from London but they'd already smashed the place up when I got here. I don't know where Finn is, the house was empty and then they came again, as you can see. They have Mam's ring that she gave me, they spat in my face and took my mobile, tore the landline from the wall; they have my watch, my designer shoes, clothes, all of it."

"Never mind your bloody clothes. What about our Finn? What did they say?"

"They frightened the shit out of him, told him they were going to rape me."

"Oh Noooo." Michael put his head in his hands.

"No, they didn't do it, Grandad, they said they didn't want to contaminate themselves by 'giving one to a half-cast smack head' like me. I've been here ever since; my brother has not been near. I'm so sorry, I thought he was with you. I'm starving, I've been living on cold cans and biscuits."

James sighed. "So, it's drugs again, Adamma, is that it?" he turned to Michael. "You know what our dad always said about her? 'That one suffers from a double dose of original sin' — I'm beginning to think he had something there!"

Adamma cringed.

"That's enough, James, talk like that won't help us now, we need to find the lad, and quickly, and we'll need to get in touch with the landlord. Wait a minute. To hell with it, James, can you see if Nellie is up? See if her downstairs lights are switched on, will you? If she is up, ask if we can take Adamma around to hers — they might come back."

"No, Grandad, they won't be back here now, they're long gone, back in London. They've cleaned my bank account out, all the money Dad left me, it's gone. It was revenge on me for turning their boss down; sexually, you know, I didn't want him; he'd let me run up a bill, promised me that he could arrange an audition for me in his next production. I'm nothing now, a scouse bitch, small fish, long forgotten."

"Then why are you still hiding?"

"I've no clobber, I'm skint, I've been going cold turkey! I've been seeing things, I haven't slept for days, I'm a mess, and I'm so sorry that I've let you all down," she wailed.

Michael was angry, livid, struggling to keep his voice steady. Swallowing his anger, he took a deep breath. "Have you any idea at all where he can be? Think! Try, Adamma! From what you and Joseph say he's been missing over three weeks, and what about Kamaria?"

"She's washed her hands of me, said until I stopped using the stuff, until I really wanted to stop, that she will help those who really need her. Oh, I don't know, I don't know about him, Grandad! But they had his money and probably his mobile too, they told me they tipped him upside down and shook it out of his pockets. He's not been back here. Oh, Granda', 'ew', quick."

A surge of vomit spewed out in a gush — the projectile flow covered them both.

"Feck! I'll get you some help, Adamma, Jaysus, I'm out of my depth here; I'll get Nellie."

Shaking violently, she clutched the blanket around her. The closeness of family made her want Robina even more, the sadness of losing her mam was like a fist squeezing her heart; teeth clenched, she made a guttural sound. How long had it been since someone had been genuinely nice to her? Michael turned towards her and held her close whilst fumbling in his pocket for a handkerchief and his mobile. The sticky wetness clung to his hands.

"Where the hell is James when I need him."

"Hello, ambulance please, I've a young girl here needing your help urgently; she's coming off drugs, I think she's having a seizure, Lord help her, come quickly."

Systematically they began their search; they rang the college, they'd not seen him for weeks; then the salvation army, churches, food halls, neighbours, students from the college, animal sanctuaries, everywhere that he had ever volunteered.

Why hadn't Finn knocked on Nellie's or Joseph's door, why hadn't he asked for money to make a call or asked to use somebody's phone?

The local police took a description, asked routine questions: Was anything worrying him? Had there been an argument? Have you rung round his friends? Any girl troubles? When was Finn last seen? They tried to reassure them. "You'd be surprised how common this is — he'll be back when his money runs out, he's nearly eighteen, we see this all the time!"

"There's something you need to know. It's not that simple," Michael protested. The officers listened, they'd heard it all before, but they listened, wearily. They could see how worried the man was. "The house was burgled, the lad was threatened, they took his card and pin number."

He gave the police the description that Joseph had given him, vague as it was, it was all they had and Adamma was not in a fit state to do so. Besides, he was wary of involving his granddaughter and didn't want to bring her drug use to their attention; all he wanted was the lad to be found, to have him home.

Shaking his hand, they took their leave, "This maybe puts a different slant on it. Try not to worry, it sounds as if the lad has been badly frightened — we'll organise a search and let the cars know. If you find anything out, get back to us straight away."

Michael and James scoured Liverpool. James drove further on whilst Michael walked the streets, around the docks, the parks and all the lonely places, revisited the churches, knocked on doors. It was December. The cold bit at Michael's arthritic fingers and feet; was Finn was outside in this?

Michael hadn't been able to tell Mary everything but after two days he knew he'd have to; James listened in as he begged her to stay put — he didn't doubt for a minute that Mary would comply with his request.

Mary was over the water the next evening after making the necessary arrangements for home. She was horrified when she saw the house, the home that Robina had loved and worked her fingers to the bone for. It was all like a horrible dream, how could Adamma have let this happen? Where was Finn? Fierce as an Amazonian warrior fighting for her young, she made a noise at the police station, refusing to listen to or accept their tired routine placations. "You'll have to do better than that."

She made a phone call to Kamaria's superior, demanding that her granddaughter be released from her duties to return home for urgent family business. She bought clothes and toiletries and made a visit to the hospital, stayed until she was satisfied that Adamma was improving, jumped in a taxi and telephoned the men to organise another search. "Take a photo of Finn to the library and make some photocopies and then ask a few of Finn's college friends to put them in the shop windows and pubs; offer a reward!"

Mary prayed, she prayed so hard that she wasn't aware of anything else around her. She begged God in his heaven, Mother Mary, dear, sweet Jesus and all the saints to help bring her grandson home to safety. She prayed for love and peace to return to her family, asked God to give permission for Robina to return from heaven in spirit to be with her son. "He's never taken a wrong turn, Lord, but he's sensitive and innocent, and the world out there is harsh; if there is any justice in this world, please help us find him, please bring him back to us, please."

Was time running out for Finn?

Their evil faces danced in front of him, they licked the blood dripping from their lips — the little white demons danced along his arms and legs. "They're waiting for you, they'll lift your shirt and you know what they'll do then, don't you," they screamed. "They'll chop off your fingers, one by one, and you'll never be able to play your music again. They will force you to give your grandparents address, and then they will find them too, and oh! You will never believe what they will do to them; they are old, they will die, they will find them and kill them and it will be your fault! You are lost, you may never go home, never!"

The two plain-clothes officers had just left the house, they'd decided to step up the search. "If you can think of anything, anything at all, then please let us know. It could lead to a new line of enquiry."

Mary was fretting — it was biting cold outside; how could they be so relaxed about it all?

"Where's Kamaria? I was assured they gave her my message, word for word! I can't believe she's not here with us now — and Michael! The police have come up with 'diddly squat'; every hour that he's out there, oh, I can't bare this — oh, sweet Mother Mary, please help us now in our need," she begged.

"We've searched the precinct, shop doorways, anywhere we think he may be holding out to keep warm; they've patrolled the docks, put the word out. All we can do now is try and get a night's rest and start again in the morning. Come on now, love," Michael pleaded.

"But I can't help thinking that we've overlooked something. We've failed him, we've failed our Robina, we should have kept him safe; he's just an innocent boy at that."

"Enough now — run yourself a hot bath — you'll be no good to him if you work yourself up to a lather like this. I'll sit up with James and if we hear anything, anything at all, I'll be straight up those stairs to tell you so. He must be somewhere and we'll find him."

She didn't answer. He hurried her on; he was sick with fear. The brothers listened as the bathroom door slammed shut and the water gushed into the bath.

James shook his head. "I'm not sure that you're right brother, this is a 'bad do' so it is. I only hope he isn't out there — it's freezing — I hope to God that he is, well, that he is still alive."

The figure was huddled under an old tarpaulin on the bench. He'd hoped to find some comfort under the branches of the horse chestnut tree; its branches were bare but they were heavy and thick and offered some shelter from the wind.

"Mam used to love coming here," he whispered through clenched teeth. "Maybe she'll be here for me soon." He tried to smile but was strangely disconnected. He began to float upwards; he was weightless, just like the snowflakes drifting around him.

Now comfortably detached from the bodily sensations of fear and the hunger that had chewed away at him for the last few hours, he peeped out from under the canvas at the snow fluttering down,

"It's all so very beautiful."

In the height of his terror, amid the clamour of the voices, Finn had heard his mam's words. "Son, God has given us all a guardian angel; he never leaves us, ask him for help," and he'd summoned every ounce of strength and shouted out prayers and he'd drowned out their voices. And, wonder of wonders, their foul screeching had stopped and the spinning demons had vanished, evaporated!

Someone told him to "get yourself moving, go back home now, you'll be safe," only in his confused state he'd gone to the wrong house, he'd knocked on the door and it wasn't his mam that opened it. They'd told him to clear off, slammed the door in his face and bolted it shut. He'd slithered down onto the step and they'd thrown a kettle of water over him from the upstairs window.

Confused, his mind blank, he'd dragged himself along the streets, aimlessly wandering until he came to the little park where his mam used to bring him when he was a small boy, luckily, he was able to go in, the padlock had been broken on the gate. He'd found an old torn canvas sheet and curled up on the bench, covering himself as best as he could.

He tried to take a deep breath, but it hurt. The sharpness of the pain pulled him back down into the heaviness for a moment — no, he heard a voice — everything was going to be fine; the swirls of snow were taking him up to heaven, he could hear voices calling him already.

"Finn, Finn, son, here; we are here!"

Someone, something was pulling him back.

"No, stop it, leave me be, I'm going to Mam, stop pulling me, Noooo!"

He shouted and struggled against them, but he was tired, so tired. All around him he could hear hushed voices. His eyelids blinked against the snowflakes, wet and cold on his eyelashes. Now someone was shaking him, rubbing his arms, his face, there was a female voice, she was crying.

"Finn, wake up." Strong arms pulled him up and wrapped him in something heavy and warm. "Thank God, here's the keys, Kamaria, help me; go and get the door open, I'll carry him. Oh, come on lad, son, stay with me, oh dear God in heaven, don't take him from me, not now, don't let him go."

Finn opened his eyes. He was slumped on the back seat of a car and he could feel the warm air from the heater blowing on his feet. A woman was sitting next to him, holding him, rubbing his hands, kissing him.

"Mam? Is that you, Mam? Am I in heaven? Do they have cars in heaven?"

"No 'soft lad', it's your sister, and the man driving the car isn't St Peter either; it's our dad, Moses."

Moses slowed down at the lights, turned his head sideways and looked into the back. "Pleased to meet you, son, it's been a long time coming. I'm taking you home."

And that's how it all began, and ended, and carried on again; a family story of births and deaths, of traumatic events, of love and betrayal, human frailty and beauty.

And the womenfolk had their hair styled at Annette's on the corner — you know, the hairdressers next to the pub — and they wore new frocks and old Joseph cheated at cards. They danced and sang together, the old and the not so old, the young, the spirits of the newly departed and not so newly departed; they held a Christmas Eve party that shook the rafters. A family party that would be remembered down the years, and Moses took photographs for the family album.

And old Michael and young Finn and James played their new song, 'Just One Life', Adamma and Kamaria sat near their dad and Mary looked on, smiling, and they all sang along together:

"When you're feeling down and it's all a bit too much,
It's a crazy world and they're all out of touch.
You want to walk away but you want to stand and fight,
If they push just a little bit too far, you just might"
So, dry your eyes,
Be yourself, just one life, make it count"

And the Angels looked on, and they joined in too;
PEACE ON EARTH, GOOD WILL TO ALL MEN.